DANGEROUS LITTLE SECRETS

SAINT VIEW HIGH #2

ELLE THORPE

For fellow reverse harem author, Zoe Ashwood.
Thank you for all the years of critiques, proofreads, daily chats,
and most of all, your friendship.

1

COLT

"You're a real piece of work, you know that?" Rafe's growl, low and deadly, was out of place with the excited gossip rippling around the shocked partygoers.

I dragged my gaze away from the doors Lacey had disappeared through and focused on my best friend. "What?"

Rafe's laugh was cold. "Cut the crap. Are you happy now? You got your way. You've finally found a way to break her. Gotta say, you've done some fucked-up things, but this is next level."

I folded my arms and peered at Rafe in disbelief. "You think I did this? From where I was standing, that was your face buried between her thighs, not mine. How the fuck do I have anything to do with it?"

Rafe lunged for me, shoving me up against a pillar. My skull hit the hard cement structure, and annoyance prickled through me. I fought off the urge to throw a punch. It was my natural instinct when threatened, but I also knew Rafe wasn't a real threat. Not to me, anyway.

"You're upset, I get that." The words were quiet, but my tone was no-nonsense. He'd get away with that sort of shit one time only. "But you're going to back off now, because it's not my problem the three of you were stupid enough to make a sex tape and then broadcast it to the entire party."

Movement at the doors caught my attention, and I narrowed my eyes. Owen. Fuck that prick. Where the hell was he going? Every instinct in my body forced me to pay attention, priming my muscles, ready to chase him down. I didn't trust that asshole as far as I could throw him. I hadn't forgotten what he'd done at the beach party last weekend. The way he'd watched her lose control. His gaze had rolled over Lacey's body tonight, lewd and possessive, until I'd wanted to ram my fist down his throat.

I sure as hell didn't like that he'd disappeared in the same direction as Lacey.

Rafe's grip on my shirt loosened, and I shoved him away. He took a few steps back, eyes still flashing with anger, his muscles coiled too tight. His expression froze my plans to run Owen down and find out why he was taking off so quick. Rafe was a ticking time bomb, ready to go off.

I grabbed his shoulders and shook him. "Hey. Knock it off. I'm not your fucking enemy. You need to go home. Sleep on it. You've been drinking, and nothing good is going to come of you hanging around, getting fired up."

Rafe was so lost to his anger I wasn't sure he even heard me. With his fingers clenched, his wild gaze bounced around the room, eyeing every person as if they were his number one suspect. The blue of his irises frosted over into something hard. Something ready to unleash at any moment and wreak havoc amongst the chaos this party had turned into.

I ran a hand through my hair. Dammit. I couldn't leave

him in this state. He'd end up in jail.

"I've got him."

I spun around to find Jagger, Aaron a few steps behind her.

"I need to go after Owen," I confided in them. "I don't trust him."

Jagger nodded. "Me neither. Go. We've got this."

She loved Rafe like I did. And Aaron had the bulk to get the physical job done, if it came to dragging Rafe out of there. He was in good hands, so I left without another word.

But I didn't get far, the crowd at the doorway was too thick. People stood around in groups, still gossiping and laughing about everything they'd seen and heard tonight. Nobody seemed interested in moving off to their cars, even though the party had come to a screeching halt.

I scanned the crowd for Owen's obnoxious head but couldn't see any sign of him. His flashy car still sat in the front row of the parking lot, though. I recognized it from last weekend.

He was still here somewhere. And so was Lacey.

My heart rate picked up, adrenaline spiking my blood. I noticed Lacey's other friend from Providence, the girl with the crazy blonde curls, and made a beeline for her. She stared off into the darkness of the beach, her jaw held rigid.

"Did you see Owen come down here?"

She blinked at me, took in my outfit, then pursed her lips into a disgusted line. "What do you care?"

She obviously knew who I was then. I stared her down, waiting for her answer.

With a huff, she let out a breath. "He went after Lacey. Banjo did, too."

"Which way?"

She shrugged. "I didn't see her run off. Banjo went that way, Owen the other."

"Fuck," I bit out. How long had it been since I'd seen Owen leave? Minutes? Ten maybe? Hell, I didn't know.

I ran down to the wet sand where it was more compact and easier to speed up. The dark night wind whipped around me, sending chilly tendrils around my skin, but all too soon I was wishing I had less layers on. Sweat trickled down from my spine, but I pushed on through the darkness. The noise and lights of the party dimmed behind me.

"Lacey," I yelled into the darkness.

I stopped, breathing hard, waiting for a reply. But nothing came. Fuck. Maybe I was way off base here. She'd obviously taken off for a reason, not wanting to be found. She could have gone back up one of the beach paths and gotten an Uber. With every cell of my body, I hoped she was tucked up in the back of a car right now, devastated, but safely on her way home.

I couldn't shake the sense that she wasn't.

"Lacey," I yelled again.

The silence was deafening.

"Fuck!" I closed my fingers into fists.

That's when I heard it. Against the roar of the ocean, a muffled cry of agony chilled me to the bone. I bolted, this time toward the sound, up to the softer sand. My chest burned as I pushed myself past my limits, the memory of the pain in that cry spurring me on.

He was fucking hurting her. I just knew it.

In the dim moonlight, a dark shape moved on the sand. Twisting, rolling. It was impossible from this distance to make out what it was, but I changed gears, finding a new speed that sent me pummeling forward.

Lacey's cries of terror met my ears before my eyes worked out what was happening.

I didn't think.

My brain shut down completely.

He had her pinned to the sand, a hand pressed to her mouth and nose while she fought beneath him.

Red clouded my vision.

Through a haze, I grabbed Owen by his jacket and hurled him off her. He landed on the sand with a thud, the wind knocked out of him, a surprised yelp escaping his swollen lips.

"Stay there," I yelled.

Ignoring his protests, I turned to Lacey, who lay on her back, gasping and wheezing, fighting to suck in air. Her dress ripped. Her skirt hiked up, panties halfway down her legs.

My stomach roiled.

I dropped to my knees beside Lacey's beaten body, yanking off my jacket and covering her. She blinked up at me through an almost completely swollen-shut eye, and I fucking lost it. He'd beaten her to within an inch of life. And probably worse.

Pure, white-hot rage uncoiled from somewhere deep inside me.

I reared back and found the coward stumbling to get himself off the ground, his fly undone, clutching at his stomach and doubled over like it hurt to breathe. I hoped it did. I hoped it was agony. But any pain he had now was nothing on what he was about to feel.

I yanked him up the rest of the way. "What the fuck did you do!"

"What?" He laughed around his split lip. "It was nothing she doesn't do with you in the slums."

I drew back my arm and let my fist fly straight into his jaw.

It cracked satisfyingly, and Owen howled in pain.

But it wasn't enough to cover Lacey's whimpers behind me. They were all I could hear. Those tiny desperate sounds, no louder than a kitten's mewling, somehow drowned out Owen's wails. I pulled my fist back again. And again.

I didn't even feel the pain explode through my knuckles. It was all buried beneath the anger at what he'd done to her. I just kept punching.

Until Lacey's tiny voice stopped me. "Colt."

It was barely more than a whisper. But that was all it took for me to drop Owen to the ground and focus back on Lacey. I scuttled across the sand, tucked my jacket around her, and lifted her into my arms.

She put one arm around my neck, barely strong enough to hold on. "Hurts," she whispered.

"I know, princess. I know. Hang on, okay? I'm going to get you an ambulance."

She thrashed in my arms, shaking her head rapidly. Her one good eye went huge, round and terrified. "No," she croaked. "No hospital. They'll take him there when he's found. He'll try again."

The growl came from deep in my chest. "The police then."

She shook her head.

It was her body, I couldn't force her, even though everything inside me screamed to get her some help. Her injuries didn't look life-threatening, but what the hell did I know? What if she had internal bleeding or something? Injuries I couldn't see?

"Please, Colt," she gasped.

Fuck. What the hell was I supposed to do? I was

standing in the middle of a deserted beach at midnight with a nearly unconscious girl in my arms. I needed help.

I yanked my phone from my pocket and dialed Banjo's number. He answered on the first ring.

"Get the car. I've got her."

2

____

LACEY

*E*verything hurt. My throat was on fire, every swallow complete torture. My eye throbbed. Ribs ached. My thighs bruised and violated.

Colt's warm chest, and his arms locked tight around me, were the only things keeping me from letting the blackness take me completely. I focused on his breaths. In and out. The rise and fall, so rhythmic.

Owen was dead. I was sure of it. The way Colt's fist had smashed into his face had turned my stomach. But I couldn't bring myself to care.

About any of it. It had all faded into insignificance with the force of my hate.

Banjo. Rafe. Owen.

The level of anger shocked me. Scared me even. They'd all betrayed me. They were supposed to be my friends, and they'd fed me to the wolves.

Colt was a wolf, too. I had no doubt about that. He'd made my life hell for weeks now, threatened to run me out of school, told me to leave and never come back, taunted me, saying I didn't belong and never would.

He was right.

I hadn't listened, but I saw it all now.

Despite the fact I was in his arms, he was a wolf in sheep's clothing.

I was in and out of consciousness, no real idea where we were, when the roar of an engine pulled up beside us. A flash of blond hair flew from the driver's seat.

Banjo stopped a few steps away and stared, his gorgeous mouth, the one I'd kissed not that long ago, dropping open in horror. "Lacey, no."

I stared back. I didn't even recognize him. He might as well have been a stranger. But then, the Banjo I'd known had never truly existed, had he? I didn't believe the shock rolling off this version for a second.

I spat out words wrapped in hate. "Get away from me."

He rushed in, trying to take me from Colt's arms. "Give her to me," he yelled when Colt wouldn't give me up. "What did you do to her?"

I clutched at Colt tighter.

"It was Owen, not me. Just drive the car. I'm not giving her to you when she clearly doesn't want that." He bundled me into the back seat of a car.

I could only pray he wasn't going to take me home. If Selina saw me like this, she'd call the cops and an ambulance, and I'd be dragged off to hospital.

What was the point? After last night, no one was going to believe me when I said Owen attempted to rape me.

Attempted.

Thank God.

I cringed, remembering the way Owen had ripped at my clothes and yanked my panties down my legs, leaving me bare and helpless. He'd muffled my screams with his hand, careless with his placement, for his big fingers had blocked my nose, too, while I fought for air beneath him.

Or maybe that had been deliberate. If he was capable of rape, then he was capable of trying to kill me.

A full-body tremble racked my body, and Colt drew me tighter.

I let him. Because his touch was all that was keeping me from floating off into the ether.

"Where are we going?" I murmured.

"Back to my place," Colt said quietly.

He smoothed back my hair from my face. It was probably the one spot on my body that wasn't in complete agony. Despite the hate I'd harbored for him for weeks, I leaned into his touch like a starving kitten, desperate for someone to show her the tiniest scrap of kindness.

Banjo stopped the car and rushed to the back doors, opening them so Colt could get me out.

"Take her to my room," Banjo said.

"Why? So you can fucking film me again?"

Banjo blanched ghost white in the darkness.

Colt's indecision filled the air. "Shit. I'll take her. Just, fuck, I don't know. Go to bed, Banjo. We'll work this all out in the morning."

Relief settled over me. I might have hated both these boys, but in that moment, I had to choose the lesser of two evils. And somehow that person was now Colt. My heart splintered at the thought. I'd fallen so hard and fast for Banjo, I could have never imagined this would be the way things would turn out. I couldn't even stand to look at him, standing there in his mussed-up costume, fake devastation written all over his face. Is this what he'd wanted? To hurt me? Humiliate me? If so, he'd gotten it.

"Seriously, Banjo. Go. If we wake up the whole street,

we're gonna have a whole new host of problems. I'll call you in the morning."

I tucked my head against Colt's chest and let him carry me up several flights of stairs, to his attic bedroom. Banjo didn't try to follow, and for that I was grateful. Colt placed me down on the bed gingerly, and I groaned in pain.

He stood back, his gaze raking over me, worry twisting his dark features. "Shit, Lacey. You're messed up bad." His voice was softer than I'd ever heard it.

Footsteps on the attic stairs had us both turning to the doorway. "Colt? What's going on? Are you hurt?"

The woman who appeared was probably in her early forties. Her mismatched flannel pajamas boasted smiling avocados on the top half and fluffy pink rabbits on the bottom. One quick glance at her told me she was Colt's mom. They both stared at me with identical almost-black eyes, though his mom's had smile lines around the corners. I doubted Colt would ever have those, since he was bigger on sulking and smirking than smiling. Her stare didn't have any of the animosity Colt usually threw at me. Instead, her eyes widened, filling with surprise which morphed into confusion.

"Is that—"

Colt cut her off with a quick shake of his head. "She's hurt. Maybe bad. She won't go to the hospital. I was about to wake you."

She shot Colt a hard stare. "You keep your sister out of here."

"You have a sister?" I croaked. I couldn't blame his mom for not wanting a young girl up here. If I looked half as bad as I felt, I wouldn't want my child around me either. I was currently the poster girl for making really shit decisions and screwing up your entire life.

Not exactly a good role model.

Colt's mom knelt at my head. "Hey, sweetheart. How are you feeling?"

"Like death," I answered truthfully.

She smiled sympathetically. "Yeah, I bet. But I want to help, okay? I'm Willa. I'm a nurse. I work up at the local hospital. Can you tell me why you don't want to go? Because I think you should."

I stared into her kind eyes and wondered how on earth she was Colt's mother. I shook my head slowly. I had a sudden urge to keep the events of this evening away from this beautiful woman. I still all too vividly remembered the expression on Selina's face after the tape had played and didn't want to see the same expression on Willa's. I couldn't bear it if another person gazed at me in disgust tonight.

"I can't," I whispered.

Willa peeked over her shoulder at her son. "Can you give us a minute?"

He wasn't happy about it, but he traipsed out into the hall.

Willa got up and shut the door behind him before coming back to my side.

She gave me a tight smile. "Anything you tell me will be kept in confidence, okay?"

"Thank you," I whispered.

"Can I examine you? I can see you've taken a beating, and while your eye doesn't look great, it probably won't kill you. I'm more worried about where else you might be hurt."

I had no idea why, but I trusted this woman wholeheartedly. Perhaps it was that I had no one else to turn to, but Willa hadn't even blinked when she'd seen me. She didn't know me from a bar of soap, and yet she was willing to step right in and get her hands dirty. That said a lot about a person. I nodded.

Willa pulled off Colt's coat, the cool air of his bedroom sending goosebumps over my bare skin. She started at my neck, pushing her fingers to my pulse point and counting the beats of my heart, while timing them with her watch. She frowned at my ripped dress but continued on, poking and prodding me, and asking questions about my pain levels. When she picked up my hands, I knew she would probably see Owen's skin beneath my fingernails.

She placed my hands down on the bed then focused back on my face. Tears glistened in her eyes. "You fought."

My own eyes welled up. "Until the end. But I wasn't strong enough. If Colt hadn't found me..."

Willa nodded and smoothed back my hair. "You should get a rape kit done."

But I shook my head. "It didn't go that far. I just need a shower and some sleep. I'm so tired."

"We can manage that." She still seemed worried, but she helped me into a sitting position and then let me lean on her to shuffle to the door. As soon as she opened it, Colt jumped to his feet.

His gaze bounced between the two of us, then landed on me. "Are you okay?"

I nodded. "Your mom said I could have a shower."

"Yeah, of course."

He went to take my hand, but Willa shooed him away. "I've got her. Get some clothes for her to wear. And change your sheets. They're full of dirt and sand now."

We shuffled down the stairs, painfully slowly, each step agony, but I was covered in wet sand and blood, and the promise of a hot shower was worth more than any amount of pain.

The little bathroom on the second floor flooded with bright light when Willa hit the switch. The tiling was outdated, a few chipped but otherwise impeccably clean. Willa drew a flowered curtain aside and turned on the water, fiddling with the taps until steam filled the small space.

I stood there limply, leaning heavily on the basin. "I'm really sorry about this," I said to her quietly. "I hope the shower won't wake your daughter."

Willa shook her head, dark hair bouncing around her shoulders. "She sleeps like the dead. It's not a problem. You should be in hospital, but I'm at least glad Colt had the sense to bring you here. And to help you."

I bit my lip. I wasn't about to tell her about all the horrible things he'd said to me before tonight. Other people had done worse, and in the face of that, Colt's sins faded into the background.

At least he'd never lied about his feelings toward me. His dislike had been right out there for the world to see from day one.

"You're going to need help with that dress, sweetheart," Willa said. "May I?"

She indicated to the laces on my back. Modesty went out the window. I knew she was right. The thought of trying to reach around and undo the straps at my back hurt.

She moved slowly, carefully, unlacing the straps and then pulling the dress away from my battered body. To her credit, she didn't gasp the way I did as I caught sight of my bruises in the full-length mirror. Ugly swollen red patches marred my ribs, my stomach, my thighs. My panties still hung awkwardly, ripped from Owen trying to get them off me in a hurry.

Tears filled my eyes again, and Willa wrapped a fluffy towel around me, giving me some privacy.

Her sad face met mine in the mirror. "I'll be outside. If you need help, call out, okay?"

I wouldn't, but I nodded anyway. I waited until she left, then placed the towel gingerly on the side of the tub. I got in the shower, still in my ripped panties and strapless bra.

The water cascaded over me, and finally, I let myself break down.

3

LACEY

The water ran cold before I was really ready for my shower to be over. Guilt flooded in over how long I'd been standing there for that to have happened. But it couldn't have been later than one in the morning, and I hoped that was sufficient time for the hot water to heat up again before Willa or anyone else might want to take a shower.

My bruises hadn't improved any, but I'd managed to wash my hair, which made me feel marginally more human. A soft pile of clothes waited on the vanity, so I toweled off and slipped them on, relishing the soft fluffiness of the sweatpants and the oversized hoodie with SVHF scrawled across the front. I frowned at it. It had to be Colt's, judging from the size. I hadn't picked him to be one to own a supporter's hoodie. Apart from his prince's costume, I didn't think I'd ever seen him in anything but black t-shirts and jeans.

Colt and Willa both waited for me in the darkened hallway.

"Thank you," I whispered to Willa. "I feel much better."

Colt didn't look like he believed me for a moment.

I ignored his scowl. "I don't know where my phone or purse are. I think probably still at the party." The realization I was stranded made me wobble. Selina would be worried about me, but I still didn't want to go home.

Colt darted a worried glance toward a closed door to our left and then moved into my side. "Can you walk up the stairs? You can stay here tonight. But not in the hallway. We're going to wake Aria."

Reluctantly, I gripped his arm. I hated I needed to, but there was no way I was getting up those stairs without his support. "I can walk."

Willa watched me hobble a few steps then made a move to her open bedroom door. "I'm right here if you need anything during the night, okay? If the pain gets too bad, you have to let us know. But I did leave some ibuprofen in Colt's room for you."

Without waiting for a thank-you, she disappeared, shutting her bedroom door behind her. Colt and I climbed the stairs slowly, me leaning heavily on his arm. My eyes drooped with each step, my entire body as heavy as lead.

"Your mom is amazing," I said softly. We entered his room, and I noticed he'd done as Willa had asked. Fresh linens covered his bed, no longer wet and sandy from where he'd deposited me earlier.

"She is." His eyes held a pride I'd never seen on him before. "She's a bit of a badass."

I smiled at the term. "Probably has to be, working at the Saint View hospital. I can only imagine the sorts of things she sees there." Yet she hadn't treated me like I was just another one of her cases. She'd genuinely cared about me. But that was what good nurses did, I supposed. They made each patient feel special and cared for. I probably got double the special treatment, since I was in her house. I was grateful for it.

I perched on the edge of the mattress and sighed. "Colt, I—"

He moved in close, crouching so we were eye height. Despite myself, my skin still prickled with awareness.

"Whatever you're going to say can wait until morning. You need rest."

He'd changed into gray sweatpants and a t-shirt while I'd been in the shower, the prince costume discarded to the floor. I eyed it now. I'd been about to thank him for his help tonight. For beating up Owen on my behalf. For getting me off the beach and bringing me to his home. For giving up his bed.

But seeing that outfit again sent a different set of emotions rushing in. I remembered the way he'd smirked at me across the party, his grin smug and knowing. Irritation prickled when I remembered how he'd been last weekend at the beach, where he'd dragged me away from the crowd and thrown my keys into the ocean. Not to mention every other shitty thing he'd said and done since I'd enrolled at Saint View.

We weren't friends.

This wasn't a truce.

He was still the enemy, and I'd come dangerously close to falling into his web.

I narrowed my eyes at the pile of clothes on the floor, and the tension in the air between us changed. "Why did you come as a prince?"

Colt sighed. "You're seriously that stubborn? You've been beat to hell tonight, but will you lie down and rest? No. You're going to give me a hard time instead."

"Wouldn't have to if you weren't always ready to stick a knife in my back."

He leaned in closer so our faces were a mere inch apart. His lip curled. "Do you not know me at all? If I were going to stick the knife in, I'd do it where you could see it. Right through your heart."

I shook my head slowly. His words had a ring of truth about them. Banjo, Rafe, and Owen had all stabbed me in the back. But Colt's hate for me had always been right out there in the open. Somehow, I believed him when he said I'd see his attack coming.

We stared each other down. My body was tired, but something inside me sparked to life. And I rejoiced in it. Rolled around in it, let it rain down over me, igniting my aching muscles. I wouldn't let this break me. These boys thought they knew me. But they didn't. I was stronger than they were, and I'd make them all pay.

"It wasn't you behind the tape, was it?"

Colt's warm breath misted over my cracked lips. "No."

"Last weekend at the beach. I was drugged. I'm sure of that now. It wasn't you who slipped something in my drink, though. Right?"

Colt's gaze remained steady in the flickering lamplight. "No."

"It was Owen."

It wasn't a question, but Colt nodded anyway.

"You knew?" I asked.

"I suspected after you nearly fell into the fire. I've seen you drink before. You have one or two. Enough to get a little buzz going, but you stop before you lose control. You were so far out of control at the beach, it was like watching a different girl."

Anger boiled up in my belly. "I can't believe that asshole

drugged me." Memories flickered dimly in the back of my mind. Owen slipping into bed behind me after he drove me home. Hands on my thighs, my belly. Slipping beneath my panties.

My insides cramped. "Oh God, I think I'm going to be sick."

Colt grabbed a trash can from the corner of the room just in time for me to hurl up the contents of my stomach. I moaned pitifully. In typical Colt fashion, he didn't try to comfort me. For which I was actually grateful. I didn't need his pity. But he did get up and leave the room momentarily, only to return with a large glass of water. He found the tablets Willa had left for me and popped a few, passing it all over to me. I took a tentative sip, but the water stayed down, so I swallowed the tablets, too.

Colt got rid of the vomit bucket, and when he came back, he crossed his large room to a tiny desk tucked away in the corner. I tracked him as he moved, his body all long and lean and sleek. Panther-like.

He pulled open a drawer and fished around in the drawer for a minute, before pulling something out and tossing it in my direction. I flinched away, but the object landed on the mattress beside me with a jangle.

It was a set of keys.

I recognized them instantly and gaped at him. "You threw these into the ocean."

He came and sat on the bed next to me. "No, I didn't. I just made you think I did."

I was sure my jaw was on the floor. "I was so angry at you."

"You were."

"I told you I hated you."

He shrugged. "That's the truth, isn't it?"

No. Yes. Fuck, I didn't know. I kept staring at the keys in my hand.

"I followed you home that night after the bonfire at the beach," he said, softer this time.

I snapped my head in his direction so fast I was sure I'd have whiplash. "What? Why?"

His solid black gaze bored into mine. "I needed to make sure you made it home safe."

I blinked, my head spinning. What the hell was he talking about? Since when did he care if I was safe or not?

But I didn't get a chance to question him.

Colt's expression went stony. "I watched Owen pick you up on the side of the road. I kept telling myself to drive away. That you weren't my problem. But fuck. I followed him right to your house, then sat at the end of the driveway in the darkness, watching the two of you. You turned the light on, and your curtains were open. I could see everything he was doing. You were a fucking rag doll puppet by that stage. Barely conscious. And he had his hands all over you."

His words took me right back to that night. "He got into bed with me," I whispered. "I didn't want him there. Kept telling him to go, but he wouldn't."

A sob broke free from my chest. God, it all seemed so clear now. Owen's attack tonight wasn't the first time he'd tried something like that. It was the culmination of previous attempts and frustrations.

Colt swore low under his breath, then grabbed my chin, tilting it so I had to face him. A tear fell from my eye, tracked down my cheek and over his fingers. He didn't seem to notice. Just stared at me with that same intensity he always did.

"Did he hurt you?"

I shook my head. "I don't think so. It's so hard to remember. He tried." I blinked, trying to remember through the fuzz. "He was interrupted by his phone."

"That was me."

I stared. "You messaged him? How?"

Colt fished out his phone and brought up his Instagram messages. Then he passed it to me. The screen showed a message to @owen.waller1 that simply said, *I know what you did.*

Owen had read it but hadn't responded.

Colt shifted, the mattress beneath us squeaking. "I saw the light go off and knew he was still up there with you. But I swear, Lacey, it took everything in my power not to run up that driveway, kick down your door, and drag that fuckwit outta there."

"I kind of wish you had."

His expression turned pained. "I would have if I'd known what he was doing up there. If I had, maybe tonight wouldn't have happened."

Shock rippled through me. "Don't do that. This isn't on you. Owen carries all the blame." I paused. "Do you think he's dead?" Worry had me tugging at my earlobe distractedly.

Colt gave a dark laugh. "Owen? Nah. He's fine. He'll have a black eye tomorrow, but he'll live."

"It looked bad."

"You looked bad. He just got what he deserved."

I gnawed at my bottom lip and then my teeth opened up a split, forcing me to stop. "I'm worried you're going to regret that. When his dad finds out what happened..."

Colt studied our hands, side by side on the mattress. His thumb moved ever so slightly, brushing over mine. "I'm not worried."

But he should be. He had no idea who Owen Waller's dad was.

He stood abruptly and strode to an armchair by his desk. "Enough of this. Go to sleep," he said gruffly.

Unable to make sense of this Colt who'd been gentle and protected me, even after I'd told him to go to hell, I did as I was told.

4

———————

LACEY

Nightmares plagued my sleep. Owen's leering face loomed, his hands clutching at me, pressing against my mouth and nose, cutting off my oxygen until my lungs were ready to burst. I thrashed, fighting back, until his face disappeared in the blackness, replaced by Colt's.

My heart rate slowed.

Colt muttered nonsense words, none of it making any sense, but it didn't need to. He was there when everyone else had abandoned me.

The first rays of dawn splintered through the tiny attic window, no curtain to hold them back. A heavy weight warmed my back, and it soothed away the last of my dreams.

Until I realized the weight was moving.

"What the hell, Colt?" I yelped, jerking away from him. Tears pricked at the backs of my eyes from the sharp movement, sending a ripple of pain throughout each of my injuries. A lump rose in my throat, but I'd already cried in front of him last night. I wasn't going to make a habit of it. But God, it hurt.

"What?" Colt mumbled sleepily.

I twisted onto my side, moving more carefully now. "What are you doing in my bed?"

He blinked open one eye and peered at me. "My bed, actually."

"Whatever!"

He shifted onto his back and stretched his long limbs out. Something in his back cracked, and he groaned. "You were having nightmares. Kicking around the bed like a fish out of water. You stopped when I lay down next to you."

I paused, remembering his face in my dreams, and the calm in knowing he was there. "I told you to stay."

He nodded. "Yeah. So I did. But sleeping around you was as uncomfortable as shit. You're a bed hog."

"Wow, is that the way you talk to all girls you have in your bed?"

A slow lazy grin spread across his handsome face. "Actually, I'm normally a whole lot dirtier with them." Satisfaction rolled off him.

"Arrogant prick." I hadn't meant to say it out loud, but what do you know, there it was.

His gaze raked over me, then landed back on my eyes. "You've got some of your fire back. Good. I didn't like seeing you the way you were last night. It's a lot more fun when you're giving it back to me."

I bristled. "Sorry if the fact I was publicly humiliated and beaten up put a damper on your opinion of me." I struggled to sit up, but it hurt so bad.

Colt rolled his eyes. "Don't be a moron. Stay where you are. I'll move. I didn't mean to fall asleep next to you anyway."

The door flew open before he could get up.

"Morning, baby. I brought coffee—" Gillian looked up from the cardboard cup tray, her gaze colliding with mine.

Shit.

"What. The. Hell." The coffee crashed to the floor, spilling everywhere.

Colt and I winced in unison, but I doubted his stomach sank the way mine did.

I was wearing Colt's clothes.

I was in Colt's bed.

And now his girlfriend was ready to kill.

Gillian launched herself across the room, and I scrambled back against the wall, out of her reach.

I needn't have bothered. Colt was on his feet and catching her around her middle, stopping her from getting too close.

"Whoa. Cool your jets." He tightened his grip on her. "This isn't what you think."

But Gillian was having none of it. She glared at me, kicking and punching at Colt. "You slut," she yelled. "Let me go." She lunged for me again, but Colt picked her petite frame straight off the floor and walked her to the other side of the room. She finally stopped struggling when she realized he wasn't going to let her get at me. Instead, she turned her wrath on him. "Take your damn hands off me."

He let her go, then raised his hands like he was talking to a wild animal. "Settle down. We didn't have sex."

I snorted at that. "He wishes."

Colt shot me a look as Gillian started up again.

Oops. My bad.

Colt let out a long breath. "Will you both knock it off?" He pinned me with a glare. "You, shut up." He turned back to Gillian. "And you, quit it. She's hurt. Can't you see that?

What would you have me do, leave her on the beach half-beaten to death?"

Gillian eyed me, this time actually taking in my swollen eye and the bruises around my mouth and neck. "Who did it?"

"Not your business," Colt interrupted, saving me from answering her. It would have been mortifying to let Gillian in on the fact that someone I'd thought was my friend was capable of doing this.

A light dawned in Gillian's eyes. Then she grabbed Colt's hand, turning it over so she could see his knuckles. I hadn't noticed, what with it being dark and wallowing in my own pain and pity, but his hands were busted. His knuckles ripped and scratched from slamming against Owen's face.

She dropped his hand like it was hot. "Owen Waller was found beaten up on the beach last night."

Colt played dumb. "Oh yeah?"

Gillian rolled her eyes. "You're an idiot. Don't you know who he is?" She laughed, the sound cold. Then she threw me a scathing look. "I hope your princess was worth a jail term. Because that's probably going to be where you end up once he tells his daddy who beat him up."

She shoved her bag farther up her shoulder then gave Colt one last scathing glare. "Get that bitch out of your bed. Don't you dare fucking speak to me until you do." Then she was gone, her car engine roaring to life outside a minute later.

Colt sighed. "Time to go, princess. Hospital or home. Your choice."

He was right. I couldn't stay here any longer. Despite what had happened last night, we weren't friends.

"Home. I'll get someone to pick me up if I can borrow your phone."

He shook his head. "I'll drive you."

"Fine."

"Fine."

We both stared at each other.

The tiniest of smiles lifted his lips, and I tried to pretend I didn't notice how cute he was. Now was not the time.

I gingerly got up from the warmth and softness of his bed while he ran downstairs and grabbed a towel to soak up the coffee mess. Mess sort of half-cleaned up, he led me downstairs.

On the bottom level, the hum of low conversation came from the kitchen. "Is your mom home? I want to thank her again before I leave."

"She wants to see you, too."

In the kitchen, Willa looked up from a mug of steaming coffee and smiled. A broad-shouldered man had his back to us, elbows resting on the countertop. He straightened and turned when Willa's attention diverted to us.

My eyes widened. "Coach Tontine." Saint View High's football coach was exactly the last person I'd expected to see sipping coffee with Colt's mom on a Sunday morning. He was so relaxed and at home in her kitchen, he couldn't possibly have been there for a school matter. Especially not at this time, on a Sunday. Colt wasn't even on the football team, anyway.

Coach Tontine shifted on bare feet, a pair of loose sweatpants tied around narrow hips. A soft black t-shirt covered his chest, a now familiar set of letters embroidered over his heart. Mine plummeted. It was that same Saint View High Football shirt I'd found in Banjo's drawer. The same one whoever had carried me from the fire had worn.

He did a double take when he recognized me, but his

surprise quickly morphed into concern and then anger. He took a step forward, hands out as if to touch me.

I flinched back on instinct, though this man had never done anything to me. I'd really never had any contact with him at all, other than watching him on the sidelines at Banjo and Rafe's games.

He dropped his hands, his anger and concern morphing into confusion.

"Drew..." Willa said quietly.

He glanced at her and then nodded before turning back to me. "I'm sorry. Willa told me you were here and that you'd been hurt. I just didn't expect... Are you okay?"

All I could do was stare at the logo on his shirt. Banjo had sworn only players had that shirt. Had that been another one of his lies? "That shirt," I croaked out.

Coach Tontine pulled out the fabric from his chest and stared down at it in confusion. Beside me, Colt's attention intensified. Willa's gaze bounced between the three of us, obviously not following what was going on.

"My shirt?" Coach asked. "What about it?"

"Where did you get it? That's a player's shirt. You aren't a player."

His eyebrows tugged together into a frown. I couldn't blame him. This was a seemingly random conversation after finding the school coach in Colt's family kitchen. Hell, even me being here was weird. I could understand why he was confused, when the one thing I was asking about was a shirt he'd probably gone jogging in. It was hardly the most interesting thing to comment on.

Except, to me, it was.

"I'm not a player anymore. But I was. State playoffs in my senior year." He shrugged as if he were a little embarrassed. "It's old, but it's comfy."

My head spun. "They don't change the design each year?"

Coach shook his head. "No, it's been the same for as long as I can remember. Colt's is the same, right?"

I whipped around to Colt, ignoring the scream from my ribs. "What? You aren't a player."

Willa walked over to my side and touched my arm tentatively, worry etched into her pretty features. "No," she answered for her son. "He's not. But his dad was. Colt has one of his shirts."

The room around me turned into a whirlwind. This changed everything. This widened my pool of suspects to a group so large I would have no chance of ever narrowing it down. How many boys had played for Saint View High in the last twenty-something years since the school had opened? Hundreds? A thousand? I couldn't even begin to do the math. All I knew was half of Saint View could potentially have that same shirt rolled up in the back of their drawers, or in their memory boxes, or shoved in the back of a closet where it had been forgotten after graduation.

And it put Colt on the suspect list.

I suddenly didn't have the energy anymore. For any of it.

"Was it you?" I asked him, point blank. My legs wobbled.

He moved in slowly and took my arm, steadying me. I knew I needed it, but I also didn't want him touching me.

"Was it you?" I repeated.

Colt tilted his head. "Was what me?"

"The fire at Providence. Someone carried me from those flames, and he wore a t-shirt just like that one." My gaze bounced from Colt to the coach.

"What?" Coach choked out.

Something instinctual told me it wasn't him. He was too surprised. Colt I couldn't read as easily. His black eyes never left mine. He didn't look shocked, but he didn't look guilty either. His face was an impenetrable mask I couldn't make sense of.

"Lacey..." Willa started.

I cut her off. I focused on Colt. "Deny it," I said, suddenly certain it was him. The pieces didn't all fit. But something in my gut yelled loudly. And I wasn't about to ignore it. "It was you, wasn't it? You were there that night?"

It was as if we were alone in the room. Colt's presence blocked everything out. I was so sure. It had to be. But that meant he was also the one who'd murdered my uncle.

A full-body tremble racked my body.

"No, Lacey," he said quietly. "It wasn't me. I do have the same shirt, but I wasn't at the school that night of the fire. Why would I be?"

Breath whooshed from my lungs, relief crashing in on me. He was right. Of course he was right. Whoever had been there that night had known my name. And I hadn't met Colt until the first day of school. It didn't fit. I was losing my mind.

"I think I need to go home now," I said quietly.

Willa put her coffee down on the countertop and came to my side. "I'll drive you."

Colt didn't protest. He simply nodded at his mother, turned, and went back upstairs, leaving me more confused than ever.

5

BANJO

*F*irecrackers went off in my head. Left and right, they bounced around, slamming against my skull, blocking my ears, sending my brain into a spin.

I squeezed my eyes tight and groaned into a scratchy cushion. I opened one eye. I may as well have scrubbed it with sandpaper. The banging started up again, but this time, I was more aware it wasn't firecrackers, and it wasn't actually inside my head. It was at my front door.

"Augie," I called, tongue thick and limp. But no response came. Either he couldn't hear me, wasn't home, or was just being an asshole. The latter was most likely.

I rolled off the couch and dragged myself across our living room, pulling open the door without checking to see who it was.

Rafe barged past me, his shoulder connecting with mine and sending me straight back into the wall. My head clunked off the drywall with a crack. I grunted in surprise, but he took no notice, storming up the stairs with a face full of thunder.

"Good fucking morning to you, too," I mumbled.

If he heard me, he didn't respond. I hauled myself after him, rubbing the back of my head and willing the contents of my stomach to stay put. Alcohol still swirled through my system.

This was not what I was expecting from my Sunday morning. I'd had big plans for last night. I was supposed to spend the night with Lacey. It was all I'd thought about through the party.

She'd said she loved me.

No one had ever said that to me, that I could recall. I couldn't really remember my parents. But I doubted parents who loved their kids abandoned them when they couldn't be bothered anymore. Augie didn't have an emotional bone in his body. He wasn't even capable of like, let alone love. The fact he had no friends and was content in his lifestyle of random women, who were only interested in him as a dick and a tongue, seemed to reinforce that. Colt and Rafe loved me as a brother. I loved them, too, but none of us went around saying it out loud.

Lacey was different. There'd been an honesty in her words that had slapped me in the face, rendering me speechless. I'd wanted to say it back. Wanted to grab her, wrap my arms around her, and tell her I'd fallen for her a little more every time we'd been together.

Except I didn't know how. Then the moment had passed, though I hadn't forgotten. I'd spent the entire party walking around with a shit-eating grin on my face, all because of the knowledge that Lacey Knight was in love with me.

And I was in love with her. So stupidly, head over heels in love with her that I'd follow her to the ends of the earth.

Then the earth as I knew it ceased to exist. That tape... Fuck. It all came rushing back through my alcohol-riddled brain. Someone had filmed us.

It wasn't fucking me.

I raced up the stairs after Rafe, head complaining with each step. By the time I got to my room, Rafe had already torn it apart. I skidded to a halt in the doorway, mouth dropping open at the carnage.

Blankets were ripped from my bed. Clothes yanked from drawers and scattered around the floor. Rafe turned for my shelves. One by one, every item was thrown into the walls, photo frames shattering, trophies snapping.

For a good long moment, I couldn't even move. I just stood there, gaping at my best friend destroying my things. When I finally clicked and my body jolted into action, I grabbed Rafe's arm. "What the fuck are you doing?"

He shook me off, breathing hard, eyes wild. "Where is it?"

"Where's what?" I narrowed my eyes. "Are you high right now? What did you take?"

Rafe's hands connected with my shoulders, shoving me back against the hallway wall. "Where's the fucking camera?"

He didn't even wait for me to answer. He picked up a surfing trophy I'd won two years ago at a local competition. The base was black marble, heavy and solid. Fuck, if he threw that, it would make some damage. Either to a wall, a window, or judging by the look on his face, my head.

"You son of a bitch," he said quietly, some of the rage going out of him. He barked out a laugh. "Why?"

I scowled at him. "You're asking me questions right now? You're the one who's out of his head."

He thrust the trophy at me but didn't let go. "I'm sober, asshole. I'm just seriously fucking pissed you made a sex tape of us. What the fuck were you thinking? Everyone saw it, Banjo. Everyone."

I moved in, getting in his face, because I was suddenly sick of his shit. I had a raging headache from the bottle of whiskey I'd downed after Colt took Lacey inside, and I was in no mood for this. "For the last time, I didn't do shit."

"Then why is there a camera on the base of your trophy?"

I grabbed the trophy from his outstretched hands, ready to tell him whatever drugs he'd taken were giving him hallucinations. But I stopped dead.

He was right.

On the base of the trophy, camouflaged by the dark stone base, was a tiny flat spy camera. I plucked it from the base, peering at it intently. Then back at Rafe, red in the face, fingers clenched at his side.

"I don't know anything about this."

"Bull," Rafe seethed.

"Swear to God. I didn't put this here."

Rafe wasn't listening. He was too caught up in his anger. "Did you and Colt plan this? The two of you together? Wow. I knew you blindly followed him, but I didn't think either of you would stoop this low."

I reached out and grabbed his arm. "Rafe. Fucking listen to me!"

"You know who's going to see that tape now? The whole fucking world. Every scout. Every college dean. Every potential employer." With one last look that seared me alive, he pushed past me. "You better hope she forgives you," he said darkly. "Because I won't."

I let him go. When the front door slammed, it sent a shudder through the entire house. I slumped down against the hallway wall and put my head in my hands. My goddamn life was spiraling out of control, and every move I made seemed to make it worse.

"Now, now, little brother. Why so pouty?"

I lifted my head. Augie stood at the bottom of the stairs that led to his bedroom in the attic. Boxer shorts hung low on his hips, showing off his carved abdomen, cut from hours upon hours in the gym and on a surfboard. His blond hair was shaved close to his scalp, tattoos snaking down his neck and across his broad shoulders.

"Don't start," I said quietly. "I've had a shit night."

"So I heard."

My headache worsened. I wished Augie would shut up and go away. I didn't need his crap this morning. He wandered past me, ruffling my hair as he went.

I batted his hands away.

He just laughed. "Cheer up. You'll thank me once this all dies down and we get to work."

I peered at him warily. "What?" My brain ticked over. I squeezed the little camera between my fingers so tightly the tiny piece of glass broke and splintered into my finger. I flinched, but I couldn't drag my gaze away from my brother.

His grin widened, showing off rows of straight white teeth. They might as well have been fangs.

"It was you, wasn't it?"

Augie put on an air of fake innocence, which confirmed my assumptions.

I pushed to my feet, anger coiling through my muscles. "You taped us?"

He shrugged. "I may have put some surveillance in your room. For your own safety, of course. I've got clients coming in and out at all times of the night and day. Surveillance keeps theft down."

"Liar," I seethed. "You would have told me if that was all it was. Not used a fucking spy camera." I hurled the broken pieces at him, but they were so small and had such little weight they just fell to the carpeted floor.

Augie's act didn't last long. He laughed, like it was the funniest thing in the world. "Fine. I put it there, hoping to get some dirt on your princess. And what do you know? Princess gets it down and dirty, and not just with one guy. Honestly, the three of you put on quite the show. Get your skills from your brother, huh?" He held his hand up for a high five.

I could only stare at him. "What the hell is wrong with you? Why would you film us? And how—no, why—would you play it at my goddamn birthday party? You weren't even fucking invited."

"I know, and that cut me real deep."

My mouth dropped open. "You did it because I hurt your tiny feelings?"

Augie's face turned to stone. He stepped in, eliminating the distance between us. I was an inch taller, but he had it over me in terms of brawn. I was cut and muscled from football practice, but Augie's business was his body. And he had the advantage of ten years of weight training on me.

He stared me down with eyes that didn't blink. "I did it because that girl needed to be taught her place. As did you. You're eighteen now. You've got a week, and then you start working with me."

I opened my mouth, but he cut me off with a glare.

"I ain't fucking asking, Banjo. That stupid girl might have filled your head with dreams of college and a future outside of Saint View. You think she's gonna want you now? After you showed her dirty little secret to everyone she knows? That's you by the way, Banjo. That's all you were ever going to be to her. Dirty. Now get the fuck out of my face and clean this shit up."

6

RAFE

The phone rang out for the fifth time in a row, and I threw my cell onto the passenger seat, not caring when it bounced off and hit the floor mats. "Dammit, Lacey," I muttered to the empty car. I'd been calling her from the minute I woke up this morning. I'd called her the entire way back from Banjo's place. And again now I'd arrived home. I had no idea where she was or if she was even okay.

Hell. How could she be okay? I wasn't.

I unclipped my seat belt and stretched across the center console, wrapping my fingers around my discarded phone.

With my head down, I didn't see my father until it was too late.

The car door swung open, and he fisted my shirt, dragging me out of the car.

I struggled to get my feet beneath me. "Dad! What the hell?"

"Get in the house," he whispered, low and deadly through clenched teeth. He glanced around, checking the neighbors weren't watching, but it was still early and there was nobody but us.

He was the king of keeping his sins behind closed doors. I knew that tone in his voice. I knew what was coming.

I let him haul me up the stairs and shove me through the doorway. My body flushed with a cold sweat.

He slammed the door behind us. My mother stood in the middle of the living room, as perfectly put together as always. To anyone else, she would have looked like the dutiful housewife and mother, ready to welcome her family home. But I saw the nervous tremble in her hands. I saw the way her teeth bit into her lip. The stress lines at the corners of her mouth.

"What did you do?" she asked me.

I didn't even get to answer before the back of my father's hand cracked across my face. Pain exploded in my cheekbone, the force of the blow sending me staggering back.

My mother let out a cry, which hit me right in the chest, but I knew I had to ignore her. My father had used her as a distraction. He was a master of that. If I let my guard down for one second, he'd have me. He didn't fight fair. My mother, my friends, and now Lacey, were my weaknesses.

He had none. Because the man cared about no one but himself. Never had. His only concern was the happy family façade we kept up and his constant pursuit of power.

"I'll tell you exactly what your son did," my dad bellowed. "In the space of one night, he went and ruined everything I've been working toward."

My mother's gaze flicked between me, clutching my cheek and trying to reel in my temper at the lucky blow my father had scored, and Dad, chest heaving, anger radiating from his very pores.

My blood boiled. "I ruined everything for you? Are you

serious right now, old man? Fuck me. My life blows up, but no, this is about you? Narcissistic much?"

Dad's eyes narrowed, and his already vicious expression darkened. "You think you know everything, don't you, Rafe? With your smart mouth and comebacks. Shame you didn't show an ounce of intelligence when you were going down on Lacey Knight with your best friend watching. We're the laughingstock of the town. Didn't you stop and think for one second how this would affect me? Or your mother?"

My mother gasped. "I don't understand."

I couldn't bear to explain. It was too mortifying. There was no reason he'd had to tell her. I hadn't come home last night, crashing on Jagger's couch instead. I knew he'd find out. I knew there'd be consequences. But he didn't have to do it like this. My mother never left the house. She had no friends. He'd put a stop to all that. The only way she would have found out was for one of us to tell her. I would have taken it to my grave. I would have saved her the pain and embarrassment that crumpled her face right now.

But he didn't care.

He never had.

My anger spilled over. How dare he? I pulled myself to my full height and went eye to eye with him. I was his image all over. Height. Looks. Build. I could never escape that I was Todd Simmons' son.

Which meant I was half evil.

Because that was the only word to describe my father. A horrible, evil, self-obsessed man. An abusive father and husband.

The man I hated with every ounce of my being.

"Do you know what a good man would do in this situation, Dad? He'd see that his son had been happy. And that a private moment had been broadcast to everyone he knows. A good dad would see that—"

"He'd see his son is a fag."

I coughed on the hateful word and the way he slung it at me like I was no better than a piece of trash. "You're really going to go there, huh? Never mind it was a girl in that video. You just concentrate on the fact Banjo was there, too."

"You made a sex tape and broadcast it to the world. Did you expect a fucking trophy?"

"No," I yelled in his face. "I expected you to be my father. To see someone betrayed me and be on my side for once. But what an idiot I am, huh? You've never been on my side. Not one day in your miserable life."

"You watch your mouth, Son. "

"I'm not your son. A son is someone you love unconditionally. You want to call me son? Tell me you love me."

His chest rose and fell, his eyes flashing.

"Tell Mom you love her."

He remained silent. The only sound was that of my mother's quiet sobs.

"That's what I thought. You're not my father. And I'm not your son."

I didn't see the punch coming. It cracked straight into my nose, sending blinding pain through my face.

But this time, I didn't just take it. I was so fucking sick of taking everyone shit. Banjo's. Colt's. My dad's.

I charged him, crash tackling him into the nearest wall, our fists flying at each other. My mother screamed, but neither of us stopped. This time, I gave as good as I got.

There was no satisfaction in any of the times my fist connected solidly with some part of him.

I was numb.

We broke apart, both breathing hard. The metallic taste

of blood filled my mouth, but I swallowed it down, not wanting to spit on my mother's perfect carpet. She sobbed in the corner. The noise so heartbreaking I could barely stand it.

Dad wiped at the blood trickling from his nose, then looked down at the back of his hand, seemingly surprised when it was smeared with red. Then he shook his head slowly, a gleam in his eye. "You won't ruin this for me."

Then he picked up his car keys and slammed his way out of the door. Instead of analyzing what he'd meant, I went to my mother's side and held her while she cried.

7

LACEY

The entire drive home, I rehearsed in my head what I'd say to Selina. I had so many things to explain. The tape. My injuries. I peered into a side mirror at my swollen eye and the bruising around my mouth.

"Do you have some makeup I could borrow by any chance?" I asked Willa.

She shot a glance at me. "You don't have to cover it up, you know. Nothing that happened last night was your fault."

"I know. I'm not trying to. But this looks worse than it really is. I want to dull it down a little, for my aunt's sake. She's been through a lot lately."

"So have you by the sounds of it."

I nodded.

"There's a makeup kit in my purse, just there." She reached out and tucked a stray strand of hair behind my ear. The motherly gesture caught me off guard, but I didn't flinch. She'd been so kind to me. I still couldn't work out how someone like Colt had come from her.

I smiled at her gratefully and set to work disguising my bruises.

With a few directions from me, Willa navigated the streets of Providence and parked at the end of my driveway. I stared up at the big house and sighed, dreading the thought of walking inside.

"Do you want me to come with you?"

I shook my head quickly. "You've already done too much. Thank you."

She didn't seem happy about that. She grabbed a pen from a pocket in the door and scribbled something on the back of an old receipt. "My phone number. Call me if you need to. Anytime. Okay?"

Impulsively, I leaned over and gave her a hug.

She squeezed me gently, being careful of my injuries, and when she released me, I got out of the car. I was halfway up the driveway before I even remembered my soiled and torn princess dress. It was still at Colt's place somewhere. I hoped they'd burn it, and that the flames would take the horrible memories of last night with them.

I swallowed down a lump in my throat. Less than twenty-four hours ago, I'd stood right here, wearing that dress, telling a boy I loved him.

Oh, how the mighty fell.

Selina pounced on me the moment I walked in the door, wrapping her arms around me.

Though I tried to hold it in, a yelp of pain still escaped me.

It was only then that Selina really looked at me. She put her hand over her mouth and gasped, her eyes filling with tears. "What happened? I got a message from Jagger that said you were safe."

I shook my head wearily, shuffling over to the couch and slumping into it. "I just can't," I whispered.

"A boy? Someone you knew?"

I nodded.

Selina's eyes went from horrified to sad to fury in the space of three seconds. "I'm calling the police."

She was right. I knew I couldn't let this go.

I drooped against the cushions, a single tear running down my face. I nodded.

She let out a shaky breath and then walked out to make the phone call. I didn't have the energy to move. I just stood there, hating Owen even more for what I was going to have to do. He'd forced this on me. Not only had he attacked me, but now I was also being made to relive it. To say it all out loud to men I didn't know. Who would judge me and determine if I was telling the truth.

Selina came back in, anger flashing in her eyes. "They can't come until later tonight. Apparently, they run on a skeleton staff on Sundays."

I read between the lines. I wasn't a priority.

"Let's get you up to bed. It's Angelique's day off, but I'll run to the store and buy all the things to make some soup. The chicken one is your favorite, right? I'll text Angelique for the recipe."

My empty stomach rumbled at the thought of rich, delicious, body-warming soup.

Selina faked a laugh, though it didn't come close to meeting her eyes. "Right, I'll get some crusty bread to go with it then. And maybe some of those cookies you like? I don't think calories count today."

I smiled weakly, though that sort of comment from her made me wonder exactly how bad I looked. Calories always counted in Selina's book.

She helped me up the stairs without commenting on the fact I was still in Colt's clothes, and pulled the covers back on my neatly made bed. I slid between the sheets, immediately sinking into the mattress. My eyes fluttered closed.

Selina's lips pressed to my forehead. "Rest up, sweetie. I'll be back soon."

I was asleep before she even left the room.

Sometime later, the beeps of the alarm being turned off woke me. My stomach growled again. "Selina?" I called out. "Could you bring me the cookies first, please? I don't think I can wait until the soup is done."

My bedroom door cracked open. "Sorry, I didn't think to bring chocolate."

I gasped at the unexpected voice.

That was not Selina.

Owen stared at me from the doorway, his face a mottled pattern of bruises, but he'd freshly showered and dressed in neat pants and a button down.

"Get out," I yelled at him. I scuttled away, but he was quicker, launching himself across my bed and grabbing my wrist.

"Help!" The scream cut off into breathlessness, icy fingers of fear wrapping around my throat.

Owen rolled his eyes. "There's no one here. Scream your lungs out. This is a big house. The neighbors won't hear."

He was right. They wouldn't. I still didn't even know where my phone was. There was a landline downstairs, but I somehow doubted Owen was going to let me go to wander down there and call the police.

"How did you even get in here? Let go of me."

To my surprise he did.

He held his hands up in mock surrender. "Okay, stop. How about a show of good faith? You unlocked the door in front of me last weekend. I knew the code and took a gamble you wouldn't have changed it. I just want to talk to you."

"You tried to rape me. And beat me half to death in the process."

"Rape? No. You wanted it. And then your little boyfriend got jealous and made mincemeat of my face in retaliation. I spent the night in the hospital, you know? They took photos."

"I wanted it?" I spat in his face. "Is that why I was fighting you off with everything I had?"

"Don't tell me you've never gotten a little rough before. I saw exactly what you've been doing with those Saint View boys. If you're up for another threesome, let me know."

"Get. Out," I seethed. My skin crawled just breathing the same air as he was.

He stood. "Fine. I'm going. But I came to tell you I'm not going to press charges against your ghetto boyfriend. But in return, neither will you."

"You don't control me, Owen."

He moved in closer, grabbing my chin and twisting it sharply. He pressed hard on the bruises around my mouth.

He smiled at my yelp of pain. "Don't I? Looks to me like I do."

He dropped my chin and made his way to the door. But he stopped before leaving. "This is our deal, Lacey. My father is real insistent I tell him who did this. You know, being the police chief, he has a vested interest in catching bad guys."

"The only bad guy is you."

"Stupid girl. Do you even realize what I'm offering you? I checked into your friend. He's eighteen. They'll try him in an adult court. You think my dad won't throw everything he can at him? He'll do time. Aggravated assault and battery.

There'll be no early parole. And the entire thing will be your fault."

The words he left unsaid hung in the air between us. *And nothing would happen to him.* They'd sweep what Owen had done beneath the rug, because he wasn't a poor kid from the slums of Saint View. He was a trust fund baby, the police chief's son, a privileged white man who got to walk away from what he'd done, simply because of his last name.

He left the room without another word. Despite my aches and pains, I got up and crept to the top of the landing, making sure he left the house. Then I ran downstairs and changed the security code.

Colt couldn't go to jail. He'd done nothing wrong. With my heart pounding, I called the police station and told them they wouldn't need to come out after all.

It was only then I let out a shaky breath. My fingers trembled, and tension, mixed with a healthy dose of loathing, coiled deep in my belly.

A serpent waiting to explode.

I screamed into the silence of the house, letting it loose.

I wouldn't live like this.

Owen wouldn't catch me by surprise again. Next time I saw him, he was going down.

8

LACEY

At some point during the next ten days, my phone—rescued from Mojito's Beach Bar by Selina—stopped accepting voicemails and flashed a message that the memory was full.

That wasn't enough for me to check it. I'd had call after call while I recuperated at home. Meredith and Jagger both rang at least once a day. Some were from unknown numbers I didn't dare answer for fear they were either the police, or possibly worse, kids from school who just wanted to gloat about the video. But by far, the most attempts came from Rafe and Banjo. The two of them were incessant, calling multiple times a day and sending text messages until I got so sick of my phone beeping I turned it off.

I didn't want to hear it.

The worst part was, I missed them. I missed Banjo's dirty-blond hair flopping into his eyes and the freckles across his nose. I missed the way my skin tingled at a single look from Rafe.

By day ten of me lying on the couch, binge-watching Netflix, my bruises had mostly healed. Nothing had been broken beneath them, so once they'd faded to a barely-there yellow-gray color, I picked up the phone and called the one person I never thought I would.

Colt answered on the third ring. "Wrong number."

Great greeting. How he got by in life with such charm and charisma was astounding.

"Not the wrong number."

"Lacey?"

"You got it."

He didn't reply, though why I had expected an easy conversation, I didn't know. Colt never made anything easy. We hadn't spoken since the morning after my party. Why would we? He didn't even have my number. I'd had to ask Jagger for his. I blew out a long breath. "How are you?"

"Quit the pleasantries. What do you want?"

"Forget it."

I went to hang up.

"Lacey..." he drawled.

Fuck. A tremor rolled through my body, coming to rest at the spot right between my legs. Damn his voice for being so sexy.

"Can you come over?" I could practically feel his eyebrows rising in surprise. "I just... I need a favor. And yes, I know what I'm asking, and before you even say anything, yes, I'll owe you a favor in return. Two now, I guess, since I still owe you from the party..."

I braced myself for his rejection.

"I'll be there in thirty."

The phone went dead, and I pulled it away from my ear, blinking in surprise before cancelling out of the call.

An unexpected round of butterflies took flight in my belly at the prospect of seeing him again.

If I hadn't just recovered from some pretty serious

injuries, I would have punched myself in the gut to get rid of them.

The phone lit up again with a text from Meredith.

Meredith: *I know you probably aren't reading these, and don't think I'm not coming over there this weekend and dragging you out of that house. But a heads-up, in case you're quietly creepin', Selina was at Edgely today.*

That couldn't be right, surely. Selina had kissed me on the forehead this morning, announced she had a full day with her trainer, a lunch, and then a tennis game. She hadn't mentioned anything about Edgely.

Lacey: *You sure?*

Meredith: *Ah. You're alive.*

Lacey: *Yeah, yeah. I'm alive. Sorry. I know I've been a shut-in, but I needed to catch my breath.*

Meredith: *Understandable. But yes, it was definitely Selina headed into the principal's office.*

Lacey: *Okay, thanks for the heads-up.*

Meredith: *Now you owe me. Lunch on the weekend. No excuses. Pick you up at twelve.*

I wasn't sure what to write back. I knew it was time to quit licking my wounds and face the world again. I hadn't given up on investigating my uncle's murder.

And now, I had my own revenge to exact, too.

Meredith: *I'll take your silence as an agreement.*

I smiled despite myself. Only a true friend would be as persistent as Meredith was, considering how badly I'd blown everybody off lately.

A little voice in my head whispered that she wasn't the only one who'd been calling me non-stop. Banjo and Rafe had been, too. I shoved my phone in my pocket.

Meredith hadn't done anything wrong.

Banjo and Rafe had. I didn't want to talk to either of them.

The door opened, and I tensed until Selina's familiar face popped around the jamb. I breathed out a sigh of relief.

She glanced at me curiously, dumping an armload of shopping onto the couch. "I bought you presents."

"Okay, why? It was only just my birthday."

"Can't I spoil you?"

Her voice was overly high and a little squeaky.

"Are you okay?"

She pulled clothes from the bag, holding them up in front of me and studying them before tossing them onto the floor, only to repeat the process. "I'm great."

She clearly wasn't, but if she didn't want to fess up yet, there was no point in pushing it. Whatever she'd done, or hadn't done, would come out eventually.

"Thanks for the clothes." I scooped them up from the floor and caught a wayward pair of jeans Selina threw across the room. "I'll put them upstairs."

With one hand on the banister, I remembered Meredith's text. "Oh, hey, Selina? Were you at Edgely Academy today?"

Selina froze.

I narrowed my eyes, a sinking feeling in my stomach. "Selina?"

She sighed and flopped dramatically into an armchair. "Fine. You caught me. Yes, I was."

"Why?"

She bit her lip. "To enroll you."

"What?"

She jumped to her feet, holding her hands up in what was obviously supposed to be a calming gesture. "Wait. Hear me out. I didn't end up doing it, you're staying at Saint View."

I breathed out slowly, but relief didn't come. There was something more she wasn't saying. Her story didn't add up. Why would she go there to enroll me but then not? "What aren't you telling me?"

Selina's mouth drew into a straight line. "They're a bunch of stuck-up snobs at that school anyway, sweetheart. And I already called your guidance counselor at Saint View, who thinks the fact you'll have a year of public school beneath your belt will be great for your college applications." Her bright and cheery demeanor changed to something softer, angrier. "So Edgely Academy can go fuck themselves."

"Selina!" I'd never heard her drop an F-bomb in all the years I'd lived with her. "They wouldn't take me?"

Selina ground her molars so hard the noise sent a shiver down my spine. She was pissed. She'd tried covering it in shopping and fake cheeriness, and God, I loved her for that. But the truth was right there in her expression. Edgely Academy didn't want the girl who'd made a sex tape with two boys from Saint View. After everything, this was a new low.

I dropped my gaze to my feet. "I'm never going to live this down, am I?"

"Rubbish," Selina said, coming to take me by the shoulders. "You're going to go off to an amazing college and forget all about these small-town fools. They're all jealous anyway. They wish they could have boys as good-looking as Banjo and Rafe."

A smile flickered at the corner of my mouth then abruptly spread into a grin, followed quickly by laughter.

The mere thought of all the stuck-up snobs in this town being jealous because I'd had a threesome was hilarious.

"What?" Selina asked, amusement in her eyes. "They are. You think Mary-Ann Waller wouldn't love a little three-way action from some young, muscled guys?"

I would have been rolling on the floor laughing if Selina had picked anyone but Mary-Ann Waller. Owen's mom. My smile fell.

Selina wrapped her arms around me.

"I'm glad," I said into her shoulder eventually. "I need to go back to Saint View. I need to finish what I started."

Selina pulled back, holding me by the shoulders. "You're a good person, Lacey. Don't you ever forget it. You hold your head high. You've nothing to be ashamed of."

The doorbell ringing interrupted our moment.

"You expecting someone?" Selina asked.

I nodded.

Selina's expression morphed into relief. "Good. I've been worried about you sitting alone in the dark. I'm glad you've invited a friend over."

I didn't mention Colt and I weren't friends.

Selina disappeared upstairs, and I opened the door.

It was like opening the doorway to Heaven.

With the crown prince of Hell standing in the way.

Colt's usual scowl was firmly in place, his intelligent black gaze leisurely wandering up and down my body. The sun behind him was blinding, casting shadows over his too-handsome face and only strengthening the effortless bad-boy vibe he had going on.

For a long moment, all I could do was drink him in. All of my lady bits went haywire, demanding I grab him, wrap my legs around his waist, and find out exactly what his body and mine could do if we were both naked.

As if he could read my mind, Colt's scowl changed to a smirk. "You gonna let me in? Or did I drive all the way over here just so you could eye-fuck me?"

Heat flushed my cheeks. Goddamn him. "One of these days someone is going to point out what a cocky asshole you are, you know?"

He pushed past me into the house. "You think I don't already know that?" He rounded on me, so he stood behind me, his mouth just above my ear. "I also know you like it."

I hated that he was right.

He sauntered off while I shut the door and let out a long, impressed-sounding whistle. "Nice pad."

"Forgive me if I don't give you a tour. I doubt your ego would fit through the doorways anyway."

My nipples tightened at his chuckle of amusement. I crossed my arms over my chest to hide it, though I suspected he knew exactly what I was doing. He always seemed to know.

"Since you're a shitty host, do you want to tell me why I'm here? It obviously isn't for Devonshire tea."

I snorted at the idea of Colt and I sitting at a little table with a lace cloth, drinking tea and eating scones with cream.

That was never gonna happen.

"I want to learn to fight."

He raised one dark eyebrow. "So go take one of those boxing classes set to music at the gym."

I shook my head. "Don't baby me. We both know those classes are for fitness. Not for fighting. I don't want cardio. I want to be able to protect myself."

"Protect yourself or kick Owen Waller's ass?"

Sometimes his mind-reading ability was a good thing. "Both."

Colt just looked at me.

I stared back.

It went on so long, neither of us saying anything. His gaze was calculating, and I could practically see his mind whirring.

"He came here," I explained.

That got his attention. His gaze darkened. "When? How? Did you tell your aunt? Call the police?"

I shook my head. "Nothing happened. He grabbed my wrist—"

A low growling sound came from Colt.

I trembled. It was hot and possessive, and it shouldn't have made me feel anything. But it did. And I liked it. I liked that the thought of Owen's hands on me pissed Colt off. It pissed me off, too. And that was exactly why I never wanted to be in that situation again.

It ended here. It ended today.

"Teach me to fight," I said again.

"What makes you think I know how?"

"Because I saw what you did to Owen. Those punches weren't sloppy. They were strong. Accurate. Deadly."

He eyed me. "You'll owe me."

"I'll pay you."

"Don't want your money."

"What do you want then?"

His gaze grew heated.

I suddenly couldn't breathe. He filled the room, taking up the space until all I saw was him. He inched closer until I had to tilt my head to look up at him.

"I don't know yet, princess. So let's call it an IOU." He spun on his heel and opened the door, striding out, his black boots scuffing on the driveway.

He paused, one hand on his car door. "We start Monday."

9

LACEY

True to her word, Meredith picked me up just before midday on Saturday. It was almost strange to leave the house. I hadn't been out since the morning after the party. Everything seemed a little brighter and louder than I remembered, but at my best friend's worried expression I tried to relax. I sank back into the plush seats of her car and smiled over at her.

Selina had talked to her about my attack. But Meredith didn't mention it now. Though the way she studied me made me think she was looking for bruises. She wouldn't find any. The last of them were easily covered with makeup.

"I'm glad you came. We need to have a powwow."

"We do?"

"Rafe called me."

I twisted in my seat, mouth gaping open. "What?"

Meredith shrugged, keeping her focus on the road. "What did you expect him to do, Lace? You wouldn't talk to him."

"So he started ringing around my friends like some stalker? There's a reason I won't talk to him!"

Meredith nodded. "I know. And I told him that. Told him to give you time..."

"You should have told him to go to hell."

Meredith bit her lip. "He was really upset. He's only just gone back to school. Apparently, Banjo hasn't come back at all."

"How the hell do you know that?"

"Jagger."

"How many other people have you spoken to behind my back? My teachers? Principal Simmons?"

Unhappiness tugged at Meredith's pretty bow mouth. "Don't be mad," she said softly. "We're all worried about you. You completely went dark on us."

I shuffled in my seat so I was facing the front again. I took a deep breath. I knew she would never deliberately hurt me. It just felt like I was the subject of everyone's gossip right now. And truthfully, I had no problem with her talking to Jagger. I was actually glad the two of them were getting along. I wanted my old life to mesh with my new one. That was what the party had been about...before it all went to shit.

"Sorry." I threaded my fingers through the strap on my purse so I'd have something for my hands to do. "I know I worried you. I didn't mean to. It was just a lot."

"A whole lot of boys," Meredith quipped. Then shot me a nervous smile. "Too soon?"

I couldn't help but laugh. She was always so inappropriate. "Yes too soon!"

"Okay, okay." A little of the tension eased out of her shoulders. "Rafe said to tell you he had nothing to do with it."

I cocked my head to one side and fought back the urge to plug my fingers in my ears and yell, "La la la, not listening."

Fact was, I was going to have to face Rafe and Banjo at some point. If I couldn't even have a conversation *about* them, how was I going to handle seeing them in person? "Did you believe him?"

Meredith nodded solemnly. "He sounded bad. Broken."

Despite how angry I still was, my heart clenched. I still cared about Rafe. If he'd been the one behind making the sex tape, and then broadcasting it to the world, would he seriously be calling my best friend to plead his case? Why would he bother? That made no sense.

A tiny bit of hope crept into my shattered heart.

Meredith reached over and squeezed my hand. "When are you going back to school?"

"Did Selina put you up to this?"

Meredith shook her head. "No. I swear. If you need more time, then take it. But this is your senior year, and you aren't going to let what happened stop you. You've had two weeks. Time to get back on the horse, don't you think?"

"Actually, I agree. I feel better. And I've got things that need doing."

"A grade point average to uphold. Parties to go to. New boys to find. Or maybe old ones to forgive?"

"Actually, I was thinking more that I need to get back to working out who murdered my uncle."

Meredith stiffened. "Really? That didn't end so well last time."

"I know. I realized I've been going about it the wrong way. My suspect list is longer than ever, thanks to some information I gleaned from the football coach. Apparently, those shirts are a dime a dozen. Half the male population of Saint View probably has one stashed away somewhere."

Meredith chewed that over. She navigated through an

intersection then brought the car to a stop in front of our favorite café. "So the shirts are a dead end. What else do we have to go on?"

"Nothing from that night that I can think of. I think we're searching in the wrong place. Uncle Lawson had to have known his attacker, right? Statistics say most attacks are by someone the victim knows. A random break-and-enter gone wrong doesn't make sense. There's no cash kept at a school over the weekend. What would they have been there for? It had to be personal. So we need to focus on the people he knew. Find out who had a motive to kill him."

"Everybody loved Lawson, though."

The headshots of Lawson that had been shoved inside my locker said otherwise. I couldn't forget the horrible words, scrawled across them in blood-red Sharpie.

Liar. Cheat. Rapist.

Those words were personal. Gillian and Colt swore they didn't know where the photos came from, but did I believe them? If they knew more, they weren't giving up the details.

I was so sick of trying to read between the lies.

I wanted some cold, hard proof.

"I need to get a copy of the police report. Maybe there are some details in there I don't know. And talk to Selina. And his friends."

"Don't you think the police would have already done that?"

I shrugged. "Maybe. But if they did, it didn't get them anywhere. Maybe something they say will trigger a memory."

Meredith gave me a patient smile. "If I say burgers and fries, will that mean anything to you? Because right now, I want to have lunch with my best friend. Searching through your uncle's life will have to wait until after my belly is full."

On Sunday night, I deleted every message from my phone without reading the multitude of unopened ones. I deleted all the voicemails, too. Going through them all was a task too big to undertake. I knew they'd drag me down to the deep, dark place I'd been in after the party, and I didn't want to go there again. Seeing Colt on Friday, and Meredith yesterday, had awakened something in me. For the first time in two weeks, I felt almost like me again. I had drive. Purpose. I knew what I had to do.

Find out who murdered my uncle. And take down Owen without landing Colt in jail. At least I had a plan for one of them.

After lunch, Meredith had driven me to a couple of Lawson's friends' houses. They'd all been happy, if surprised, to see me and had answered all my questions about Lawson patiently. But no one had said anything out of the ordinary. According to them, he was the Lawson I knew: father, husband, school principal, player of golf, drinker of whiskey. If there were skeletons in his closet, his closest friends didn't know about them.

But on Sunday, my thoughts turned to school. I laid my clothes out for my first day back, checked I had all my books and pens, and then I texted Jagger to let her know I'd be returning to Saint View student life. She called immediately, squealing into my ear.

Her excitement did little to calm the nausea in my stomach, though. It plagued me all night, and when my alarm went off on Monday morning, I was still tired. For half a second, I thought about rolling over and burying my head in the sand some more.

But I was better than that. I lifted myself from my bed

and forced my feet toward the shower. Thirty minutes later, I was ready and headed downstairs.

Voices babbled in the kitchen, and I poked my head in, wondering who Selina had over at this time of the morning. Her friends rarely rose before ten.

"Lacey!" Jagger screamed, launching herself across the kitchen. She caught me unaware, and both of us tumbled to the tiled floor with a thump.

"Oh my God. Ow, Jag." I struggled beneath her. "I don't have time for any more injuries."

She kissed my cheek and hugged me anyway. Despite the fact she was half on top of me and squishing my legs, I hugged her back. She scrambled to her feet and then pulled me up.

"You okay?" Selina asked, worry in her voice.

"Fine, Mom."

Selina grinned wide. She loved it when I called her that. It made me happy, too.

She handed me an overloaded bag of food, which Jagger immediately pounced on and riffled through.

Selina nudged it back in my direction. "So you don't have to eat cafeteria food on your first day back. I figure it's probably going to be a little rough, you don't need an upset stomach as well."

I kissed her goodbye, and then Jagger grabbed my hand and led me out to the driveway where her car sat in the morning sun. I shivered at the drop in temperature since the last time I'd been out at this time of morning. I'd manage to hibernate right through Halloween last week, and before long, we'd be staring down the barrel of Thanksgiving.

Jagger chattered happily all the way back to Saint View, while I got more and more nervous with each mile that rolled by. My stomach lurched as we drove into the parking lot, and I saw a familiar face waiting by the school entrance.

"Did you tell him I was coming back to school today?" I hissed at Jagger.

Rafe's ice-blue eyes drew my gaze. He seemed anxious, but he didn't look away.

"He's been there every morning since he came back to school, just in case you showed up. He's been waiting for you."

"Why would he do that?"

"Because he didn't want you walking in alone. Today isn't going to be easy, Lace. You know that. So does he. He had to deal with it all last week, by himself."

I let my gaze run over him. His dark, neatly brushed and styled hair. Black glasses perched on his nose. Long-sleeved T-shirt with the logo of some obscure band I'd never heard of. He strode to my door, a man on a mission, his gaze never faltering from mine. His intensity sent awareness through my entire body.

"Gotta face him sometime, babe." Jagger got out of the car but leaned back in the open door. "I'll give you two a minute and meet you by the gate."

I knew she was right. I slowly climbed out, straightening until I was face-to-face with him.

His gaze burned. It was hot and fevered, tracing over my features rapidly, as if reassuring himself I was okay. Or maybe that I was there at all.

I couldn't breathe. It hurt too much. All the shame and embarrassment from that night flooded back.

"Dammit, Lacey. You scared the hell out of me. I didn't think you were coming back."

"Would you have even cared?"

He looked as if I'd punched him in the gut.

"Of course I care. You're all I've thought about for the past two weeks. Didn't you listen to my messages?"

"No," I replied honestly.

He stepped in, and damn my stupid hormones, just the nearness of him had my heart rate up. I hated how badly I wanted him.

He dropped his voice so only I could hear. "Then let me tell you again. To your face, so I know you heard it. I had nothing to do with that sex tape. Not the making of it or showing it at the party. I was as shocked as you were."

I pressed my fingers against the metal of Jagger's car, trying to keep myself steady. "How am I supposed to believe that? Banjo is your best friend."

"Not anymore. I went over there and found the camera. Haven't spoken to him since."

A dull throb echoed through my heart for their broken friendship. But also for me. A tiny part of me had always whispered that Banjo wasn't capable of this.

But now I had the proof he was.

Rafe reached out one hand, linking his pinky finger around mine. "I swear it on my life, Lace. I didn't do it."

There was pure, unfiltered honesty in his words. I stared down at our entwined fingers. "I believe you."

Rafe put his fingers beneath my chin and tilted my head up.

His eyes were full of hope. I almost hated myself for what I was about to say. "But I lost that trust, and I don't know how to get it back."

Rafe visibly deflated in front of me. His breath rushed from his chest on a devastated exhale.

"I'm sorry," I whispered. And I truly was. Because this was hurting me as much as it was hurting him.

Eventually, he nodded and pulled his shoulders back.

"I'm not." His voice took on a strength it hadn't had before. "Because this isn't it. You're what I want, Lacey Knight. You're *who* I want. And I was *this* close to having you. I'm not giving up."

I shook my head. "How are we supposed to come back from this? I just don't believe we can."

"Then I'll believe for the both of us. I'll show you, Lacey. Every day. I'll show you I'm the guy you thought I was. And that starts right now. I'm walking into that school by your side."

"Not trying to eavesdrop or anything," Jagger called. "I'll be on your other side, but we've got five minutes until the bell. Let's roll."

I glanced between the two of them. Jagger's gaze was encouraging. But it was Rafe's I focused on. He looked ready to kill anyone who dared say a word to me.

Without resolving anything, we walked into the wolves' den.

10

LACEY

*P*osters for an upcoming 'Fall Ball' lined the halls and classroom doors, but I paid them little attention. A school dance was the last thing on my mind. The whispers in the corridors were harder to ignore. I quickly got used to conversations stopping every time I entered a room. It wasn't even restricted to the other kids. Teachers eyed me, some with pity, some with disdain. Both hurt.

A crappy video someone had managed to catch at the party was doing the rounds. I saw the other kids on their phones, peering up from them whenever I walked by. A few times, I'd been unlucky enough to hear some of the audio and I'd wanted to crawl into a pit of snakes.

I hovered at the doorway of the cafeteria, remembering when all I'd been worried about was finding out who'd pulled me out of that fire. I still desperately wanted to know, but I wasn't here for that reason anymore. Now I was back because I refused to let these kids think I was ashamed. I'd use the emotion building inside me, not just for surviving school but also for the revenge I needed to take on Owen.

Not that I could bear the thought of being near him at the moment. But his time would come.

First though, I had to deal with lunch period. I took a deep breath and pushed open the door. It wasn't my imagination that all conversation came to a screeching halt and a hundred sets of eyes swiveled in my direction. I clutched my pre-packed lunch to my chest and searched the room for Jagger, before I remembered the text message she'd sent me earlier. She'd gone and gotten herself a detention, so she wasn't going to be here. *Shit.* I was still sort of avoiding Rafe, though I would have been happy to see his face right now. But there was no Rafe either. Hell, I might have even tried my luck with Colt, but he was also noticeably absent from his usual spot beside Gillian.

Gillian's smile was vicious. She stared me down, but then someone called me, and I turned away to see a blonde girl I vaguely recognized from my gym class. She sat with a mixed group of girls and guys. I frowned. I didn't think we'd ever spoken before, but her smile was wide, and after the frost positively rolling off Gillian, a friendly face was welcome, even if I couldn't remember her name.

The girl stood as I approached. Marnie, I realized with a jolt, proud of myself for recalling her name. I smiled tentatively at her.

She grinned back. "Hang on a second, I'll clear you a place."

I glanced along the table full of students. "It's okay, there's no free seats—"

Marnie laughed, shoving trays out of the way. "But you don't need a seat, do you? Just something to lie on? Here you go, hop on up." She patted the tabletop, while the others burst into laughter.

Embarrassment heated my cheeks.

One of the guys jumped up on the table instead, spreading himself so he lay facedown, head closest to me. Bracing himself on his forearms, he gyrated his hips against the laminate, simulating sex while Marnie moaned and carried on behind him.

Their laughter echoed in my ears, and all I could do was stand there in shock. The boy stared at me as he air-humped the table, his eyes half-lidded in what was probably supposed to be a sex face. "That how you like it, baby?" he purred.

Something inside me snapped. My lunch slipped from my fingers, the brown paper bag spilling its contents all over the floor. It hadn't been purposeful, but it distracted the group long enough. I grasped both sides of the boy's head and then slammed his face down as if it were a basketball.

His nose hit the table with a crack, blood spurting everywhere.

His scream of pain cut through the laughter and Marnie's fake moans.

For a moment, there was pure silence. Pure peace.

And I reveled in it, all while staring at what I'd done.

The boy scrambled to get off the table, clutching at his busted nose, blood dripping down between his fingers. "You stupid bitch," he screamed.

He came at me, and I backed away, heartbeat thrumming against my chest. *Shit.* That had not been a smart move. I was alone in a crowd of people who hated me. But I hadn't even thought about it. I'd just acted on impulse.

"Apologize," Rafe's voice came from behind me.

I spun around, my mouth dropping open. So much for having my back. "What? I'm not apologizing for anything."

He grabbed my hand and pulled me slightly behind him. Tingles shot up my arm before I could pull it from his grip. I could still see the other boy, his seething anger pouring from him as quickly as blood ran from his nose. Rafe took another half step in front of me, cutting off the other boy's path. A hush came over the entire cafeteria.

"Not you, Lacey. Him. Apologize. What the fuck even was that? Did you threaten her with sex? You fucking piece of shit."

Rafe was a ball of barely concealed rage. His entire body coiled tight, his fingers clenched at his sides. I flinched at another big, male body moving in behind me, but breathed a sigh of relief when it was Aaron, Jagger's sort of boyfriend, and Rafe's teammate on the football field. One by one, the other football players got out of their chairs and pushed their way into the aisle, standing behind me and Rafe.

A lump built in my throat.

The boy lost his bravado. "Sorry."

Rafe leaned in. "You pull that shit again, to *any* girl, *ever*, and I'll come for you. You remember that. Now get the fuck out of here. You're getting blood on my shoes."

I glanced down. Rafe's shoes were as clean as I'd ever seen them. I wondered if he'd borrowed that line from a Mafia movie. I smiled at the thought.

Marnie and her crew backed off, most leaving the table and scuttling out the big glass doors that led to the quad. Rafe didn't let go of my wrist as he turned us to face the football team. He nodded at them, and they slapped him on the shoulder, heading back toward their seats.

Aaron put his arm around my shoulders and squeezed. "You okay, kid?"

I assured him I was fine, and then he was gone too, leaving me alone with Rafe. But I could still feel the eyes of the room on us, even if they were now wide with shock and fear.

"I need to get out of here," I whispered.

He linked his fingers through mine, and this time, I didn't pull away. We left the cafeteria behind us, and I followed him through the quiet corridors to the library.

The monitor looked up from behind her desk. "You can't be in here during lunch... Oh."

Rafe gave her a nod, and she sat back down. Ah. The power of the Untouchables, the boys who ruled the school. I'd almost forgotten about that. As much as I still thought that sort of thing was ridiculous, it came in handy when I needed a quiet place to hide.

The library was one large open room. Tables for studying in groups were over to the right, while the left side boasted shelves full of books. Rafe led me to the back of the room, then pulled me behind the shelves, out of the librarian's sight.

I slumped against the solid metal structures and the books sitting neatly atop them, suddenly completely exhausted.

He grinned at me. "You're such a badass."

I shook my head. "Not exactly. If you and the team hadn't rescued me..."

"Not rescued. Backed you up. That asshole deserved everything he got."

"You saw it all?"

Rafe's gaze was full of fiery anger. "If you hadn't slammed his head into the table, then I would have. You did good, princess. Stuck up for yourself. I'm proud of you."

I gave him a weak smile, still shaken.

"It made me realize something, though," Rafe said.

"Oh?"

"I owe you an apology, too."

"For what?"

He tugged me down to the floor, and we sat side by side, backs leaning on a row of encyclopedias that were older than I was. "I told you I didn't know about the tape. And that's the truth. But after it came out... I should have gone straight after you. Instead I was too busy focusing on who did it. I nearly punched Colt out over it. I was so riled up Jagger and Aaron had to force me into a car and drive me home." His lips lifted in a small smile. "She's surprisingly strong when she's protecting someone she loves, if you hadn't noticed."

I knew exactly how headstrong Jagger was when she wanted to be. "It's okay. I'm glad she was there to look out for you. And all the rest." I shrugged. "It wasn't your fault. Nobody knew what Owen was capable of."

He brushed a lock of hair out of my eye. "I'm still sorry."

"Then I forgive you." There was nothing to forgive, but I knew he needed to hear it, anyway.

A little of the stiffness eased from his muscles. "I missed you. That night we were supposed to be together..."

Me. Him. Banjo. The thought of it tightened my nipples.

He inched closer, his gaze dipping to my lips. "I still want you, Lacey. So bad."

My breath hitched. I believed him when he said he'd had nothing to do with what had happened. He'd had my back just now. And he'd apologized. That went a long way to gaining back my trust. Butterflies rioted around my belly. They remembered what it felt like to kiss Rafe. To be in his arms. They remembered the intense attraction that had never been fully realized.

And so did I.

"I can't," I whispered. "Not yet."

Rafe nodded. "I know. And it's okay. We went slow once before, I can do it again."

I threw him a bone in the form of a tiny smile. "Not too slow, okay?"

He grinned, and it was contagious.

"Tonight?" he asked. "A date?"

I went to say yes then remembered I couldn't. "Shit. I want to, I swear. But I can't. Colt is coming over."

Rafe's eyes widened. "To your house?"

"He's teaching me to fight."

I waited for some sort of reaction from him. I was well aware the thought of me fighting, when I was barely coordinated enough to tie a shoelace, was laughable.

"Why are you staring at me?" Rafe asked eventually.

"I'm waiting for you to tell me fighting is a terrible idea."

"Why would I do that? You already proved today what a badass you are. If Colt can help you with that some more, then I think it's great."

"You're making it hard not to kiss you right now."

His eyes twinkled. "I wouldn't mind if you did."

But I shook my head. "Tomorrow? My place, after school. We'll hang out. Or something."

"I like the idea of 'or something.'"

So did I. But we'd see how I felt tomorrow. Today had been one huge step in the right direction for Rafe and me. But if I'd learned anything recently, it was tomorrow was never a given. Especially not in Saint View.

11

LACEY

Colt never showed. By eight, I'd quit checking my phone every five minutes, wondering if he was going to at least call to cancel. That was hardly Colt's style. But I couldn't shake my disappointment. I'd wanted this training session to learn what he knew. I wanted to stop being a victim.

I wanted Colt.

I ground my teeth together and sat in my window seat, staring out at the dark night beyond. From our vantage point on the top of a hill, my bedroom overlooked the valley. The lights of Providence, and Saint View beyond, gleamed like jewels.

A flash of headlights at the end of my drive caught my attention. My muscles tensed as the lights cut out, leaving the car in a pocket of complete darkness. Dread crept down my spine. It had been awhile since I'd heard anything from Owen, but I wasn't naive enough to think he'd forgotten about me. I reached for my phone, ready to dial nine-one-one, when it rang in my hand. The shrill noise scared me, and I fumbled to catch it, while trying not to look away from the car. Had the driver gotten out? I couldn't tell. I glanced down at the phone.

"Colt?"

"Quit gawking at me and get down here."

Instant relief loosened my muscles. I peered into the darkness once more. If I focused really hard, the shape of the car could have been the same as Colt's. But I had to be certain. "Why are you outside my house at this hour?"

He blew out an impatient sigh, obviously irritated with me. "You wanted to train. I said Monday. It's Monday. So get down here. Or did you chicken out?"

I narrowed my eyes, though I knew he wouldn't be able to see it. "Who trains at this time? My aunt has already gone to bed."

"What is she, eleven?"

I didn't reply. Outside, the headlights flicked on and the car's engine roared to life. Definitely Colt's car.

"Leaving in two minutes, princess. Get your pretty ass down here, or forget it, deal's off."

I hung up without saying goodbye. In a whirlwind, I raced around my bedroom, pocketing my phone, keys, and jacket. Thank God I was still dressed. I raced down the stairs, grabbing my boots from beside the front door and opened it quietly, slipping through. Hopefully, Selina wouldn't notice I was gone. I slowed my pace in the driveway, not wanting Colt to think I'd been running around at his beck and call.

His car began to roll down the street.

"Wait," I yelped. I took off after him again, running along the passenger side. I thumped a fist against the trunk, but Colt just looked over his shoulder lazily and raised a condescending eyebrow.

Oh, fuck him.

I put on a burst of speed and yanked the door handle. The door flew open, and I threw myself inside, slamming the door closed behind me.

"'Bout time. You're fitter than I thought you'd be. That's something at least."

I glared at him. "You couldn't have waited an extra ten seconds before taking off?"

"Where's the fun in that?"

"I hate you."

"Yeah, yeah, heard that before."

I pulled my seat belt on and crossed my arms over my chest. God, he was infuriating. I shoved my feet in my shoes while he navigated out of Providence and back to Saint View. The houses grew smaller and shabbier with every passing mile, until we were in one of the poorest parts of his neighborhood.

"Where are we going?" I asked, the edge of nerves in my voice. I itched to reach over and lock the doors. Though logic told me the monster I should be most scared of was sitting right beside me.

"The industrial area."

"Want to explain why? I thought we were training?"

Colt spun the wheel, making a sharp right-hand turn. "We are. Sort of. This is where your training starts. You need to know what you're in for."

"What's the industrial area got to do with it?"

He didn't answer. Just pointed ahead.

"Whoa."

In front of us, a crowd gathered in a huge empty parking lot. Old factory buildings lined the wide road, but most looked abandoned. There was a gas station with the lights on a way down the road, but otherwise it was completely deserted. Cars formed a horseshoe shape around the parking lot, headlights all pointing inward to make a pool of light. The cars' occupants all seemed to be outside though, mingling in groups, a mixture of men and women.

Colt parked his car on one end of the horseshoe and took his seat belt off, getting out of the car without a word to me.

I scrambled to follow, not wanting to be left behind. I shifted close to his side.

He chuckled. "Scared, princess?"

"No."

He stopped and grasped my chin, forcing me to look up at him. Any lingering sign of humor evaporated. "Cut it out. For one, quit lying to me. You're scared. Admit it. Feel it. Then let it go. Nothing is going to happen to you here tonight. Not while you're with me."

I let out a shaky breath. There was a security in his gaze. I believed him when he said nothing would happen to me with him by my side. And I liked the way that felt. I let go of the nerves, and the uncertainty, and nodded.

"Good. Now let's go."

I walked beside him to the crowd, making sure my head was held high and there was confidence in my step. I took in the other women as I passed. None paid any attention to me. Some were dressed as if they were going to a club—heels and skinny jeans and full faces of makeup. Others were dressed more similarly to me in sneakers and hoodies. Some hung around their men. Others stood in little groups, laughing with friends.

At the edge of the pool of light, a burly guy had stripped down to a pair of athletic shorts. He jogged on the spot, then threw a few air punches after jumping up and down and rolling his shoulders.

"What is this?" I asked quietly.

"Street fight. Organized. We do this every Monday."

I gawked at him. "We? As in, you fight here?"

He shrugged.

An older guy, bundled up in a jacket and beanie, spotted us and disentangled himself from the woman he'd been talking to. He trotted up and slapped hands with Colt before pulling him in for a man hug. Then he turned to me, confusion etched into his features. "Who's this?"

Colt let me answer for myself.

Despite the nervous energy coursing through my system, my upbringing had me holding my hand out for him to shake. "Lacey Kn—"

The man cut me off with a sharp noise from the back of his throat. "I'm Buck. We don't do last names here. Better we don't know them if the cops question you."

My eyes widened. What the hell were they doing here? Why would the cops need to question anyone? I shot a panicked look at Colt, but his calm expression reminded me of what he'd said a moment before. Feel it. Let it go. I breathed out, reminding myself he'd promised to keep me safe.

I still believed he would.

The older man lost interest in me and turned back to Colt. "Need you to fight tonight, bro."

My heart stuttered.

But Colt shook his head. "Nope. Just watching."

Buck's face turned pleading. "Please, man. Joey pulled out last minute, and there's a big crowd here that are gonna be pissed if I don't put on a show."

"You fight then."

Buck shook his head. "Can't do that no more, man. Got a baby at home now."

"No shit?"

The man smiled softly. "Yeah." His expression hardened again. "But you don't. And I need you."

Colt sighed and eyed the man warming up. "He good? I don't recognize him."

Buck nodded. "One of the best."

A slow grin crossed Colt's handsome face. "Better than me?"

Buck shrugged. "There's a good chance he'll kick your ass, yeah."

"I'm in."

"What?" I choked out. Was he deaf?

Colt shot me a warning look.

"That guy is huge."

"We came here to see if you could handle it, princess. You want to back out now, you can go sit in the car and we'll forget the whole thing. You can go right on being scared of your own shadow. Or you can stand over there with Buck and the others and watch me take this guy down. And then tomorrow, I'll teach you how I did it."

I stared at him for a long moment, then held my hand out. "Give me your keys."

He raised an eyebrow. "Seriously? You want to go sit in the car?"

"No, I want them because you're a cocky son of a bitch. And if that guy kills you, I still want to be able to get home tonight."

Buck chuckled.

Colt's lips curled upward. He leaned in, lips brushing the shell of my ear. "It's seriously fucking hot when you talk like that, you know?"

I shoved him away. Because it was his presence that got me hot. In more places than one. He grabbed his keys from his pocket and made a show of dropping them into my hand. Then shrugged out of his leather jacket and tossed it at me.

It hit my chest and slid to the ground. "You want me to hold your shit? Ask."

Amusement danced all over his face. "You're such a fucking firecracker. Please, Lacey. Will you hold my things while I go kick this guy's ass?"

I held my arms out. Colt crouched, sweeping his jacket from the ground, his gaze burning over my thighs and belly as he straightened. He placed the jacket in my arms before pulling off the t-shirt he'd worn below it.

My brain short-circuited.

I didn't even try to pry my gaze from his body. His broad shoulders were sculpted from pure muscle. A solid chest led down to abs cut from steel. V-lines dipped either side of his hips, a light dusting of dark hair beneath his navel.

A body made for sin.

One I instantly wanted to do bad, *bad* things with.

"Ah shit," he mumbled.

I had to drag my gaze off his tanned skin to even notice he was looking over my shoulder. His body tensed and, as if we were somehow linked, mine did as well. I turned, expecting to find some other gigantic man Colt would stupidly agree to fight.

Instead I found a petite blonde cheerleader.

Who was somehow scarier.

"What are you doing here, Gillian?" Colt asked.

She completely ignored the fact I was standing right there, holding half his clothes. She strode up and placed her hands on his chest possessively, stretching up onto her toes to kiss the corner of his mouth. He didn't respond.

A tiny thrill raced through me at that.

If Gillian noticed, she didn't let on. "I came to watch my man fight."

He picked up her hands and gently pushed them back toward her. "You haven't spoken to me in two weeks. I'm not your man anymore. You know that. It's why you haven't called."

Gillian's face hardened. "Are you serious?"

"As a heart attack."

Breath stalled in my lungs.

"That's really what you want?"

He shook his head. "Sick of being your plaything, Gilly. I ain't got time for the drama."

Her laugh was bitter. "But you do have time for hers?"

He didn't deny it.

Holy shit.

"She's fucking your best friends! What are you going to do, jump in on that, too?"

My fingers clenched into Colt's jacket. But Colt's calm expression didn't change.

I tried to mimic it. Gillian, of all people, was not worth getting upset over.

He was better at it than I was. "Who I fuck, or don't fuck, is none of your business anymore."

Her mouth pulled into a tight line. "That's a two-way street, you know."

He shrugged. "I gotta go warm up. See you around."

Gillian glared after him. Then whirled on me. "You want my sloppy seconds? Take them. But remember, princess. I had him first. And he'll be back. We both know it."

She flounced off to a group on the other side of the lot. She sidled right up to a guy who had to be a good ten years older and pressed up against his side, pulling his head down to whisper something in his ear.

I looked away and back to Colt before I could see the guy's reaction.

A hush came over the crowd, and Colt entered the makeshift ring, made by the horseshoe of headlights. He rolled his shoulders once and tilted his head to one side, cracking his neck. A sudden flurry of movement and conversation sparked around me. Money exchanged hands as people laid down bets.

"You want to put some money on your boy?" Buck asked me.

Colt watched me from the center of the circle. I locked on to his gaze but reached into my purse and produced two crisp hundred dollar notes from my wallet. I held them up so he could see, one eyebrow raised in challenge, then I handed them over to Buck.

Buck grinned and snatched the money from my fingers.

The smug smile I loved to hate curled Colt's lips. Buck handed me a slip of paper, and I shoved it into my pocket without glancing at it.

"Don't lose," I mouthed.

Colt shook his head and went on with his warm-ups. Across the circle, Gillian had her tongue down her new friend's throat. I grimaced. That hadn't taken long. The little looks she shot Colt's way told me it was all for show, but I hoped he didn't notice.

I didn't care about the money I stood to lose, but I didn't want to watch Colt get his ass handed to him either.

A shiver coursed down my spine. It was cold enough that our breaths fogged in the night air. Without thinking about it too much, I pulled on Colt's jacket and tugged it tight around my smaller frame.

His familiar scent hit me in the face. His cologne mixed with a clean, fresh soap smell tantalized my nose. It was the same scent as the hoodie he'd loaned me when I'd stayed at his house. The one I still hadn't given back because it smelled of him. His scent was as alpha as he was. Powerful. Possessive. Dangerous.

"All right, all right," Buck called, walking into the center of the circle. "Let's get this show on the road. Betting is closed. You all know the rules. Tap out or knock-out. Nothing in between. Colt on my left, Loch on the right. You two wanna shake hands or some bullshit?"

Neither fighter showed any such sportsmanship.

Buck smirked. "Get on with it then."

A cheer went up from the crowd and Buck jogged out of the way. My heart thumped unevenly, my gaze pinned to Colt. He had a lazy, smug expression on his face as he and Loch circled each other, both men taking their time. They were both tall. I suspected Loch might have been early twenties, but his body was no more filled out than Colt's. Unlike Colt, who practically strolled around the ring, Loch bounced lightly on his toes, eyeing his competitor carefully.

With a speed that surprised everyone, Loch bounded forward and cracked his fist against Colt's jaw.

Colt didn't even try to duck. He just took it, his head whipping to the side with the force of the blow. Around me, a chorus of 'oohs' rang out, and I flinched, twisting away from the sight.

When I forced myself to look back, Colt was grinning, as if he'd enjoyed the punch that was already coloring his cheekbone.

Crazy asshole.

But that burst of pain seemed to get him in the game. Loch threw a few more punches, and I watched with my mouth hanging open. Colt ducked and weaved, somehow avoiding them all. Blood trickled from a cut that had opened up on his cheekbone, but he didn't seem to notice.

Loch, frustration rising with the lack of punches connecting with anything but thin air, put all his weight behind his next hit. It sailed toward Colt's already busted cheek, but at the last second, Colt slammed his forearm against Loch's, blocking the punch. His free arm shot out and delivered a double jab to Loch's throat.

A combination of surprise and pain morphed the older man's features, but my heart soared. Loch's next punch was slower.

Colt ducked, the punch sailing over his head and leaving Loch's side unprotected. He followed up with a hard blow to the man's ribs.

Loch howled in pain, one of his ribs cracking.

Everyone, me included, winced at the noise.

Loch doubled over, gasping for breath.

"Tap out," Colt said, breathing hard.

Loch shook his head.

I cringed, foreseeing what was coming.

Colt sighed. He spun and let loose with a roundhouse kick to Loch's temple that sent the man sprawling to the ground.

He didn't move.

Buck wandered in, peered at the unconscious man on the ground, and slapped Colt on the back. "Didn't think you had it in you, kid." He raised Colt's left arm, and the crowd, at least the half who'd bet on Colt, let out a loud cheer.

Me included.

Gillian stared daggers at me from across the lot. She stormed away from her plaything toward her car, and took off, her tires kicking up gravel behind her.

Colt wandered over, too close to me, but I didn't back away. The glint in his eye was wild.

I couldn't help but grin at him. "Nice job."

"Nice?"

"What's wrong with nice? What do you want me to say?"

"That was more than nice. That was a thing of beauty."

I snorted. "You and your ego. If it was more than nice, he wouldn't have landed that first punch. You want an awesome? Next time, don't go getting your cheek split open."

Colt touched his hand to his face, interest morphing his features when it came away with blood on his fingers. "Shit. Didn't even feel that. It bad?"

I peered at it. "Could probably use a stitch or two."

He groaned. "Get your money from Buck."

Buck moved through the crowd when he saw us coming and pushed a wad of bills into my hand without me even producing the ticket stub he'd given me earlier. Then he handed Colt an even bigger stack. A *much* bigger stack. My eyes widened.

"You need to come back and start fighting again. I can get you on the roster."

Colt shook his head. "Told you. Not right now. Got other things going on."

Buck gave me a sidelong glance. "Talk some sense into your boy, would you? He makes me a mint every time he fights."

I didn't say anything. I should have set Buck straight. Told him Colt wasn't mine to convince of anything. But I didn't, because dammit, something deep inside me enjoyed the way it sounded.

Colt eyed me, that knowing look on his face again, like

he could read all my deepest, darkest secrets. His cut was getting blood everywhere.

I fished through my purse and came up with a package of Kleenex. I pulled some out and handed them to Colt who pushed them to the cut on his cheek, wincing.

"I'll be fine in a minute," he said.

Remembering the way he hadn't pushed me about going to the hospital after Owen's attack, I didn't argue. But his blood was soaking through the tissue already. That cut needed attention. I glanced up the road toward the gas station. "They might sell those little Band-Aid strips up there. If you're lucky, that might hold it closed without stitches."

Colt balled the blood-soaked tissue and raised an eyebrow. "You could just come out and say you want to play doctor with me, you know, Lacey."

I was so shocked he'd called me my first name I didn't even manage a smart-ass comeback before he was striding toward the gas station.

12

COLT

*A*drenaline pulsed through my veins. I hadn't expected that tonight. It had been a while since I'd fought, but hell, it felt good to get out there and use those muscles again. The roar of the crowd when I won still vibrated around my skull, Lacey's cheers the loudest.

Fuck.

I didn't know what I was doing with her. Ever since that night of the party, I couldn't get her off my mind. Hell. That wasn't even really true. She'd been on my mind before that, too. I'd tried so hard to fight every instinct I had. Tried to mask it. Tried to get rid of her. Because even now, I knew there was no chance of a future with her. But she was a boomerang. She kept coming back, no matter what I threw at her. She was tougher than she gave herself credit for. Tougher than *anyone* had given her credit for, myself included. It was damn addictive. And while she kept coming back, my feelings never changed.

I wanted Lacey Knight like I'd never wanted anyone before.

My fingers twitched as we trudged side by side up the hill to the gas station. I walked closer to her than I needed to. My fingers brushed hers every now and again, just to see what she'd do.

If she was as affected as I was, she wasn't showing it.

Damn.

Maybe I'd pushed her too far. I knew I was an asshole. But Gillian had always kind of liked it. I thought Lacey did, too. I played the part well. Lacey and I bounced off each other, and I couldn't imagine suddenly stopping all that and being...nice. Fuck that. It wasn't me. I had to get her out of my system. It didn't matter that her hair always smelled amazing. Or that her curves drew my eye wherever we were. The urge to see what she had beneath all those layers of clothes was strong.

But there were things she didn't know. I had to protect my family. That was my job. I'd promised my father on his death bed that I'd look out for Aria above all else. She'd been a kid when he'd died. Hell, so was I. But his death had aged me. In an instant, Aria had gone from my annoying kid sister to someone I needed to protect at all costs.

While Lacey Knight might not know it, she had the potential to destroy my sister.

She had the potential to destroy me.

That didn't stop me from wanting her.

Lacey pushed open the gas station door, a little bell ringing over our heads as we made a beeline for the tiny selection of medical supplies. I eyed the cashier, but if he knew about the street fight, he didn't care. He casually flipped through a magazine, without noticing one of his customers had blood dripping down his face.

Lacey riffled through the products on the shelf and

seemed miffed when she only came up with a box of Band-Aids and a bottle of disinfectant. She strode up to the cashier and placed her items on the countertop. "Do you have any gauze pads?"

The cashier lifted his head from his magazine and shrugged. Lacey grabbed a pile of napkins from a dispenser. "Never mind. These will do." She fished her wallet from her purse and pulled out a credit card. She tapped it against the machine without really paying attention, her frown trained on my cheek instead. She winced.

"Do you have a bathroom?" she asked the attendant.

He tossed her a key and jerked his head toward the door. "Outside and to your right."

Lacey thanked him, and then, without checking to see what I wanted, marched toward the other building.

She was so damn bossy.

But I liked it.

She screwed her adorable nose up at the public bathroom door and then took a deep breath before pushing it open.

"Oh," she said on the other side. "It's not so bad."

I was as surprised as she was. The light was bright, the tiles white and clean, apart from the floor where people had walked in mud. Even the sink top was clear, and the place smelled of disinfectant. Not normally a pleasant smell, but considering where we were, I'd take it.

Lacey set her purchases down on the counter then looked up at me. She wasn't short. She was a hell of a lot taller than Gillian. But I still towered over her. She reached up and took the Kleenex, throwing it in the trash can, but then frowned at me. "I can't see what I'm doing. You're going to have to sit down."

I dropped the lid on the throne and sat my ass down. She added some disinfectant to one of the napkins, then dabbed at the cut on my face gingerly.

I hissed at the burn. *Son of a bitch.*

She raised one eyebrow. "Really? You, of all people, are going to whine about a little sting?"

"Perhaps it's not the disinfectant but your shitty bedside manner that hurts?" I sniggered when she rolled her eyes.

It was hard for me to keep focus on her face, though, with her tits right at eye level. And damn if they weren't perfect. A high, tight handful I longed to touch. Stroke. Suck.

My cock stirred. Shit. Now was not the time for that. This always happened after a fight. The adrenaline took hours to go away. Normally I'd call up Gillian and fuck her hard and fast wherever we met up. I wasn't going to do that tonight.

I was done with Gillian. I'd seen her making out with that guy. I knew it had been for my benefit. A big *fuck you.* But I'd felt nothing. No jealousy. No longing. She hadn't spoken to me since the day she'd walked in and found Lacey in my bed. I'd made no effort to talk to her either. My heart wasn't in it anymore.

It hadn't been since Lacey had come back into my life. And I think both Gillian and I had known it.

I squeezed my eyes shut, pushing out those memories.

"Okay, it's mostly stopped bleeding." Lacey's hair fell down her back in waves. Dark strands, silky and smooth. Long enough to wrap around my fist while I fucked her.

I stifled a groan, but she heard it.

"Seriously, you are such a cry-baby."

She'd completely misinterpreted it. The cut was the least

of my worries. Getting my libido in check was a much bigger problem.

She ripped open the Band-Aids, put two across my cheek, and stood back, grinning. "You're ridiculous, but hey, it's better than it was."

Her warm breath misted over my lips. I squeezed my eyes shut and tried to inhale deeply. Tried to think about something other than the soft swell of her breasts, visible above the neckline of her shirt.

"You look good in my jacket."

She glanced down, fingering the zipper.

I stood, but she didn't move back. We were so close now our chests brushed.

"I forgot I was wearing it. Here."

She shrugged out of it, tugging at the sleeve with one hand and then held it out to me.

"Keep it. It's cold out."

"And leave you in a t-shirt? No, I'll be fine."

"Just keep it."

A muscle ticked in her jaw. "Just take it."

I let out a low growling noise. "Are you always this annoying?"

"Are you?"

She dropped the jacket on the tiled floor, leaving me to scoop it up or lose it for good. She swiped the leftover first-aid supplies into the trash.

"Fuck, Lacey. Typical rich kid. They were almost full."

She eyed the trash can, pink coloring her cheeks. "Fine. I'm a rich kid. We all know how much you hate that."

She yanked open the bathroom door and stormed out.

Oh, hell no.

I stomped after her into the cold night air. With longer legs, I caught her before she'd taken more than a handful of steps. I circled my fingers around her wrist and yanked her back. She stopped, eyes flashing in anger as I rounded on her.

She was sexy as sin when she was angry. Tits rising and falling with her rapid breathing. Eyes narrowed. Jaw set like she wanted to punch me in mine. Hell, I almost hoped she did. I crowded in on her until she took a step back, her body pressing to the cinderblock wall of the bathroom.

"I never once said I hated you because you had money."

"Then why?"

Because your uncle isn't who you think he is. Because you're not. Because I'm not. Because everything you think you know is a lie.

I slammed my lips down on hers.

She gasped in surprise, and for the tiniest moment, she didn't move. But then she moaned, her body melting to mine, and it was on. Our lips parted, tongues tangling. My dick gave up any pretense of staying under control, kicking to attention and reveling in the fact it was now up tight against Lacey's warm body. I still had one hand gripped around her wrist, and in between hard, fast kisses, I found the other hand, drawing them both up over her head and locking her in place with my fingers.

Our mouths moved in unison, devouring everything the other had to offer.

"Colt," she gasped when I moved my lips to her neck. Her head dropped to one side, giving me better access, but I couldn't stay there long, even if hearing her moan my name like that was the hottest thing I'd ever heard. I went back to her mouth, claiming it for my own once more.

I loved public sex. Had always gotten off on it. But public sex with Lacey was off the charts in terms of hotness. I ground on her, drinking in her gasp of pleasure. I put my lips to her ear. "Want to taste you, Lacey. Want to turn you around and sink my dick between your legs, right here, right now."

Her moan of pleasure told me everything I needed to know. I let go of her hands and spun her, so her face was to the wall. Her fingers forced to it, and her head twisted to one side, allowing me to claim her mouth once more as I ground over her ass.

Fuck. The thought of taking her there had moisture beading at the tip of my cock.

"Kiss me again," she whispered.

She didn't even open her eyes, but I was on her mouth, getting in as much of her as I could. When we broke apart, both of us opened our eyes. For the longest moment we just stared at each other. I raked over her gorgeous face. Her big eyes, framed with dark lashes. The long dark hair that looked even better a little mussed up. Her slightly swollen lips I hadn't had enough of kissing. I doubted I'd ever have enough.

"Colt?"

"Yeah, baby?"

Her half-lidded, come-fuck-me bedroom eyes opened fully. She straightened and pushed off the wall, forcing me back. She gave me a slow, shit-eating grin that told me she knew exactly how much power she had over me in that moment. "Training is done for the night."

"What?"

She took her phone from her purse and chuckled at me while she waited for her call to connect. "Jag? Can you come pick me up? Gas station in the industrial area."

I raised one eyebrow, trying to play it cool.

She mimicked the action.

"You're seriously leaving?"

"You seriously thought I'd stay?"

She stepped in again and pushed her chest to mine. Fuck, she was a siren. So tantalizing, even with the simplest of moves. All I could think about was how much I wanted her.

"You know more than you're telling me."

"A lot," I agreed.

"But you aren't going to fill me in."

That annoyed her. And I had to admit, I kinda enjoyed it. I really was an asshole. "Nope."

She shrugged. "Then that's as far as this goes."

"You blackmailing me? Sex for info?"

She laughed. "No. Sex was never on the table. But now kissing is off it, too. Tell me what you know, maybe I'll reconsider."

"What if you don't like what I have to say?"

"That's my decision to make, isn't it?"

I ran my teeth over my bottom lip. Thing was, the secrets I held weren't mine to tell. So even though all I wanted to do was wrap myself in Lacey's tight, warm heat, I pulled back.

Neither of us moved until the headlights of Jagger's beaten-up ride bounced over the gravel road, blinding me temporarily. I put my arm up to shield my eyes from the light.

She hit the brakes and got out of the car, a baseball bat clenched firmly in her hand, ready to use it as a weapon. Then she squinted at me and dropped her arm. "Colt?"

"One and only. Want to kill those headlights?"

"Don't bother," Lacey interrupted, slipping around me. "Colt and I are done here, right, Colt?"

She strutted to the passenger side of Jagger's car. I would have sworn her hips swayed more than they normally did.

But I dragged my gaze away from her ass and focused on her words.

"We're done," I agreed. "For now."

Those last two words held a promise I knew she'd heard. A tremble ran down her spine, and I smiled to myself. It was a promise I intended to keep.

13

BANJO

Filling my lungs with oxygen, I plunged beneath the cold waves. Water rushed around me, swirling and turbulent, invading my ears and blurring my vision. It was a relief. The quiet drowned out Augie's incessant noise. For a long moment, I contemplated letting my body sink to the ocean floor.

Inevitably, though, my lungs burned, and no matter how hard I tried to ignore it, the need for oxygen won out. I pushed off the sandy bottom and broke through the surface, gasping for breath.

"What the hell is wrong with you today?" Augie snapped. "That wave was tiny. I could have ridden it when I was five."

I didn't respond. There was no point arguing with him. He'd dragged me out to surf this morning, and I'd agreed to keep him happy. I couldn't afford to be on his bad side right now. I'd managed to dodge his not-so-subtle requests to join his business for the last week. Instead, I'd picked up extra shifts with the catering company to get Augie half the rent and utilities he now claimed I had to pay, since I'd turned eighteen. He still wasn't happy, but he didn't have a leg to stand on when I'd pushed a wad of cash into his hand. I had ten months left before college. If I could get in, that was. College meant going back to school. But school meant I couldn't take day shifts, which meant not enough income to pay my half.

Rock meet hard place. It was easier to just stay beneath the waves.

Ignoring Augie's taunts, I turned back for the beach. It was getting too cold to be out here anyway, plus the beach had lost some of it's magic. My gaze kept straying to the caves, my body still remembering the last time I'd been there, a few weeks ago with Lacey. I squeezed my eyes tight and tried to forget. It wasn't just what we'd done there. Though the thought of that got me hot under the collar. This beach was also where I'd lost her. Where I'd let that creep Owen nearly kill her.

All of that was my fault. My stomach churned every time I thought about it. I couldn't face her, but I'd tried calling. I'd sent her messages and voicemails explaining what had happened. That it was Augie who'd placed the camera and ruined her life. But either she hadn't read them. Or she didn't care. I couldn't blame her either way. I'd let her down.

A guy running along the beach stopped as I walked from the water, board beneath my arm. My wetsuit did little to insulate me from the wind whipping off the ocean. I gave him a polite nod, but he gave me a broad smile in response.

"Banjo, right?"

I nodded. "You a surfer?" I didn't get recognized all that often, but every now and then someone who followed the local tournaments would stop me and ask me how it was going.

"Hey?" the man asked, then shook his head. "Oh no. Not me. I can barely swim."

"How'd you know my name then?"

He looked surprised for a moment, but the expression quickly morphed into casual nonchalance. "Oh, I saw you in a competition once."

"Yeah? Which one?"

His smile widened, but it was strained. He pointed to the sports watch on his wrist. "Gotta keep going. It's telling me my heart rate is slowing."

"Sure, of course."

He ran off to continue his exercise. I watched after him for a moment, but then the wind picked up again, forcing the man from my thoughts in favor of my towel and dry clothes. Augie was still out in the ocean with no sign of coming in anytime soon. Couldn't blame him, really. The waves were ripping this morning, and I suspected a storm might roll in later today.

Our house wasn't far from the beach, so I walked home. Colt was just getting in his car when I arrived. He tossed his books onto the passenger seat then leaned on the open door.

I walked past him without saying hello, up the side of my house to place my board on the racks we kept there. I was all too aware that he followed, his heavy boots scraping over the concrete behind me.

"You ever gonna talk to me again?" he asked.

"Didn't realize we were ignoring each other." Though I kind of did. We hadn't really spoken at all since the night of the party, where he'd refused to let me help Lacey. In hindsight, I knew he'd done the right thing. But it still ached.

Colt ran his hands through his hair. "Listen. I need to

talk to you about something. You probably aren't going to be happy about it."

What was one more thing to add to the shit list that had become my life? "Spill it then."

"I kissed Lacey last night."

A low growl vibrated through my chest. "You what?"

"You heard me."

"I'm just giving you a chance to take it back before I punch you in your smug face. You can't stand her! And what about Gillian? Since when are you a cheater? That's never been your style before."

Colt sighed. "It's still not. Gillian and I are done."

Well, that was new. "For good?"

It took Colt too long to answer.

I shoved my hands in the pockets of my hoodie and shook my head. "Yeah, that's what I thought. You two are never truly done."

"This time we are," he said quietly. "Kissing Lacey wasn't some way to get back at Gillian."

"Was it to get at me then? Rafe? What the fuck did we do to you? You know there's feelings there. At least on my side." I cursed beneath my breath and decided to dump the truth on him. "I'm fucking in love with her, Colt."

He froze. "What?"

"Did I stutter?"

"You never told me that."

"Maybe I would have if you'd spoken to me in the last two weeks."

He groaned and buried his face in his hands. "How the hell did this happen? How did we all end up chasing one girl?"

I knew the answer to that. It was because of who Lacey

was. She was a ray of fucking sunshine in this gloomy-ass town. It didn't surprise me that we'd all noticed her.

But I'd done more than just notice. I'd fallen for her each and every day we'd spent together. I'd been so caught up in her I hadn't even noticed how far gone I truly was until it was too late. "Just tell me one thing. Do you even like her? Because she's not the sort of girl you fuck around with. She's not Gillian."

Irritation flickered in his eyes. "I never fucked around on Gillian."

"I know, but your heart wasn't really in it either, was it? She's hot. You were comfortable, sure. But did you ever see yourself settling down and marrying her? You know that's what she wanted."

He didn't say anything.

I shook my head. "You're such an asshole."

"I know." But this time he didn't sound as if he were proud of it.

"Look. I have no claim over Lacey anymore. She's made it really clear she doesn't want me in her life. But that doesn't mean I'm going to stop trying. Because I wasn't playin' when I said I'm in love with her. But all I want is for her to be happy. And if that means she's with Rafe, or with you, or both of you, then that's what I want." I eyed him, a muscle ticking in my jaw. "But you better step up and give it to her. Don't fucking break her heart, Colt. Trust me. I've done it. And it feels like shit."

Colt mused over that for a minute. "I'm teaching her to fight."

"Good."

"You need to come back to school."

"I need the money. Can't work if I'm at school."

He shoved me on the shoulder. "Nah, bro. You need

Lacey. And me and Rafe. Football and a fucking education. You ain't gonna get none of those by dropping out of school."

I knew he was right. "Augie wants me to work with him."

"Dealing? Fuck no, man. You can't do that."

It wasn't the dealing Augie wanted me to do. But I couldn't explain the rest to Colt. He wouldn't understand. It was easy for him. He had Willa. She always had his back, no matter what. If Augie kicked me out, I'd have no one. Willa would let me sleep on their couch, but that wasn't a long-term solution. I was eighteen. I needed to be independent and stand on my own two feet. I'd pay my way with Augie *and* finish school. Somehow. An athletic scholarship was the answer to getting out of this shithole town. The only way out.

Colt was still waiting for my reply.

"Give me two minutes to have a shower, and I'll be down."

"You're coming back to school?"

"Looks like it."

Colt grinned and slung an arm over my shoulder. "The gang will be all back together. You. Me. Rafe."

"And Lacey in the middle?"

He went quiet. So did I. That was a problem I didn't have a solution to.

14

LACEY

$\mathcal{R}$ain pelted my bedroom windows, the storm clouds overhead dumping more water than I'd seen in a long time. It was coming down so thick and fast I flicked on the television in my room and found a news channel. As I'd suspected, there were severe storm warnings for the coastal areas.

Great. This house was full of glass windows, and it was too late to board them up now. The best I could do was make sure I knew where the candles were.

I got up to do just that but stopped when my phone buzzed.

Selina: *Staying at Pamela's until the storm passes. Will you and Angelique be okay? Heat up the pasta she made soon, in case the power goes out. See you later tonight. I hope. Love you.*

I'd already sent Angelique, our hired help, home. I'd seen those clouds rolling in on my way home from school and told her to go the minute I got in the door. She had little kids who would be scared if she didn't make it back to them on time. And I was more than capable of taking care of myself for one evening.

So I assured Selina I'd be fine, and then went in search of candles and flashlights, just in case.

"Jackpot," I murmured in the utility room. Selina, or more likely Angelique, had an emergency stash in a drawer. There was also a small first-aid kit, as well as a list of emergency numbers to call for if we needed help.

Very thorough.

I pulled the lot out and dumped it on the kitchen countertop so it would be in easy access if the storm worsened.

Someone thumped at the door, and I jumped a mile, my heart rate tripling in the space of a second. Despite the fact I'd changed the security code on the alarm system, I was still always on alert, always wondering when Owen was going to make his next move.

He'd been quiet, but I knew him. He wasn't done.

Neither was I. But I had to keep him at arm's length until I was ready with a plan.

Reminding myself that knocking wasn't Owen's style, I tiptoed to the heavy wooden door and peered through the peephole.

Rafe stood hunched over on himself, rivulets of rain running down his face and neck, his clothes already drenched from the short distance between the car and the entranceway.

"Oh my God." I yanked the door open.

He looked up, his dark hair plastered to his face, wet shirt clinging to his muscles.

My brain short-circuited. He should have been modeling on some catwalk. Or in one of those fancy perfume ads, with glamorous women and men too handsome to be real. Not standing on my steps in a storm. "What are you doing here?"

Water dripped in his eyes, and he blinked it away. "We had a date?"

The corner of my mouth tipped up. "We had an arrangement to hang out. I wouldn't call that a date. And I figured it was off because normal people don't drive in this sort of weather."

He grinned. "Normal people would let a guy in before he catches pneumonia."

Oh shit. Yeah. I opened the door wider and scooted out of his way, closing it behind him and resetting the security alarm.

Water puddled at his feet on the white tiles.

"Okay, we need to get you dry. Follow me." I took off down the hall that went past the stairs to the second level. Around a corner, toward the back of the house, a large linen closet took up most of one wall. Beside it was the closed door to Lawson's study. I ignored that and went through the cupboard, pulling out thick, fluffy towels and a white bathrobe from the top. I handed Rafe the towels and waited while he got out the excess water from his hair and clothes, while I debated what to do next. Lawson's study kept drawing my attention.

"Why do you keep eyeing that door and gnawing on your bottom lip?" He reached over and popped my lip free from my teeth. "Stop. It'll fall off."

I hadn't even realized I'd been doing it.

"That's my uncle's study. There's a gas heater in there, and the room isn't as big as the rest of the house. It's the fastest way to get you dry and warm. But I haven't been in there since..."

"Since he died?"

"Since he was murdered."

Rafe flicked his wet hair back off his face. "We don't need to go in there. I'll be fine."

But I could see the shivers racing over his big body, and the goosebumps covering his flesh. He was wet and freezing.

Rafe was here. He was alive. And there was nothing in Lawson's study but memories.

I opened the door, expecting a wave of them to hit me in the face. I expected the smell to be familiar. Expected him to somehow still be here, a presence in this room, even though his body had left the earth.

But there was nothing. It was just a room with a big mahogany desk in the middle and a couch pointed at a big-screen TV. One wall was lined with bookshelves, Lawson's entire library neatly stacked within.

"You okay?" Rafe asked, coming up behind me.

I clutched the folded robe a little closer to my chest. "Yeah, actually. It's weird. I thought this would be hard. But I made it worse in my head than it really was."

"It's just a room."

I nodded. "I barely ever came down here. This was kind of Lawson's man cave."

Rafe gazed around and out through the large-glass windows that overlooked the back yard. The storm hadn't worsened any, but that rain was constant. "It's a real nice man cave. I'm surprised he ever came out of it." Rafe eyed the big-screen TV. "You want to watch a movie or something?"

I nodded and thrust the robe at him, swapping it for his wet towel. I strode over to the gas heater and pushed in the button to ignite it. Immediately, heat radiated from it, and I motioned Rafe closer. "Get dry. I'll find us something to watch."

I turned away and busied myself with the TV remote. From the corner of my eye, though, I watched Rafe pull off his wet shirt and drop it on the floor. My mouth watered.

Nothing had changed in the few weeks we'd been apart. He was still as long and lean and muscled as he'd always been. He still made my heart skip and heat bloom between my legs.

He undid his pants before I forced my eyes closed.

Rafe chuckled. "You don't have to turn away, Lacey. It's nothing you haven't seen."

But only once. On the way to the football game when I'd sucked him off. Oh God. I couldn't think about that. It had been one of the hottest moments of my life. Hell, all my moments with Rafe were hot. *He* was hot.

The old Lacey would have insisted on turning away. But I wasn't the same girl anymore. And this girl knew what she wanted.

He'd invited me to watch him.

I wasn't going to miss the opportunity.

He sucked in a breath, realizing I was no longer pretending I wasn't interested. He kept his front to the heater, giving me an awesome view of the muscles cording his back. I longed to trace my fingers down his spine, but instead, I sat on the couch and pressed my palms to the buttery suede. Anything to anchor me to the spot and keep me from closing the distance between us.

Rafe pushed his soaked pants down over his ass, and laid them in front of the heater to dry. I couldn't help but grin when he glanced over his shoulder at me.

"It's like my own private strip tease."

He cocked one eyebrow. "You want me to dance for you, princess?"

"Wouldn't say no."

He chuckled, pulling the robe over his arms and covering up without so much as a sway of his hips. He knotted the belt at his waist before turning around.

I pouted.

"Don't give me that face. You're the one who wanted to take it slow."

Past Lacey was a moron. Past Lacey had forgotten how good Rafe looked without clothes on. Current Lacey wanted to punch Past Lacey in the lady balls.

He wandered over, rubbing the soft cotton of the robe as he came to sit beside me. "Why do you have random spare robes in your linen closet?"

He spread his arms and legs wide, then motioned for me to move closer. I did, and he dropped an arm around my shoulder.

"I don't really know. They get used sometimes if we have guests over to swim in the pool. I think Selina and Lawson might have stolen them from a hotel they stayed at. Or knowing the type of hotels they stay at, they could have been complimentary."

He snorted at that, and we both stared out at the pool. It was well and truly overflowing, the fat raindrops dancing over the surface. It was going to be muddy as hell out there after the storm passed.

"Did you pick a movie?"

I shook my head. "I was too busy staring at your ass."

"Fine, perv. I'll choose."

He grabbed the remote and flicked through the endless list of Netflix movies, finally settling on an old *Die Hard*.

I snuggled against his chest and tried to focus on the movie while it grew dark outside. But my gaze kept flicking around the room, bouncing from one of Lawson's possessions to the next. When I glanced over at Rafe, he stared at a spot somewhere to the left of the TV, seemingly lost in his own world, too.

"Penny for your thoughts?"

He looked like a little kid, caught with his hand in the cookie jar.

I raised one eyebrow. "Man, that bad, huh?"

He shook his head with a sigh. "Can't stop thinking about Banjo."

"He's been on my mind a lot lately, too."

"Did you talk to him at school today?"

"No." I squinted at Rafe. "I kind of avoided him. That will be impossible tomorrow, though. We have music in last period. And we're partners."

"Will Miss Halten let you swap?"

I shrugged. "Doubt it. Everybody has been working on their pieces in pairs since the beginning of the year. No one is going to want to stop and swap now. They'd have to start all over."

"Damn."

"I have to face him sometime."

"I'll walk you to class tomorrow. For moral support."

I smiled at him, but it was a sad smile. "Why do you think he did it?"

Rafe shook his head. "He says he didn't."

"But the evidence..."

"Yeah."

I squeezed his leg. "I'm sorry. This is worse for you than for me, I think. He's your best friend."

"You love him, too, though. Don't you?"

There was no denying it. After everything he'd done, I still loved him. It was hard to forget your first love so quickly. Even if he had done something unforgiveable.

Rafe peered over at me. "I told you mine, you tell me yours. What's got you all distracted this afternoon? Apart from how good I look without clothes on."

"I'm thinking about my next move in my uncle's case.

The football t-shirts were a dead end. We're never going to narrow the field down like that. "

"It was a long shot anyway."

I nodded. "But it was all I had. I was telling Meredith last week that I think that was the wrong way to go about it. Instead of searching for a needle in a haystack, I have to look at what's right under my nose."

"You want to look at your very kissable lips?"

I smirked at him. "Keep on track, will you? I need to investigate Lawson. I think whoever murdered him was someone he knew. It had to be. But his friends all say he was the nicest guy to ever live."

"Do you think your uncle could have been involved with something? A gang?"

I bit my lip. "I almost hope it is something like that."

"What's the alternative?"

"That the words on the photos they shoved into my locker are true."

Liar. Cheat. Rapist.

Rafe swore. "Shit."

I shook my head. "I can't believe it. I seriously can't. Not without proof. It's too impossible to comprehend."

"But if we could find some sort of proof...maybe things would start clicking into place?"

"I want to be wrong," I whispered. "I want to know who wrote those horrible things, and I want to make them say they lied... But what if they didn't?"

His arms tightened around me, and I let myself be enveloped by his embrace. When he let go, he clapped his hands twice. "Right. Let's get on with it then." He pushed to his feet and went to my uncle's bookshelf. "No point sitting there, thinking about it, Lace. On your feet. You take the desk. I'll take the shelves. Here's as good a place as any to start."

He was right. I'd been putting off coming down here, dreading his ghost, but this had to be done. And with Rafe here to back me up, there was no better time.

We worked in silence for the next thirty minutes. Rafe painstakingly went through each and every one of Lawson's books, flipping through the pages and shaking each one out, convinced he was going to find some sort of tucked-away note inside one of them, while I tackled Lawson's desk drawers. I worked slowly and methodically, sorting through every item, opening every folder, reading over every bit of paper that might have offered some sort of clue.

Eventually, Rafe wandered over to my side and peered over my shoulder. "Your uncle kept a lot of crap down here."

I smiled at him. "You're telling me. There's receipts here older than I am."

Rafe moved in, dropping a cheeky kiss on the side of my neck. "You know what would make this more fun?"

I raised one eyebrow.

"If you had less clothes on."

My breath hitched. I was still all too aware how very naked he was beneath that robe. "I'm kind of busy here, you know?"

"Busy not finding anything." He came in closer, his fingers touching lightly to my hips and lifting the hem of my t-shirt. "How long until your aunt gets home?"

I glanced toward the window. The storm still raged on. The wind whipped the trees around, and rain came in at all different angles, pinging off the glass. "Sometime after that stops." Thunder rumbled in the near distance.

"Sounds like it's about to get worse, not better."

Another kiss was placed on the other side of my neck. A full-body shiver ran over me.

Rafe made a humming sound behind me that told me he knew exactly what he was doing to me. "Topless, Lace. That's all I'm asking for."

I snorted on my laughter. "That's all huh?" But a tingle moved through body, an achy need wanting to be scratched. New Lacey was bold. She took this sort of situation by the horns. She got what she wanted.

And what she wanted was getting hard right behind her.

I tucked my fingers beneath my long-sleeved t-shirt and peeled it over my head, grateful I'd put on a pretty pale-blue lacy bra that morning. I dumped the shirt on the floor then went back to riffling through Lawson's desk, pretending to look for the next file to go through.

My bra clasp snapped apart with a quick flick of Rafe's fingers. He pulled it from my shoulders, dropping it with the other clothes on the floor.

I had all intentions of teasing him longer, carrying on the game of pretending to go through the desk drawers one by one, but then his big hands snaked around from the back to cup my breasts, and all ideas of game-playing went out the window. I leaned against him, my back to his chest, and gasped when his fingers pinched my nipples.

Pleasure shot straight through me, down to my core, a beat thrumming there like an incessant drummer. I reached behind me, nudging aside his robe, and took his hard dick in my hand. With a roll of my wrist, I stroked his length, refamiliarizing myself with how big he was.

One-handed, he rolled my nipple, keeping up a wicked rhythm that had my breath stuttering, while the other hand slipped beneath the band of my yoga pants. Rafe wasted no time, pushing my thong aside and placing one finger over my clit.

"So much for slow," I moaned.

"You want me to stop?"

"Are you insane?"

He kissed my neck and went back to working my clit, rubbing it in small, slow circles that had my insides clenching with need.

"We skipped a step in this reunion." I twisted my head so I could see his gorgeous blue eyes. They locked on mine.

Without saying anything else, he lowered his mouth.

Rafe's lips were strong yet soft, and he stole my breath all over again. Our lips parted, our tongues seeking. There was none of the hard urgency of my kiss with Colt last night. This kiss was entirely Rafe. Sweet, yet sexy. Familiar, yet it had been weeks since we'd done this, and that sent a whole new excitement through me. Instantly, I was right back to where I was that night of the party. Pressed against the wall, promising to give him everything when we got behind closed doors.

We were behind closed doors now.

I hooked my fingers in my pants, dragging them down my legs, taking my soaked panties with them.

Rafe let out a hiss. "Put your hands on the desk, princess."

A whimper left my lips, but I did as I was told. Rafe kissed his way down my spine and over the curve of my ass. His hands followed, smoothing over my back and my cheeks, dipping between my legs and pushing them wide. "Stay there," he murmured in my ear before disappearing momentarily. He was back in seconds, robe discarded, a condom fished from the pockets of the jeans he'd been wearing.

"Presumptuous much?" I asked, peering around at him.

"Prepared, not presumptuous."

I watched over my shoulder as he popped a finger into his mouth, making a show of sucking on it. My core clenched in anticipation. One hand squeezed my ass, the other pushed me over the desk more, opening me up so he could stand between my widespread legs. I rested my torso on the cool wood desk, my nipples hardening beneath me.

His wet finger trailed between my ass cheeks, over my asshole, and lower, stroking through the wetness at my core. A whole-body shudder rocked me.

His fingers swiped between my lower lips, gathering my arousal. He rolled it over my clit taking me higher, bridging the gap to where I wanted to be. Pleasure coiled from my nub and spread outward. His fingers swiped back to my ass, taking me by surprise, but then he bent over me, kissing my neck hard, sucking the sensitive spot behind my ear. Then he went back to my pussy, driving me mad by stroking but never entering.

I moaned, grinding back against him, showing him with my body what I wanted. He was hard, and I wanted more.

Two fingers speared inside me, and I bucked against him. "Rafe!" I yelled.

I jerked back again, rocking on his fingers. But he removed them, and my attempts at getting him where I wanted met nothing but thin air. I moaned in frustration, built so high. I needed him.

When he grabbed the condom, I could have wept in joy. "Hurry," I moaned.

His answering chuckle had me clenching my thighs together. I swear, that noise alone had the power to make me come. The wrapper crinkled, and a moment later, the tip of Rafe's cock nudged my entrance.

God, he was big. Thick and long. I yearned for the stretch I knew was coming. I needed it.

"One hand between your legs, Lace. Rub your clit."

Yes.

I wasn't sure whether I'd said it out loud, but I brought myself up on my elbow, and gave my other hand a little more room to work between my thighs. Rafe pressed in as I took over, rubbing hard and fast at the bundle of nerves that drove me wild.

"More," I breathed out.

Rafe grabbed my ass cheek, squeezing it roughly, but it didn't hurt. Hell. I liked it. He squeezed it again, and thrust the full length of his cock inside me, stretching me so deliciously my legs near gave out. If the desk hadn't supported most of my weight, I would have been a puddle on the floor.

He withdrew before pushing back in. Again and again. He fucked me, bent over the desk, while I mewled out my needs.

On the next slide, he pulled right out. I yelped, needing him back, so ready to fall off the edge with him. His fingers drove in again, only maddening me further because it was good, but not as good as his cock.

I made a frustrated noise in the back of my throat, but then his dick was back, filling me so deliciously I could scream.

His wet finger found the puckered star of my asshole, massaging my own arousal over it.

Fireworks went off in my body. I ground back onto him —his dick and his finger—wanting more of both. He fucked me harder, his hips slamming against my ass, his finger on my back entrance never entering, but the mere touch of him there had me screaming his name. "Rafe!" I collapsed down on the desk while he rode me until he found his own edge.

His groan of ecstasy when he came had me flying all over again. Those same sparks that hadn't even let up from my first orgasm ignited once more, sending me hurtling into an abyss I wasn't sure I ever wanted to come back from. Outside, thunder cracked over the house, the rain pelted the large windows, but all I could do was white-knuckle the corner of the desk and have my mind blown by the most beautiful boy in the world.

He collapsed down over me, both of us sated and sticky and sweaty. We panted in time with each other, while my internal walls clenched around his cock.

"Oh my God," I groaned from beneath him. "Oh my God. Oh my God. Oh my God."

Thunder boomed again, the noise so earsplittingly loud I jolted, jerking my head in the direction of the windows. Lightning lit up the yard, as bright as day.

A scream ripped from my throat at the hooded figure staring back at me.

15

———

LACEY

With my arms locked around my knees, I was still frozen in place when the cops arrived. They bashed on the door, and I cringed away from the noise, my heartbeat too fast in my aching chest. Rafe squeezed my leg and got up to open the door without asking if he should.

"The code is one-nine-eight-two," I said quietly. "Put the alarm back on once you let them in."

"You got it." He disappeared into the entranceway, and a moment later, deep male voices and the shuffling of coats and boots being removed filtered back.

Rafe returned to the living room with three men. Two officers I didn't recognize and...

"Chief Waller. What are you doing here?" My stomach flipped.

Owen's father stood at the front of the trio. As tall as his son, but wider, more heavy-set, and a beer gut spilling over his too-tight belt. He'd lost the athleticism Owen possessed, but there was no doubting this man was Owen's relative.

They shared the same eyes, small and slightly too close together. Chief Waller's thin lips pressed into a firm line as his gaze swept over me, huddled into the couch.

"Miss Knight. I wish I could say it's a pleasure to see you, but under the circumstances, it's not." He frowned at me, his expression hard. "Your name has continually been brought to my attention lately. And now you're calling my men out in the middle of a raging storm, so I assume this is a very serious matter. I thought it best I come down myself and see what the problem is."

I ground my molars, irritation prickling at me. I uncurled myself and stood so I was closer to the man's height. Rafe moved in beside me, taking my hand. His tiny squeeze of support reminded me I wasn't alone in this.

"Somebody was in our yard just now."

Chief Waller raised one eyebrow. "Pretty dark out there. You sure it wasn't the wind?"

I reminded myself to keep calm and polite, even if his tone was condescending as fuck. "Yes, I'm sure. The lightning was bright. It lit up the whole yard."

Chief Waller's gaze flicked to Rafe. "You saw this intruder, too?"

Rafe cleared his throat. "No. I was...distracted. I wasn't looking out the window when the lightning flashed. And by the time I got out there, he was gone."

"If he existed at all," Chief Waller mused. "These are all unfounded allegations right now. We have no evidence this wasn't a trick of the light."

My mouth dropped open. I'd known our police force was incompetent, but this was more than laziness.

Before I could say anything, though, Chief Waller crossed his big arms over his chest. "So you saw this alleged intruder from this room?" He peered toward the doors. "Were those blinds down? Or did you drop them afterward?"

"They were like that. We were in my uncle's study."

"You best show us the way then."

I let out the breath I'd been holding and led the way down the hall and around the corner to the back end of the house. Still feeling the terror that had shot through my body when I'd seen the figure outside the windows, I had to force myself down the stairs. Rafe stuck close to me, and I was grateful for it.

"He was out there," I said, pointing to the windows. "On the other side of those trees."

The two officers didn't budge from the doorway, leaving the chief to wander the room. He moved to the window, as casual as a Sunday stroll. He pulled a flashlight from his pocket and shone it through the windows, cupping his hand around his eyes and pressing his face to the glass to peer through. "No one out there now."

"Not really the point, is it?" I ground out, my patience evaporating. "He was hardly going to hang around after he'd been busted."

The chief pinned me with a glare that reeked of arrogance. "You've had police training then, have you? What do you need me for?"

"We need you to do your job," Rafe spat out. "You know? Protect and serve? Perhaps actually go out there and investigate?"

"Watch your mouth, boy."

I squeezed Rafe's fingers, urging him to be quiet. Chief Waller wandered around, coming to a stop at the desk. To my horror, I realized the condom wrapper was still sitting on top of it. We'd grabbed our clothes and hightailed it to the living room, Rafe disposing of the condom in the trash can in my bathroom. But neither of us had remembered the condom wrapper. I snatched it from the desktop, balling it inside my fist.

Chief Waller chuckled. "Well, that explains your distraction," he said to Rafe.

The other two officers chuckled as well.

Rafe didn't.

Neither did I.

"Putting on a show for your neighbors, huh?"

The neighbors couldn't see into our yard, and Chief Waller knew it. He was just trying to piss me off now. And he was succeeding. "That's not your business."

He stepped in closer. "It is my business when you're wasting my time with false allegations. Boys, we're done here. I'll meet you at the door."

The two officers nodded and abruptly turned and disappeared from view, their stocking feet quiet on the tiled floors.

A muscle in my jaw ticked, and I suddenly wondered if he were even still talking about tonight. Did he know about what Owen had done to me? Did he think I was making that up, too? My temper soared, and words fell out my lips. "Where's your son tonight, Chief Waller?"

I knew I'd made a mistake the minute the words echoed around the quiet room.

The big man whirled on me, his glare as hard as stone. "My son? What would he have to do with any of this?"

His voice was hard and flat. The warning in his tone as clear as day.

I didn't say anything.

Chief Waller's lip curled into a sneer. "He told me about your party."

I sucked in a deep breath.

"About how you made a fool of yourself, playing the wrong tape. You sure showed everyone what sort of girl you are, didn't you? Can take the girl out of the trailer park, but..."

A low growl came from Rafe's chest, and I pulled his hand harder.

Chief Waller laughed in his direction. "Settle down, Saint View. Before I arrest you for threatening an officer."

I lost my patience. I was so sick of the Wallers throwing around their weight. I didn't give a shit that this man was the Chief of Police. All I saw when I looked at him was the man who'd raised a rapist.

"Oh, that's rich. Of course, you'd have absolutely no problem arresting an innocent man, would you? How about a guilty one?" It was on the tip of my tongue to hurl his son's name at him again, but the promise I'd made with Owen, and the threat of him having Colt arrested, hung around my neck like a noose. So instead I went down a different path, unable to get a grip on my anger. It needed to be unleashed in some form. "What have you done to find my uncle's killer? There's been nothing but radio silence from your incompetent goons. Did you even investigate at all? Or did you put it in the 'too hard' basket, along with your ABC's and elementary school addition?"

Rafe snorted on his laughter but then clamped his lips tight.

Chief Waller's eyes flashed with hate.

Good. I hated the old prick as much as I hated his son.

Chief Waller had no smart comeback. His fingers

hovered over the handcuffs on his belt, and I could see him itching to whip them out and slap them on me.

Part of me wanted to dare him to do it. But the smarter part of me warned I'd already pushed this as far as I could without landing myself in a cell.

Rafe pressed his fingernails into my palm, a silent urge to calm down.

I had to force my words between gritted teeth. "Chief Waller, I think we're done here. I'd hate to waste any more of your valuable time."

"I think you're right. Send my regards to your aunt."

I stayed put, my feet frozen in place. Shock held me in its grips, refusing to process everything that had just happened.

Rafe dropped my hand, following the officers to the door, and a moment later the alarm reengaged with a series of beeps.

I was still standing in the same spot when Rafe came back and engulfed me in his arms. It was only then a tremble took over, shaking me violently. "Did I just imagine all that?"

"I wish. We've known for years the police around here are corrupt as fuck. I had no idea he was Waller's dad. I didn't even put two and two together until you said it. I nearly launched across the room and strangled him."

I shook my head, deep breaths forcing oxygen along with some clarity into my rage-fuddled brain. "He isn't Owen."

"So what? He raised him. He knows what he did, and he's done nothing about it. He's covering for him."

"I never made a formal complaint."

"What?"

"I couldn't. You saw the way he acted. He wouldn't have

believed me, and Colt would be in jail for attacking Owen on my behalf."

Rafe flopped down on the couch and buried his face in his hands. "Fuck."

I sat beside him, picking up his arm and draping it over my shoulders. I couldn't stop looking at the window and remembering the shadowed face of someone staring back at me. "Let's put the movie back on. Or go back to making out. Hell, anything that makes me forget about everything that just happened."

Rafe held me tighter and went to grab the remote from a side table where I'd tossed it earlier. His hand hovered over it, without picking it up. Instead, he lifted a coaster bearing the East Shores University logo. He turned it over in his hands, studying it curiously. "Did someone go to ESU?"

I glanced over. "My uncle. I was going to apply there as well. I know that would have pleased him."

Rafe huffed out a laugh. "And I avoided applying there for that exact reason. My father went there, too."

"No way?" I got off the couch and wandered to one of the bookshelves Rafe hadn't gotten to when he'd been searching. "What year did he graduate? Maybe he knew my uncle."

Rafe squinted. "Doubt it. He's never said anything."

I found what I was searching for. Lawson's yearbook. I took it back to the couch and sat, flipping through the pages until I found the photo of Lawson. I pointed it out to Rafe. "It's so strange, seeing him all clean-shaven. I don't ever remember him looking like that, though he couldn't have been more than five years older when he adopted me."

Rafe didn't say anything. Instead, he flicked a few pages and tapped a photo. "Shit. That's my dad. They graduated the same year."

I stared at the younger version of Principal Simmons

and laughed. "Wow, what a trip. Do you think they knew each other?"

Rafe shrugged. He flipped to the front where there were messages penned from other students.

We both sucked in a breath. The biggest message, the one right in the middle of the page read: To the guy I'd call if I needed bail. Always by my side. Best four years ever. Todd.

"I think that answers my question."

16

LACEY

Early morning light streamed in the windows of my bedroom, but it was the overexaggerated coughing that woke me. I blinked one eye open and twisted to the doorway.

"Hey, you're home," I greeted Selina. "Did you only just get back from Pamela's?"

She tapped her perfectly manicured fingernails on my doorframe. "Looks like I wasn't the only one who had a sleepover."

My eyes widened, following her line of sight to the other side of my bed where a half-naked Rafe lay sprawled, somehow still sleeping.

Oops.

I slipped from the blankets, pulling a robe over my pajamas and hustled her out the door, shutting it behind me. In the kitchen, all the emergency supplies from last night still lay scattered over the counter, and I picked up a candle, poking at the wax. "Sorry," I said quietly. "I know we've never really talked about boys staying over. I'm eighteen, though..."

"And still living in my house. But I don't kid myself by thinking you're a virgin, sweetheart."

After that video, the whole world could safely assume I wasn't. But at least Selina didn't bring that up.

"A conversation would have been nice, though. I don't want you bringing random men into the house at all hours."

I opened my mouth to argue Rafe wasn't a random hookup, but Selina held up a hand in a stop motion. "But that's not what I'm even concerned about here. That boy broke your trust. Put you in a horrible position at your party..."

"It wasn't him. He was as much a victim as I was."

Selina blew out a long breath. "And you swear to me he had nothing to do with the beating you took that night? I agreed not to push you to go to the police, but I need to know that wasn't him."

I shook my head. "I swear to you, it wasn't any of the boys from Saint View."

That seemed to trouble Selina more, so I hurried to change the subject before she stumbled upon the truth. That couldn't come out. After last night, I knew that better than ever.

"Lawson had finished college when you met him, right?"

Selina cocked her head to one side. "Odd question for a Wednesday morning."

"I just wondered if you'd ever met any of his college friends? Or if he'd ever spoken about them much?"

Selina refilled the water in the coffee machine and set it to brew while she pondered my question. "No, not really. He always said he lost contact with them all once he finished and took a job at Providence. He shot up through the ranks there so quickly, he always said he didn't have much time for friends."

"You never went to a reunion?"

"If there was one, Lawson never told me about it. Why the sudden interest in your uncle's college years? Oh! Did you do your college application? It must be due soon?"

"Already sent it weeks ago. Rafe and I realized last night that Lawson and Rafe's dad went to college together. I think they might have been friends."

"Lawson and Todd Simmons?"

I leaned on the counter. "Is that weird?"

She shrugged. "Maybe a little. Todd must know, right? That you're Lawson's niece? And I'm his wife. He never said anything at that dinner we went to together..." Her forehead wrinkled, but then she flapped her hand around. "No point rehashing ancient history. You and Rafe are going to be late for school. Go wake that boy up and get him moving."

"You aren't mad he stayed here last night?"

She kissed my cheek. "Motherly instinct tells me you could do a whole lot worse than Rafe Simmons."

"You've changed your tune about him."

She shrugged. "I saw the way he looked at you at your party. That boy really cares about you, Lacey. Banjo, too. I find it very hard to believe either of them had anything to do with that tape. At least not the showing of it."

My smile fell. I hadn't told Selina Rafe had found the camera in Banjo's room. I turned away and ran back up the stairs before she could notice.

Rafe glanced over as I came in, shutting the door behind me. I rested back against it, admiring how his dark hair contrasted with the stark white of the pillow beneath his head. He was shirtless, though nothing else had happened between us during the night. He'd simply crawled into bed with me and tucked his body around mine.

I'd actually slept last night, with Rafe there beside me. It was one of only two good nights since the party, the other being when Colt had shared his bed with me. I was already dreading tonight, knowing I'd be back to sleeping alone.

He motioned for me to come to him, and I did, lying on top of him and fitting my mouth to his.

"Mmm. Morning, beautiful," he murmured over my lips.

"My aunt is home. And guess what? She approves of you."

"No shit?"

I dropped a kiss to the corner of his mouth. "Yep, so let's not change her opinion just yet. We need to get moving or we're going to miss homeroom. Takes a little longer to get to school from here, remember?"

He groaned and flipped me onto my back, reversing our positions so he was on top. His erection pressed against my core, and I wrapped my legs around him, wishing we had fewer clothes on.

"What if we skip school and I take these pajamas off you? I can give you a follow-up on last night."

Everything we'd done on that desk downstairs came rushing back. Heat bloomed all over my body, and I lifted my hips to grind on Rafe, teasing him while he claimed my mouth again. "There's desks at school, too, you know...."

"Fuck, you're gonna kill me, Lacey."

We both looked down at his erection, straining through his underwear. With a reluctant mumble, he rolled off me and grabbed his clothes from the floor. He pulled them on with jerky movements, not that his pants did a great job of hiding things. He picked up his car keys from my desk and came back to kiss me again.

"I am most definitely finding us an empty classroom ASAP," he whispered in my ear. "I'm going to be thinking about fucking you in it all day until we get the chance to do it for real."

My insides clenched at the thought. He gave me one long, last lingering stare as he left the room, calling goodbye to Selina before he went back outside to his car.

I went to my bathroom, ready for a very cold shower.

---

*E*very class I shared with Rafe that day was a combination of hilarious and torturous. The two of us continually sneaked glances at each other, and there was much suggestive head tilting toward the teacher's desk whenever we thought we could get away with it. Our attempts at not dissolving into hysterical laughter weren't very successful. Every time we were apart, I kept expecting to be ambushed in the hallways, dragged into a darkened classroom, bent over a desk and... Heat flushed my cheeks. The anticipation kept me on my toes all day, until I was so horny I was ready to blow off last period and, well, go blow something else.

Rafe walked me to music class, as promised. Banjo hadn't been at lunch, and I wondered if he was going to skip to avoid me. I wasn't sure whether I wanted that or not. On one hand, I needed to sort out our assignment. Now that I knew I was at Saint View for the rest of the year, I had to start taking my studies more seriously. The work level might not have been the standard I was used to at Providence, but that didn't mean I could afford to flunk an entire assignment. And aside from that, I wanted to perform at the concert. I wanted that solo. Partially to rub it in Gillian's face, but partially for myself, too. I enjoyed performing. Or I used to. I had to wake up that part of my brain again. I hadn't even touched an instrument in weeks.

Rafe's arm tightened around me.

Banjo had arrived. His gazed raked over me, worry etched into his expression, as if he were assuring himself I was there and in one piece.

I was there, but my heart wasn't intact. It squeezed painfully at the sight of him.

"Lacey..." His focus switched to Rafe, and the depth of pain in his gaze took my breath away. Banjo had never been jealous over me and Rafe before. But that was when he'd been with me, too.

It was different now.

Tension vibrated between the two of them, and suddenly I wished I hadn't let Rafe walk me to class at all. I needed to sort out my problems with Banjo alone. Just like he did.

I twisted in his arms and reached up on my toes to kiss him softly. "Don't wait for me after class, okay? Let me deal with this."

Rafe's eyes narrowed, telling me he wasn't happy about this decision, but he didn't argue. He simply snaked his hand to the back of my head and pulled me tight, crushing his lips against mine. His kiss was branding. A show I normally would have been irritated by, but after everything that had happened, I understood it. I watched him leave for his own class, hoping he was okay.

"He really hates me, doesn't he?" Banjo said sadly.

I blew out a breath as the bell rang, signaling the start of class. Banjo and I walked side by side into the classroom and took our usual seats at the front of the class. I didn't know what to say. And Banjo was quiet, too.

"You not talking to me?" he whispered while we waited for Miss Halten to start the lesson.

I darted a glance at him. His green eyes begged me from beneath his flop of dirty-blond hair. He looked paler than normal. Dark circles marred the skin beneath his eyes, and his cheekbones seemed sharper, as if he'd lost some weight.

Worry flickered in the back of my mind, but I pushed it away, trying to focus on what he'd done. "You put a camera in your room, Banjo. What the hell did you think was going to happen?"

Pure, honest anger shone in his eyes. "That was Augie."

I stared, wanting to believe him. But it made no sense. "Why would he do that?"

He lifted one shoulder in a shrug. "Because he's an asshole?"

"He is, but there's got to be more to it than that."

Banjo dropped his gaze. His fingers gripped the edge of the desk like it was a lifeline and he was drowning, his knuckles white with the force of his hold. "I want to tell you. I do. But I can't. Not here. It's bad, Lace. It's really fucking bad. Can we meet somewhere? After school and talk about it?"

I blew out a long breath while I tried to gather my thoughts. "I need some time to process this."

He glanced up. "You don't believe me either."

"I'm finding it really hard to believe in anyone lately, Banjo. Did that once, got burned pretty bad."

"There's a game on Friday night. It's a big one. Scouts are coming to watch. Will you come? Maybe we could get something to eat afterward, and I'll explain everything."

"The truth? All of it?"

Banjo swallowed hard, worry flickering in his eyes. But

then he nodded. "You probably won't ever want to see me again when I'm done. But I'm so sick of secrets."

So was I. He had no idea how much.

17

LACEY

*I*n the parking lot after class, Colt leaned on my car talking to Augie, who had stopped his dark-green sedan illegally beside my convertible. Not that Augie seemed to give a shit about obstructing the flow of traffic. He and Colt chatted as if they were long-lost friends.

I stiffened.

So did Banjo. "Shit, sorry. I don't know why he's here. I told him to stay away from you."

"Hey, little brother. You're finally here. And you bought your princess, too."

"Not anyone's princess," I threw back at him.

Augie chuckled. "Not anymore, huh? Crown too tainted? They take it off you?"

Banjo shoved him hard in the shoulder. "Shut the fuck up. Let's go." He murmured something about seeing me on Friday night then slipped into Augie's car.

I shivered as Augie's gaze crawled all over me before he put the car in reverse and left in a screech of tires.

I shook off the uncomfortable feeling Augie left in his wake. He wasn't worth it.

Colt raised an eyebrow at me. "You didn't object when I called you princess in between kisses the other night."

My breath stuttered in my lungs while I fought for a smart comeback. Dammit. Why did he have to be so devastatingly handsome? Or so quick-witted? He was forever catching me off guard. Screw it. Honesty it was.

"It wasn't the name-calling I liked."

Colt just stared at me. Huh. Apparently, he hadn't expected flirty. Neither had I, but hey, if it gave me the upper hand, then so be it.

"You've been avoiding me," he declared, breaking the awkward silence we'd descended into.

"Not avoiding. Just busy."

"Thought you wanted to train?"

"I do."

"Then open your car and let's go."

"Now?"

"Why? Got other plans? Sucking Rafe's dick tonight?"

I glared at him. "Jealous?"

"Completely."

Aaaand I was back to off-kilter. *Fuck!* I fumbled with the keys.

"Give them here. I'll drive."

"Not a chance in hell," I shot back, finally getting my fingers to work properly. I dumped my bag in the back seat and slid behind the wheel.

He flashed me a white-toothed grin and got into the other side, settling his backpack at his feet.

I started the engine, letting the purr muffle the sounds of my slightly too-fast breathing. "I need to go home and get changed."

"Nuh. You're good as you are. What's the probability of getting jumped while wearing workout clothes?"

"Considering I work out once in a blue moon, probably not high."

"Exactly. What you're wearing will be fine."

I glanced down at my outfit. Jacket over a cute top. I could lose the jacket, the top was fine, though a sports bra might have been nice. "I'm wearing a skirt if you hadn't noticed."

Colt's grin was wolfish. "I noticed."

On reflex, I slapped my hand across his chest.

Big mistake. One, his chest was deliciously solid. Two, he caught my wrist all too easily on the rebound. His fingers smoothed across the soft skin there. The energy in the car became charged. He leaned in. "I can't wait to see you train in that skirt, Lace. Been thinking about catching a glimpse of what's underneath it all day."

My breath caught in my lungs, but I patted his chest like he was a good dog. "I've got my gym shorts in my bag. So sorry, but any dirty little thoughts you've been having are going to stay right there in your head, keeping your massive ego company." I pulled my hand back and challenged him with a single raised eyebrow. "Now, do you want to tell me where we're training? Your place?"

"No," he said too quickly.

Well, okay then. I guess I'd worn out any welcome I might have had at his house. The sharpness in his tone told me he didn't want me anywhere near his personal space. That was fine. I didn't really want him in mine either. Colt had a habit of taking up all the air. I already couldn't breathe around him.

"There's an old gym in the industrial area."

"Where we were the other night?"

"Yeah, not far from there. I'll direct once we get close."

We were one of the last to leave the parking lot, and so

we cruised out onto the main road without having to wait behind a line of other students. Neither of us said anything on the ride over. Colt spent too much time staring at me, while I made a point of never looking in his direction. I focused straight through the windshield, driving carefully, but there was no denying his gaze on my body. It took everything I had not to crash the car in distraction over the way his gaze heated my blood and sent my skin prickling with awareness.

I cracked open a window, letting in some of the cold autumn air, and he made an amused noise in the back of his throat like he knew exactly why I needed a breather.

I'd never been so glad to see the sight of run-down buildings and abandoned factories.

"Over there." Colt pointed to a driveway across from the lot the fights had taken place in the other night.

I put my blinker on and turned in. A row of eight identical units sat side by side, though only a few seemed to be in use. One guy had a handful of cars parked outside his mechanics business, but other than that, there was no one around. Colt indicated a unit to the left of the driveway, and I parked the car beneath a faded sign that read Amos Health and Fitness.

We both got out, and I took a few steps toward the darkened-glass windows, peering inside. "There's no one in there."

Colt tossed me my backpack and pulled out his own. "I know." He riffled through his pockets, producing a key. "Figured you wouldn't want an audience for your first attempt."

"That's unexpectedly thoughtful of you."

He shrugged. "Maybe I wanted to get you alone."

I deliberately played dumb. "So we could train?"

His warm breath brushed over my neck. "If that's what you want to call it."

I forced my feet toward the door. "Let's get on with this, huh? There's only so much of your sexual innuendo I can handle before I—"

"Before you succumb to it?"

"Before I hurl." I grabbed the single key from his hand and unlocked the door, preventing him from saying anything else.

I was all talk. I really did need him to quit it or I might jump on him. Nothing about Colt was vomit-worthy. Not one little thing.

The lock clicked, and I pushed the door in, a slightly musty odor hitting the back of my nose. "It smells like stale sweat and dirty socks in here."

Colt flicked on a ceiling light that lit up the dingy place, then headed for the back of the huge room. "It's a fighting gym. What did you expect? Flowers in vases and potpourri? Nobody comes in here much anymore. Not since they opened that new budget place in the middle of town." He cracked open two windows, letting in some fresh air.

"How do you have a key?"

"I know it's a foreign concept to you rich kids, but out here, we have these things called part-time jobs. This is mine."

"You teach aerobics? Gotta say, I'd love to see you in a leotard." I put on a fake, high-pitched voice. "And one. And two. Lift those knees! Grapevine!"

He shot me a barely amused glare.

A boxing ring sat in the center of the room, various cardio machines and weights placed neatly around it. There was a space by the windows with padded mats that Colt headed for. I wandered around, running a finger over an ancient-looking rowing machine and then dumped my bag by Colt's. I eyed the mats. And then him. "Why do I have a feeling this is going to hurt?"

He chuckled. "Nothing good comes easy, princess." His gaze lingered on me, sweeping my body. "Trust me, I know all about fighting for what you want."

There he went again, sucking the air right out of the room and throwing me off-balance. I pulled the zipper on my bag and found my athletic shorts, then headed toward the bathrooms.

Anything to avoid the expression on Colt's face and the way my body instinctively reacted to it.

The bathrooms weren't any prettier than the gym, so I hurried to get changed, pulling on my gym shorts and shrugging out of my jacket. At least I'd worn my Converse sneakers.

Colt had ditched his boots by the time I came out. He eyed me from across the room, watching while I put my discarded clothes into my bag at the edge of the mats.

"Shoes, too."

I toed them off and placed them neatly beside our back-packs, then straightened to face him, tiptoeing onto the squishy blue surface.

"All right, princess. Show me what you got."

He closed the distance between us, stopping about a foot away. He held his hands up, blue boxing pads covering them.

I eyed them. "Am I supposed to punch you or something?"

"Unless you'd rather make out?"

I slammed one closed fist into his waiting palm.

"Whoa. Okay. Wasn't expecting you to have any power, but that wasn't bad."

I smiled sweetly. "I imagined it was your face."

We did a few more punching drills, and I found myself loosening up and enjoying the smack of my fist against the pads. Colt took me through a few different punch combinations and then got my feet involved, making me move around the mats, dancing out of his way as he threw slow punches back at me.

Somewhere along the way, I forgot we hated each other. I forgot the attraction between us. My muscles burned, not used to this sort of exercise. Or any sort of exercise, really.

"Good," Colt encouraged when I squatted to go underneath his pad. "Get lower, then spring back. Hands up, protect your face."

For once, I didn't argue. This was one place I didn't mind taking Colt's orders. He was full of a confidence I'd never seen in him before. It came without any of his usual bravado or ego.

With my chest aching from lack of breath and my thighs burning from too many squats, I was near dead when Colt called a drink break. I dropped my guard and put my hands to my hips, breathing hard. Colt pulled a bottle of water from his backpack and passed it to me.

"You know what you're doing." I sipped my water. The cold liquid helped soothe the ache in my chest, and I tried to slow my breathing.

Colt shrugged.

"Have you been coming here long?"

He took the bottle of water from my hands and chugged down half of it.

I wrinkled my nose. "Ew, Colt. My saliva is all over that."

"Your saliva was all over my tongue the other night. What difference does it make?"

He had a point.

"And to answer your question, yeah, I've been coming here for years. Started after my dad died. Mom thought I needed a 'safe' way of releasing my aggressions."

"Does she know about the street fights?"

He screwed the cap onto the bottle slowly, his fingers twisting the little red piece of plastic while he mused over his thoughts. "Not officially. But she stopped asking why I was coming home with beat-up knuckles and black eyes. So I think she suspects something less than legal." He threw the bottle down. "Break's over. Let's work on takedowns before you get cold."

I was still huffing and puffing, and our break had been all of about two minutes. So I suspected his desire to get back to training was born more out of a reluctance to talk than me getting cold.

I glanced over at him dubiously. "You're almost a foot taller than me. There's no way I can take you down."

He blew out a frustrated breath. "Owen's a big guy, too. You gonna say that to him next time he lets himself into your house?"

I blanched.

Colt didn't give a shit.

"Teach me."

"Good. Get fired up. At me. Or Owen. Whatever. Then come in close."

I jumped up and down on the spot a few times, the way Colt had the other night before his match. I channeled the terror I'd felt when Owen had waltzed right into my bedroom. The revulsion I still felt when I thought about what he'd tried to do to me on the beach. I shuffled a few steps toward Colt so we were about the same distance apart while we'd been sparring.

He rolled his eyes. "When I say close, I mean close. You

can't do a takedown from all the way over there." He put his hand to my hip and jerked me forward until our chests were flush.

My nipples hardened beneath my tank top at the impact. *Shit.* We were as close now as when we'd been kissing outside the gas station.

"Right hand to the back of my neck."

I pressed my fingers to his nape, my palm flattening over his pulse. It thumped beneath my touch.

Huh. He'd barely done any work. Perhaps I wasn't the only one affected by how close we were.

"Not the side of my neck. The back. Get your palm right round."

I focused and did as I was told.

"Other hand grasps my biceps. Thumb in, get your fingers right over to press into my triceps."

Permission to touch any sort of 'cep' muscle Colt possessed? Yes, please.

"Good," he murmured. "Grip tight. Pull down. Try to move me around."

To my surprise, his big body did actually move where I pulled it.

"You aren't trying," I accused.

"You're still learning. It's a powerful grip. Combined with other moves, you'll get me down. Now, keep your elbow in. When I come at you, you throw it up and duck behind me, underneath my arm."

I focused on the hand that was on his biceps. When he lunged for me, I jerked my elbow up. We were so close, the elbow caught him in the fleshy part beneath his arm, lifting it and giving me room to duck around him.

"Good! Grab me around the waist."

"Like a bear hug?"

"Exactly. But lower. Above my hips, around my abs. Use your smaller height."

Hug him around the waist, cop a feel of his abs, try to keep my hands from going any lower. Sure. No problem. I could do that without self-combusting.

"Tighter, Lacey. Don't let me break your grip."

His abs were solid rock. I linked my hands together, squeezing him tight from behind.

"Now one leg between mine. Your other knee takes out mine. Push all your weight to that side."

I hesitated. Being this close to him was torturous. His distinctly masculine scent was inescapable with my cheek pressed to the small of his back.

"Do it," he yelled.

One leg between. Other knee to the back of his.

And down we both went, hitting the mats hard.

Holy shit. I'd done it! I let out a whoop and stretched my hands up over my head, fist-pumping the air.

"Don't lie there celebrating. Get up and run!"

Oh. Right. Of course.

I scrambled to my feet and had taken two joyous steps, completely filled with pride, when his hand shot out, gripped my ankle, and yanked it out from beneath me.

I came down as hard as a sack of potatoes, crashing into the mat, my knees and hands taking the brunt of the fall. "Ow!"

Before I even knew what was happening, he flipped me onto my back, his big body covering mine, pinning me down.

I yelped, trying to push him off me, but he grabbed my wrists, pinning them to the mats.

His face hovered an inch away from mine, both of us breathing heavy, our chests rising and falling in unison.

I glared at him. "That was a dirty move. You don't play fair."

He stared back, his gaze growing hot. "Neither should you. There's no rules in street fighting. Throw your opponent off-balance however you can."

Silence fell over us.

Then I strained up and pressed my lips to his.

His response was instant. He let go of my wrists, dropping onto his forearms, the full force of his weight crushing me into the mats while his tongue delved inside my mouth. It was only then I realized how easy he'd been going on me, but I welcomed his weight, grinding up on him, feeling his instant erection swell and prod at my thigh. The kiss was rough and hard, adrenaline coursing through me as I grabbed at his face, his hair, pulling him closer, needing more. His hips rolled, and I got my legs out from under him, wrapping them around him so his dick was where I wanted it most, fitted to my core.

"Fuck, Lacey," he whispered between kisses. "I want you."

I moaned into his mouth. Like they had a mind of their own, my fingers clenched into his t-shirt, ripping it upward, scrabbling to get it off him.

His mouth tore away from mine momentarily so he could get the shirt off, and then he was back, kissing me again, his tongue moving with mine, stroking and sliding, heat building inside me while I scratched my nails down his gloriously muscled back. My eyes drifted shut.

His cock rubbed at my core again, and I rocked with him, moaning over the building pressure there, desperate and begging for a way to release it. Colt's body was a fucking masterpiece. Built specifically for sin. I was desperate to get naked with him. To feel his skin on mine, to feel his dick slide between my legs, and to quench that thirst between them.

"I want you, too," I whispered back, kissing him harder. "Please tell me you have a condom."

Without stopping the kiss, he scrambled over our heads, and there was the sound of the zipper on his backpack sliding loose. I writhed beneath him while he sorted through his bag, blindly looking for condoms.

A beat of silence followed.

Then something cool pushed against my temple.

I blinked my eyes open.

His face was hard as he flicked off the safety of the gun he held to my head.

18

LACEY

*I*ce-cold shards of fear put out the fire in my blood instantly.

Colt pressed the gun a little harder into my head, and a whimper left my mouth. My heart hammered so hard, I was sure it was going to explode. Tears pricked the backs of my eyes, and a desperate scream lodged in my throat.

"Fight, Lacey!" Colt yelled in my face.

Gulping on a sob, I finally kicked my muscles into action. I thrashed beneath him, twisting and turning until the pressure of his weight eased. I rolled to my side, stumbled to my feet, and swiped my backpack from the mats. Without stopping to get my shoes, I ran for the door, horrid, racking cries escaping my throat.

He'd let me go.

Somewhere in the back of my mind, I knew that. From the vulnerable position I'd let him get me into, there was no way I could have fought him off so easily.

He'd let me go.

Running across the parking lot, pain stabbed through

my bare feet, the gravel and tiny bits of glass piercing my skin. But I didn't stop.

The feel of the gun at my temple wouldn't go away.

The sound of the click as he'd released the safety, ready to shoot.

I fumbled for my keys, dropping them in my haste to get away, and frantically scrambled to pick them back up and open the door.

I threw myself behind the wheel, simultaneously trying to start the engine at the same time, but when I tried to pull the door closed, it wouldn't budge.

A scream ripped from my throat when I realized it was because Colt was holding it.

"Get away from me!"

His expression was completely calm. The guy from the other unit still worked on his car and didn't even blink at the fact I was screaming and trying to get away from Colt. He carried on like this sort of thing was an everyday occurrence.

Colt produced the gun, and I cringed away.

"It's not real," he said quietly.

"I don't believe you," I bit back. It was the most real-looking gun I'd ever seen. Not that I knew one end of a gun from the other, but this was certainly no two-dollar squirt gun from a convenience store. The black metal gleamed in the dying afternoon light, and I still all too clearly remembered the noise it had made, cocked it against my temple. Nausea rolled my stomach.

He tried to hand me the gun, but I shoved it away. He sighed, impatience radiating off him as he threw it in my back seat.

I twisted around to gape at it before turning back to the madman holding me hostage. "Are you insane?"

He squatted so he was slightly lower than my eye height. His expression was fierce, full of attitude. "No. But I do want you to be safe. That," he pointed to the gun in the back seat while he eyed me firmly, "I bought for you. You feel how scared you were back there in that gym with the gun held to your head? That's how Owen will feel if the day ever comes when you need to pull it on him."

"You're a fucking asshole."

"Never said I wasn't."

I sucked in a breath and tried to hold it. Tried to let it calm me while it spread oxygen through my terrified body. "It looks real."

"Of course it does. It'd be no good to you if it didn't."

"I don't want a gun. I won't shoot anyone. Not even Owen."

"And you don't have one. What you have is a movie prop that might save your life one day. Even if it only buys you a minute, that's a minute you wouldn't have otherwise, right? You pull that gun, and you get yourself out of the situation before he realizes it's not real. It's small enough to fit in your purse, so carry it everywhere."

A single tear dripped down my face, the culmination of terror and relief mingling. "I hate you," I choked out.

For half a second, I thought I saw disappointment dull Colt's eyes. But then his hard determination was back.

"I don't care." The words ground out from between his teeth. "I'm not here to be your friend. I'm here to teach you how to save your life."

I couldn't face him anymore. I put the car in drive and got the hell away from Colt as fast as I could.

19

LACEY

 ithout really thinking about where I was going, I found myself in front of Rafe's house. I parked on the street and then checked my appearance in the rearview mirror.

I looked awful. Tears had smeared my mascara down my cheeks in dirty black trails, and my eyes were wide and red from crying. It was as if I'd swallowed shots of coffee in quick succession. My fingers trembled, and my leg bounced uncontrollably.

I twisted, hoping the gun had disappeared from the back seat on the drive over, but it hadn't budged from its landing spot. It stood out against the lighter colored seats like a leech. Damn Colt. I didn't want a gun, fake or not. But I couldn't leave it sitting on my back seat for any random person to spot if they happened to stroll by while out dog walking or something. I snatched it up, surprised at how heavy it was for a small pistol. I turned it over, testing the weight, then shook my head and shoved it deep into my backpack.

Fuck Colt. And fuck me. I was an idiot for letting my

guard down around him. God. Had I really been about to have sex with him? Had I seriously been anticipating him pulling out a condom? What an idiot I was.

Shame heated my cheeks, which then morphed into rage. I got out of the car and shut the door so hard the resounding crack would have been heard streets away. I stormed up the path to Rafe's place, trying to calm myself but failing miserably. I prayed he was home. Because I didn't know what to do with all this pent-up aggression and frustration by myself. I ran up the front steps and raised my hand to knock on the door.

"No, Todd. Please don't, I didn't—"

The muffled yells and the crash of glass breaking stopped me, my fist hovering in midair.

Rafe's dad said something undeterminable, and then the sound of crying echoed back, clear as day.

That rage I'd been carrying for Colt suddenly morphed into a dagger for the man inside, currently terrifying the woman he called his wife. Fucking asshole! What was it with these guys? I was so sick of men thinking this sort of shit was okay. It wasn't.

I slammed my fist into the door, over and over until it disappeared from beneath my fingers, swinging open.

"What," Principal Simmons yelled.

I'd never seen the man so disheveled. The fitted, pale-blue shirt he'd worn to school was half untucked from his navy suit pants, his tie discarded, and the buttons undone halfway to his navel. His hair was a tangled mess, as if he'd been running his fingers through it.

His face changed the instant he saw it was me. He shot a look back into the house, but the crying had already stopped.

It didn't matter.

I'd heard it.

I went to move past him, into the house, but he blocked the gap with a quick sidestep. "Lacey. What are you doing here? Now isn't a good time."

I raised one eyebrow. "Seems like a great time to me."

A sniffle came from behind him, but the woman who stood there smiled brightly at me. "Lacey? I've heard so much about you. Rafe isn't here, but please, sweetheart, won't you come inside?"

I shot a triumphant glare at Principal Simmons, who seemed ready for steam to shoot out of his ears. But what could he say now?

"I'd absolutely love to."

Reluctantly, Principal Simmons dropped his arm from the doorjamb and cleared his throat. "Of course. Come in. Rafe is due back any moment."

I ignored his nice guy act. I wouldn't be buying that ever again. I'd always known something was off with the man, but everything I'd just heard confirmed it. Principal Simmons was not the upstanding school leader he made himself out to be.

There was evil behind those fake smiles and neat suits.

I turned to Mrs. Simmons and smiled at her brightly. She was a stunning woman. She was tall and slim, dressed impeccably yet modestly. I snuck a look beyond her to the kitchen and noted the tiny sparkling shards of glass that littered the tiled floor.

Mrs. Simmons noticed the direction of my gaze and shot a tiny, worried glance at her husband. He shook his head imperceptibly, but I saw it. I narrowed my eyes.

"I dropped a glass," Mrs. Simmons said, taking my hand and squeezing it.

Her gaze met mine, and the plea in her eyes was unmissable.

Please don't say anything.

I squeezed her fingers back.

Relief settled over her, and she led me toward the couch, perching on the edge of it while Principal Simmons watched us from the doorway. He still hadn't closed the door, like he was half expecting he might walk out of it.

Or perhaps throw me out of it.

I couldn't stand looking at him. I knew what I'd heard. I'd seen Rafe's black eyes. I now knew where they'd really come from. My blood boiled all over again.

I might have silently promised Mrs. Simmons not to say anything about what I'd heard. But there were other things Principal Simmons needed to explain. I stared at him, refusing to back down from the way he glared at me, his big frame imposing and formidable.

"Did you know my uncle?" I asked.

A shadow passed by the windows at speed, and Rafe skidded to a stop behind his father.

Principal Simmons and I ignored him, too busy locked in a silent battle with each other.

"Why do you ask?"

He was being deliberately cagey. He knew Lawson. I already knew he did. Why wasn't he coming out and saying it?

Rafe pushed past his dad and stopped between us, spinning back to face his father while simultaneously reaching out a hand for me. "We were talking about it the other day. With both you and Lacey's uncle being school principals, we wondered if you'd met each other before. At inter-school functions or whatever. Anyway, it doesn't matter. Lacey and I have homework to do, right, Lace? We'll be upstairs." He jerked his outstretched hand deliberately then rolled his fingers in a 'come here' gesture.

I frowned behind Rafe's back but stood to take his hand. His fingers clamped around mine, and then he towed me up the stairs so fast I practically tripped over him. I didn't even get to say goodbye to his mom.

He took a turn to the right, pulling me into what had to be his bedroom, and shut the door behind him. He spun on me. "What are you doing?" he hissed, eyes wild. They raked over me, up and down. "Are you okay?"

"Of course."

"You can't be asking my dad about your uncle."

I jerked back at the insistence in his voice.

"Excuse me? Why not? He might know something."

"That's what I'm afraid of."

I folded my arms across my chest. "If he knows something, I need to know what it is."

He ran a hand through his hair. "Lacey, shit. You aren't Nancy Drew. You don't know my dad." His voice lowered, and he stared at me with pain in his eyes. "What if he doesn't just know something, Lace? What if he knows *everything*?"

I swallowed hard. "You mean...?"

"What if he did it? What if he's the one who killed your uncle?" Rafe's expression held a mixture of emotions. Confusion. Anger. Fear.

The air punched from my lungs. "But why? That doesn't make any sense."

"Doesn't it? I've been thinking it over. They went to college together. Presumably, they had all the same classes since they both went on to do the same job. Yet your uncle landed at Providence, with that beautiful big historical school to reside over, and a gorgeous wife and big house in the nicest part of town..."

"While your dad landed at Saint View..."

Rafe sank onto his queen-sized bed, pulling me down beside him and snuggling in close. He buried his nose in my hair and breathed in my scent, as if using it to calm himself. His lips brushed over the space below my ear.

"Do you really think he's capable of that?" I whispered, without looking at him. In a rush, I understood so much more about Rafe. He was the son of an abuser, but despite the terror radiating off him, one thing was clear—he wasn't afraid of his dad for his own sake. No, it was all for mine.

I felt more than saw his answering nod. "My father isn't a good man." He paused, the silence hanging over us cold and laced with tension. "I think he's capable of anything."

20

———

LACEY

Rafe and I talked long into the night, cuddled together on his bed while he confessed about how abusive his dad was, and I confided everything that had happened with Colt.

Including the kisses we'd shared.

I wasn't about to lie to Rafe. Or anyone. The kisses with Colt had been a mistake, I knew that now. But when I said as much to Rafe, he'd gone quiet.

"What?" I asked him.

He shrugged. "It sounds more like he cares about you. I know he scared you. And trust me, I'm gonna kick him in the balls for that."

I giggled a little, and he kissed my nose, pulling me tighter. "But I think he was trying to teach you something. In his own, fucked-up, Colt-ish way."

I sighed. "Doesn't matter anyway. It won't happen again."

Rafe kissed me, slow and sweet, his tongue stroking mine. "It's okay with me if it does. I know what we have isn't exclusive."

"Banjo isn't in the picture anymore."

Rafe looked a little troubled by that, and I frowned at him. "Did you forget what he did?"

He shook his head. "No. I just...fuck, I dunno. I miss him, you know? Hell, Lacey, you're amazing. And I'm so into you. But I enjoyed what the three of us had going on."

I laid my head against his chest. "I did, too," I admitted. Then I lifted my head. "So, you'd be okay with me seeing Colt as well?"

He rolled me over and pressed me into the mattress, raining kisses down my jawline. "I'm good with whatever you want. If that means we bring Colt in on this, then...actually, that's kinda hot."

I kissed him back then laughed against his lips. "You kinky fuck."

He grinned and kissed me harder. "I know. I've got issues."

"I like your issues."

I broke my curfew, getting home at one, but managed to sneak in without Selina noticing.

I blew off school the next day after waking up tired and emotionally drained from the day before. Selina hovered over me for a little while, but when I confessed I wasn't sick and just needed some downtime, she resumed her normal plans and left the house to go shopping with Pamela.

I watched Netflix for a while and then tried to read, but my attention kept drifting. My gaze inevitably fell to my walk-in closet, and eventually, I got up off the bed and opened the doors.

I skimmed past the racks of hanging clothes, most of which I hadn't even worn, and the rows of shoes that shone with their newness. Such a waste. All of it. Who needed this much stuff? Most of the kids at Saint View wore the same four or five outfits every week. And I'd followed suit, mixing and matching the handful of clothes I'd bought with Jagger during my first week of school. Those outfits had become my uniform. One I felt more comfortable in than I ever had in our preppy Providence School for Girls uniforms.

But I wasn't in the closet for my clothes. I eyed the keyboard, tucked away in its black fabric bag, and lifted it from its resting spot. I laid it on my bed while I put the stand together, testing it was sturdy on the thick carpet before fitting the keyboard to the top.

It had been weeks since I'd played. But suddenly, my fingers itched to fly across the keys.

I closed my eyes and let loose.

It took me a minute, but then muscle memory kicked in, and the music fell from my fingertips, soaring through my heart and filling me with the calm I'd been missing for so long. For months now, really. The last time I'd truly felt that magic was the night of the fire.

I had no idea what I was even playing. Bits and pieces of a song I thought I knew came together, and I hummed along, not entirely sure where the melody had come from.

Somewhere in the back of my mind, I think I heard the door downstairs open and Angelique greeting whoever was on the other side. But then I was quickly pulled back, too lost in my own world to care if a package had been delivered, or if a repair guy had come to fix the leaking faucet in the downstairs bathroom.

The knock at my bedroom door made me pay attention, though.

"Lacey?" Angelique called through the door.

I paused, my fingers hovering in the air above the keys. "Yeah?"

She cracked the door open an inch and peered in, her big blue eyes a little squinty with worry.

I frowned. She was normally super smiley and bubbly. "What's wrong?"

"Banjo is here," she said quietly. "He asked if I'd let you know. He didn't want to just come up and spring himself on you. Not that I would have let him," she added on in a rush.

I smiled at her, the thought of her tiny five-foot frame trying to block the Saint View High quarterback completely ludicrous. She was a good friend.

Banjo, on the other hand, was not. I was tempted to tell him to leave.

But something stopped me. Instead, I turned off the keyboard and followed Angelique to the top of the stairs.

Banjo stood at the bottom, staring up at me through his floppy blond hair.

My heart squeezed painfully. "You ready to talk? Really talk?"

He hesitated then shook his head. "I will. Friday night, after the game. I promise. I just need time to get my thoughts together. I need to work out how to say it right, so I don't make things worse between us. I'm not ready yet." His expression turned desperate. "Please, Lacey. Don't force this. I can't fuck it up any more than I already have. I'm terrified of losing you for good."

I fought back my annoyance and the urge to say he might have already done that. But I didn't want to make things between us any worse either. "Then what do you want?"

"We missed you in music class today. Wasn't sure you'd answer my calls or texts, so I came to tell you that Miss Halten wants a final song choice from every pair by tomorrow."

My mouth dropped open. "We haven't even started."

"I know." His hands fluttered around his sides in uncertainty before he shoved them in his pockets. "I don't have training this afternoon. I thought maybe we could work on it? If you aren't busy, that is?" He jerked his head toward a bag on the floor. "I brought my portable kit in case you were available."

Ugh. I hated the way we spoke to each other now. With him standing there at the bottom of my stairs, it was so easy to remember the first time I'd seen him. To remember the way he'd made me feel that day, and all the days after it.

But things changed. People changed.

Or maybe I never really knew him at all.

But we did have an assignment to do, and I wasn't about to blow my grade point average because I couldn't work with the boy who'd broken my trust. And my heart.

"Fine. Come up."

Angelique tutted under her breath, and I gave her an amused smile. She ignored me and shot a dirty look in Banjo's direction instead. She'd been at my birthday party. She knew all about what he'd done.

Banjo passed her on the staircase with a wary smile in her direction, which she didn't return, and I motioned for him to go into my bedroom. I closed the door behind him.

"I don't think she likes me much."

"Can you blame her? She's my friend."

He bit his bottom lip. "I know. But I swear, Lacey—"

"Yeah, yeah. It wasn't you. Can we work on the assignment?"

Banjo's wounded puppy dog expression ate at me. I needed to get him out of here as quickly as possible. "Did you come up with any song suggestions?"

Banjo withdrew a piece of paper from the back of his pocket and passed it to me.

I wrinkled my nose, unfamiliar with the three songs he'd scrawled out.

If he was insulted that I didn't love his song choices, he didn't show it. "What about you? Did you have any?"

I realized suddenly what song I'd been playing earlier. I snorted on a laugh. "How about 'One More Night' by Maroon Five. You know it?"

Banjo frowned. "Yeah, I know it well. It's about a dysfunctional couple who are terrible together but keep reuniting for one last night." He eyed me. "Fuck, Lacey. Is that how you see us?"

I shook my head. And that was the truth. That song had a whole lot more to do with me and Colt than me and Banjo. But that was safer. Everything Colt and I felt for each other was so wrapped up in our mutual hate. That provided a barrier. A safety net that meant we never got too close.

There was none of that with Banjo. His feelings were out there for the world to see. And mine were just as raw. Just as frayed. Just as broken.

I still loved him. That wouldn't go away.

But that didn't mean we could be together either.

I couldn't tell him the song I would have picked for us. "Don't Speak" by No Doubt was the first song that came to mind. Gwen Stefani performed those lyrics with such soulful pain, any attempt to recreate them would destroy me. That song was Banjo and me all over. I didn't want to hear his words. His explanations. He'd hurt me, and it was too hard to hear him say it.

"Miss Halten never said it had to mean anything. That song will be pretty cool with just a piano and a beat from the drums."

"'One More Night' it is then," Banjo agreed. "You already know it?"

"Bits. I'll search for some sheet music." I grabbed my laptop, got us the notes, and then we sat side by side, listening to the song on repeat for a while.

Banjo ditched his sheet music pretty quickly, making me wonder if he actually knew how to read it, then closed his eyes to tap out the beat on his leg. When I thought I knew the rhythms, I shifted to the keyboard and picked it up in the chorus, singing along beneath my breath. Banjo got up and went to my desk, tapping it out louder, his strikes against the wooden surface confident now.

At the end of the song, we both looked up and grinned.

My heart fluttered. It had been too long since I'd seen that smile on his face. "That sounded awesome," I said quietly. "For a first attempt, anyway."

"You're good. You picked that up so quick."

"You, too."

A sudden wave of longing crushed over me. Tears pricked the backs of my eyes, but I blinked them away. Dammit. I was not going to cry over him. Not again. I'd already done so much of that. Instead, I moved to my laptop. "I've got recording software on here. Do you want to get your kit out and play it properly? So we can get a feel for each other? Then we can practice alone."

Banjo's expression fell. "Uh, yeah, sure. Whatever you want."

I nodded. It was what I wanted. We needed to practice a lot between now and the recital. It was inevitable we'd have to get together at some point to do that, but I couldn't do this every day. It was too hard. My chest would break in two, I was sure of it.

I busied myself with the recording program then realized Banjo would need a copy, too. "Hey, throw me a USB stick from my desk, would you? It'll probably be a big file, it'll take forever if I upload it somewhere."

"You don't mind? I can give it back to you at school tomorrow," he said politely.

I glanced at him. "It's a five-dollar USB stick, Banjo. It's not a big deal. Just grab one. Top drawer."

He opened the drawer and tossed me a little portable stick. I shoved it into the port on my computer without even glancing at it, clicking the relevant folders when the computer recognized it. "Gotta check I don't have anything important on here before I wipe it."

I opened a folder that was simply called New Folder, like I'd been too lazy to actually give it a name, and a screen of thumbnails appeared. Banjo came to sit on the bed beside me, still tapping out the beat absently on his thigh.

He glanced over my shoulder and raised an eyebrow. "Why do you have porn on a USB stick?"

I shot him a look. "I don't."

"I'm a guy, Lace. I can spot porn in thumbnail from a mile away, even if you can't."

I double-clicked the first thumbnail and blinked at it in surprise.

Banjo cocked his head to one side. "Amateur porn, but porn all the same."

I elbowed him. He was exaggerating. It wasn't exactly porn. But it was a woman in lingerie. Lacy black panties and bra set, beneath a floaty silk cover-up. The photo cut off above the swell of her breasts. I sorted through the photos, my finger moving faster as each shot became more and more risqué. The cover-up disappeared. Then the bra, though most shots remained tasteful, almost arty. I paused on a suggestive shot where the woman pulled the top of her panties down, revealing a script tattoo. *Forever*, it read, placed along the top of her pubic bone.

I closed the folder. "This isn't mine." I tugged the USB stick from the port and turned it over, wondering where it had come from.

Realization slammed through me.

I jolted, dropping it on the floor like it had burned me.

Banjo bent over and retrieved it, holding it out for me to take.

I shook my head.

"It's not mine," I said again.

I remembered exactly where I'd last seen that stick, its distinctive orange stripe differentiating it from the others in my drawer. I got up and rushed to the door. "Angelique!"

She appeared almost instantly, as if she'd been hovering by the doorway.

I spun and pointed at the USB stick in Banjo's hand. "Do you know how that USB stick got in my drawer?"

Angelique peered at it, then nodded. "It was in your laundry. Some months ago now. I found it when I was washing your clothes and put it in your drawer. Did you not want it there?"

I shook my head and thanked her, closing the door again and leaning on it. Banjo looked so confused.

"That USB is Lawson's. It fell off a pile of paperwork he was carrying into school the night of the fire. I caught it and shoved it in my pocket for safekeeping. I completely forgot about it."

I crossed the room and sank down onto my bed, closing the laptop and wishing I'd never seen those images. My mind whirled.

"Lace?" Banjo asked carefully. "I'm not sure what the big deal is? I'm not trying to diminish your feelings or anything, but your uncle was a guy. Guys watch porn. This isn't that big a deal."

Hope sparked in my chest. "You think that's all that was?"

Banjo shrugged. "What else would it be?"

"Proof Lawson had a mistress? That definitely wasn't Selina. She hates tattoos. There's no way she'd get one, even a hidden one like that."

Banjo's mouth formed a little O shape. "Shit, you think?"

I shrugged. "No, not really. It wasn't his style. But I don't know. Those photos were kind of personal..."

But Banjo shook his head. "I don't think so. The woman's face was never shown. That says to me it's porn and the woman didn't want her face being broadcast to the world. If these were photos from a mistress, her face would be in them. You want to see the face of the woman you're screwing around with, you know? That's more personal than random body shots."

I nodded slowly, mulling that over. "Lawson loved Selina."

Banjo's fingers inched toward mine. "Are you going to say anything to her?"

Horror raced through me, and I shook my head sharply. "Oh God. I can't. It would kill her. And what if you're right and it is nothing? Hell, she'd be upset just knowing he had porn. I always thought that was why she spent so much of her time at the gym, and eating healthy and dressing nicely, you know? I always thought she was a little insecure and never wanted Lawson to look anywhere else."

"That's not a fun way to live."

I heaved a sigh. "He never would have, though. He was committed to her. I'm sure of that."

Banjo nodded and folded the USB stick into his palm.

"Then don't worry about this. The man is dead anyway. What good will come of you showing her any of this and putting doubt in her mind?"

"None."

"Exactly. So let's forget that we saw your uncle's secret stash and get on with our practice, okay?"

I nodded and offered him a small, grateful smile. "Thank you."

"For what?"

I shrugged. "Being a voice of calm when I was about to lose it?"

"I think I owed you one."

I didn't say anything.

"I hate that I hurt you."

I glanced up at him. "I know you do."

But the damage was already done.

21

LACEY

The next afternoon, I met Meredith and Jagger at the mall for some much-needed girl time. Meredith immediately herded us in the direction of the nail salon, claiming all of life's problems could be solved over a good mani-pedi.

She wasn't wrong.

We settled into big, comfortable armchairs, side by side, and the moment my feet plunged into the warm water of the foot spa, I let out an indecent groan.

Meredith and Jagger both swiveled to look at me, eyebrows raised.

My cheeks went hot, and I let out a laugh as I defended myself. "Leave me alone. It's really good."

"That's what he said," Meredith quipped.

"When it comes to Lacey, though, which 'he' said it?" Jagger waggled her eyebrows at me.

"Hey, hey, no slut-shaming."

Jagger grabbed my arm. "Are you kidding? No shame from me. Girl, I'm hella jealous of what you have going on and I want all the details."

Meredith bounced excitedly in her chair. "Tell us everything that's been going on. Quick, before the technicians come over here and start scraping at your nasty feet."

I slapped her shoulder. "My feet are not nasty."

Meredith waved a hand around like that was unimportant. "Spill it. What's been happening with Banjo and Rafe?"

"And Colt," Jagger added.

Meredith stared at Jagger, then back at me, her mouth forming an O shape. "No! You added a third guy to your love...square?" She shook her head. "Damn, Lace. I didn't think you had it in you."

I gave her a disparaging look. "It's not a love square. It's not even a triangle anymore. It's really just me and Rafe."

I shot an apologetic glance at Jagger and chewed my bottom lip. "Sorry I didn't tell you yet. It only sort of happened the other day."

I was a little worried about how Jagger might take the news I was with her ex-boyfriend. But before the party, she'd known this was where Rafe and I were headed. We might have taken a detour, but we'd found our way back.

Jagger gave me a reassuring smile. "You and Rafe are two of my best friends. All I want is you both to be happy."

"And to have hot sex," Meredith quipped. "It was hot, right?"

I tried to remain neutral, but it was a losing battle. My grin spread wide. "You have no idea." Then I glanced at Jagger. "Well, maybe you do..." I buried my face in my hands, and the three of us dissolved into laughter.

"And Colt?" Jagger asked. "You two were kinda cozy when I picked you up the other night."

"Yeah, and then he went and pulled a gun on me."

The laughter and smiles came to a screeching halt.

Meredith made a choking noise. "Say what?"

I shrugged. "It was fake. But he's an asshole. I lost my mind for a bit there, thinking he was something he's not. That's on me."

"Fuck," Jagger whispered. "Intense."

If any word described Colt, that was it.

Meredith changed the subject. "And Banjo? You back in the sheets with him, too?"

My heart plummeted.

Meredith reached over and squeezed my hand. "I hate seeing that expression on your face."

I swallowed hard, battling down the feelings that always threatened to overwhelm me when I thought about Banjo.

Jagger gripped my other hand. "At the risk of sounding unsupportive, you forgave Rafe. Why can't you do the same for Banjo?"

I blew out a long breath. I'd wondered the same thing myself. I blinked back tears. "Because I wasn't in love with Rafe. It wasn't his bedroom. His bed. Banjo swears the camera was planted by Augie, and I believe him. But I know there's more going on that he's not telling me. He's got walls up, and I can't let mine down until I know he's being honest with me."

Meredith took her hand back and scraped her curls into a high ponytail, fastening it with a thick black elastic from her wrist. "Well, if he can't get his act together, he isn't worth your time."

I nodded, but Jagger gave me a knowing look. Deep in my heart, I knew Banjo was worth it. He was worth waiting for. I had to hope he could get past whatever was going on with him and let me in. It was the only way we were ever going to get back to where we were.

"I'm having a party on Saturday night," Jagger announced, changing the subject abruptly.

Thank God, because I wasn't sure I could talk about my own messed-up love life any longer.

Meredith clapped her hands excitedly. "Do you think that guy from the beach party will be there? What was his name again?"

"Trenton," Jagger and I said in unison.

"That's it. I wouldn't mind doing a little more than kissin' with him this time." She reached across and tugged on Jagger's shirt. "Make it happen, Jag. Please."

Jagger flashed her a thumbs-up. "Aaron and I are hosting together. So the entire football team will be invited."

"Oooh," I singsonged. "Your first co-hosted party. Does this mean you two are an official couple now? You in love?"

She smiled softly and stared down at her hands in her lap.

I froze. "Holy fuck. You are!"

Jagger's eyes lit up. "He's amazing. He's so sweet and kind—"

"And hot as fuck," Meredith jumped in. "I bet his dick is massive."

Jagger giggled and lowered her voice again. "The sex is off-the-charts amazing. Like, multiple-times-a-night mind-blowing."

Meredith let out a hoot that had the entire salon turning in our direction. "Good for you!"

Jagger and I both shushed her.

The technicians obviously thought it was about time to get us out of their salon, because three of them arrived at once, taking our feet from the water and drying them off on a towel.

"So you guys will come?" Jagger asked.

"Wouldn't miss it for the world," I agreed.

I just had to get through Friday night's football game and whatever it was Banjo needed to get off his chest first.

22

BANJO

Nerves were normal before a game. I'd played enough of them to know that. Normally I relished them. They helped me focus. Helped me calm my breathing and keep my eye on the prize. I never wanted to feel completely confident going into a game. That meant I'd gotten cocky. And cocky players weren't good players. Nerves had their place. They showed you'd kept your head and you still cared about the outcome. That you were a team player and you wanted the best for your teammates as well as yourself.

But the anxiety that swallowed me tonight was next level. Not only was I scared Lacey wouldn't show, I was also terrified about what I was going to have to tell her later. I knew the sort of judgment my confession could attract. I didn't think I could bear it. Not from her. I'd managed to hold Augie off, scraping up the rent money each week, but his requests to join his business were becoming more and more frequent and more demanding. Last night, I'd lain in my bed listening to the sounds of Augie's 'work' in the room above me. I loved my brother. No matter what, he was the only family I had. He'd come for me, saving me from that shitty group home, like my very own knight in shining armor. He'd taken me in, barely old enough to look after himself, solely because we were brothers. He might not have ever been able to tell me he loved me, but his actions spoke louder than words.

Even if some of his actions lately had been misguided.

I didn't want people judging him for what he'd had to do to support me when I was too young to bring anything to the table. I didn't want their judgment for Augie *liking* what he did. We weren't some typical family, with a mom and a dad and a white picket fence. That had never been my life, and it probably never would be.

But I could have more than I had now.

I could have more than the life Augie was offering me.

And that all started tonight. With the scouts in the crowd. And with Lacey after the game.

I was going to get it all back on track. I was ready. I needed it. And nothing was going to stop me.

I jumped up and down on the spot and scanned the home team crowd who cheered in the stands. The two scouts from East Shore University were right behind the team benches, special guests of Coach Tontine. Willa and Aria, Colt's family, sat beside them, Willa playing the dutiful coach's wife role, even though she and Coach were just dating. Even still, she'd become a fixture at these games, and I waved to her now, a pleasant feeling settling over me when she gave me a proud smile back. She leaned in, saying something to one of the scouts, then pointed in my direction. My helmet hid my smile. I kinda loved that Willa would be talking me up through the game. She was the best surrogate mom I could have asked for.

My gaze wandered a little higher in the stands, to Gillian

and Colt who seemed to be having a heated conversation, if their stiff body language was anything to go by. But that was nothing new for the two of them. They were always fighting. Whether they were together or not.

I finally spotted Lacey, sitting with Jagger and Meredith, a dusty-pink beanie pulled low over her forehead, scarf tucked around her neck. These games were definitely getting colder as the season progressed, but that never stopped our supporters from coming out to watch. Rain, hail, or shine, Saint View turned up for us. I loved it.

Almost as much as I loved Lacey.

After the game, I'd take her somewhere quiet to give her the letter I'd written. I didn't trust myself not to screw it up, so over the last week, I'd spent hours pouring out all my truths, as well as my feelings on to sheets of bright-white paper. My heart and soul, all right there for her to read and destroy. Or to read and tell me she understood. I prayed it would be the latter. It had to be. I'd been ashamed of what Augie did. What he wanted me to do. And bound by my loyalty to him. He might have been an asshole, but he was all I had. He was the only one who'd wanted me when the rest of the world had turned their backs. It wasn't easy to betray that.

But Lacey had loved me once. I had to tell her everything.

"Get your head in the game," a gruff voice came from my side. Rafe stared across the field at the other team, who were doing the same thing we were, warming up and taking in the crowd. "They're good. And they know those scouts are here, too. You think they don't want it as bad as you do? You're wrong. Stop thinking about Lacey and start thinking about your future."

"She is my future," I said quietly.

Rafe glanced at me.

"I'm in love with her, Rafe. That hasn't changed."

He blew out a long breath and nodded. "She's easy to love."

"So are you."

He looked at me sharply.

I shrugged. "It's written all over your face. Tell her how you feel. She might feel the same way, you know."

"Is it that obvious?"

"Only to me. I'm your best friend."

"Were."

"Still here, Rafe. Still want your friendship." I darted a glance around, checking there was no one else in earshot. I dropped my voice. "Still want you."

Rafe sucked in a deep breath. "Don't fucking do this now."

He was right, my timing sucked. "After the game? I'm taking Lacey out, to talk. You should be there, too. Everything I need her to hear applies to you as well."

The ref blew the whistle, cutting our conversation short.

Then the game of my life started, and I had no time left to consider what would happen after it.

23

LACEY

Cold wind whipped around my face, and I snuggled a little closer to Jagger, who had her teeth pressed so hard to her bottom lip I was surprised she hadn't drawn blood. I nudged her with my elbow. "Aaron is going to do great. Those scouts would be insane not to consider him."

She didn't even look at me, just kept her eyes trained on her man as he warmed up on the field, stretching in front of us. "Can I tell you a secret?"

"Of course."

"I'm a shitty girlfriend."

"What? You are not."

She turned to me, her forehead lined with worry. "This morning, I was thinking about how next year, he'll go off to play college ball. While I stay here in freaking Saint View. And for the tiniest moment, I hoped the scouts wouldn't notice him tonight." She bit her lip again, her eyes going glossy with unshed tears. "See? I'm awful."

I squeezed her knee reassuringly. "Or maybe you're human? You care about him. The thought of being separated is scary."

"It makes me sad to think there's an expiration date on this thing with him."

"You still have ages together. And anyway, who says you aren't getting out of Saint View?"

She rolled her eyes. "You've seen my grades. The community college wouldn't even take me."

"So study?"

She snorted on a laugh. "Books and I don't get along."

"Then you'll get a job in a fashion store. Or you'll design your own clothing line and sell it online. All of that you can do from wherever Aaron is, if that's what you really want."

She brightened then gave me a coy smile. "I think it is. And gosh, Lacey. Can you imagine? I'd get some cute little apartment near his campus, and he could come stay with me whenever he wanted. We could have sex on every available surface and never have to worry about one of our parents or siblings walking in. You have no idea how good you have it, only having one parent." She clapped her hand over her mouth. "Oh my God. I'm so sorry. That did not come out the way I meant it to."

I waved my hand, knowing she'd meant no harm. "It's okay. Selina has been surprisingly good about everything. Even the whole two-guy thing."

"Did you run the three-guy thing past her yet?"

I elbowed her again. "Stop it. Colt and I are nothing. Look." I pointed across the bleachers to where he and Gillian were in some sort of passionate discussion. "He's probably back with her already."

Jagger squinted in their direction. "They're at each other's throats. They are not back together."

I glanced over again, and damn, my stupid heart. It skipped a beat when I realized she was right. For half a tiny second, I'd been a little jealous at the thought he might have gone back to her. Not that anything Colt did was my business. Never was. Never would be. If he and Gillian wanted to make each other miserable for the rest of their stupid lives, then that was their prerogative. "Let's just watch the game."

For the next two hours, that's what we did. Jagger made herself hoarse from cheering for Aaron so loudly. Despite the fact she practically deafened me, I let it go, because I knew she was feeling guilty over her fleeting feelings about Aaron leaving her to go to college. I clapped and cheered the regular amount—both for Rafe and the team in general. But my eye kept going back to Banjo.

"He played so good," Jagger said when the final buzzer sounded. She sank down on her seat in relief. "I can't believe they won."

"Aaron's touchdown was amazing."

But she shook her head. "I meant Banjo. You barely took your eyes off him all night."

I offered her a tight smile. "I can't stop thinking about meeting him. I'm nervous."

She squeezed my arm. Around us, the bleachers began to empty out, but neither of us made a move, knowing we'd have to wait around for the guys to get changed anyway. Jagger laid her head on my shoulder. "You aren't the one who needs to explain herself. That's on him. All you have to do is listen."

I buried my face in my hands. "Sounds so easy when you put it like that." My words were muffled, but Jagger seemed to understand.

We sat there for a while longer, but eventually we had to move.

She tugged me to my feet. "Time to face the music. Can't hide up here forever."

Jagger and I took our time descending the stairs, letting

the last of the crowd trickle out ahead of us. "I want to forgive him, Jag. I do. I miss him."

"I know. But just think, you guys could be back to normal within the hour. I really hope you are. I want you both to be happy."

"I am happy," I protested. "Rafe is amazing."

She shot me a sidelong glance that told me she wasn't buying my bullshit.

"Okay fine," I agreed. "He's amazing. And I'm falling for him hard. But there's something missing between us."

"And that something is Banjo?"

"I think so."

Jagger's grin widened. "I'm totally shipping the three of you as a couple...er, trouple? Trio? Hell, I don't know what the hell to call you."

I didn't get to answer before I spotted Rafe shaking hands with one of the scouts. He watched the man walk back to his car for a moment, then came bounding over to us and picked me up, spinning me around. I squealed and flung my arms around his neck, taking in his freshly showered scent. He was damned delicious with his glasses back in place, a light cologne mixing with his soap.

"They want me," he whispered in my ear.

I pulled back as he put me down and I stared at him with wide eyes. "Are you kidding?"

His grin was ear to ear. "Not even for a second. He said he's had his eye on me since last year and if I keep playing the way I did tonight, then to expect an offer from him to play ball at ESU next year."

I flung my arms around him again, holding him close. "Are you good with that? I know you were a bit wary because your dad went there..."

Rafe shrugged. "If it means I don't have to rely on my

dad for college, then I'm all-in with any school that wants me. Whatever gets me the hell away from him."

"I'm so proud of you," I murmured to him.

In response, he tightened his arms around me.

We stood that way for longer than we should have. But Rafe's relief and joy all mingled into that embrace, and I let the hug drag on, intuitively knowing he needed it. He needed a moment to be still. To be held. I knew what that felt like. To have everything shift around you, and to just need someone to hold on to, someone to ground you.

Good moments could be as earth-shattering as bad ones.

I kissed his mouth lightly, and he pressed against me, slicking his tongue over my lips. The kiss deepened until we moved in a slow, steady rhythm, my heartbeat picking up. But after a few seconds, I moved away, not wanting to ruin the moment by turning it into something sexual.

The hunger in Rafe's eyes said he'd already gone there in his head.

I swatted his shoulder. "Stop."

"I didn't do anything."

"Yeah, but you want to."

"Damn straight." He gazed around the diminishing crowd. "Where's Banjo? We need to get this thing on the road so we can take our girl home."

My heart tripled in size. I tugged his hand. "Do you want that back? The three of us?"

Rafe nodded. "I'm too happy to be angry anymore. Are you, though? Still angry?"

I shook my head.

Rafe grinned, and we linked our fingers together. Jagger had disappeared somewhere, probably to the back seat of Aaron's car, and the other players were leaving the field, too.

"There," Rafe said, pointing across the parking lot to Augie's green sedan.

Banjo's brother was nowhere to be seen, but Banjo and Coach Tontine were discussing something by the driver's side door. I tugged Rafe in that direction, but he pulled my hand, stopping me.

"Wait."

I looked back at him questioningly, but he simply flicked his head in Banjo's direction. "Give them a minute."

I nodded, reining my excitement in. We'd been apart for weeks. A few more minutes wouldn't kill anyone.

I was so wrapped up in my own little bubble and imagining having both my boys by my side that it took me a moment to realize that Coach Tontine wasn't happy. His expression was full of disappointment and sadness, and when he clapped Banjo on the shoulder, my heart sank at the fatherly gesture.

Banjo threw his hand off and yanked open the car door, hurling himself inside and gunning the engine. Coach went to the window, shaking his head, his mouth moving rapidly, but we were too far away to hear what he said.

"Banjo," I yelled, jerking away from Rafe and running toward the parking lot.

It was a losing battle. The distance was too great for me to catch him.

Banjo peeled out of the parking lot in a screech of tires and angry black smoke.

"What?" I asked Rafe helplessly. "Where is he going? We were supposed to meet up."

Rafe ran over to the coach, and I followed close behind.

"What happened?" Rafe demanded.

Coach Tontine eyed him wearily. "You know."

Rafe's jaw dropped open. "No. Not possible."

My gaze darted between the two of them, but nothing they were saying made any sense. "Can someone please fill me in?"

Rafe jolted, like he'd forgotten I was there, but he kept his questions addressed to his coach. "The scouts weren't interested?"

Coach Tontine shook his head angrily. "Fools. He's the best quarterback around. They wouldn't know talent if they tripped over it." Then he shot Rafe an apologetic look. "Sorry. I know they're interested in you. And I'm real proud of you, Rafe. But I'm disappointed for Banjo."

"There'll be other scouts, won't there?" I asked hopefully.

Coach nodded. "That's what I was trying to tell him. But he's upset, understandably."

Rafe sighed and scrubbed his fingers through his hair. "He needs a scholarship. There's no other way for him."

Coach nodded sadly. "This is a setback, no doubt. I was pretty confident those guys would have made him an offer tonight."

All the good things I'd been feeling deflated completely. "We need to go find him."

Coach nodded. "He could use friends around him right now. Let him know this isn't the end, okay? Don't let him get dark on himself again. He can't afford to miss any more school or games. Now more than ever."

I swallowed hard. He'd missed class because of everything that had happened with me. If nothing else, Rafe and I could at least let him know we were ready to move on and be together again.

We just needed to find him first.

24

———

LACEY

afe and I stopped outside Aaron's house on Saturday night, and for the longest time, the two of us sat there in the car, staring at the front door. It opened regularly to admit those coming in from the cars parked around us, and the steady bass thump of the music filtered through to us, even over our car radio that played softly.

"I don't feel like partying tonight," Rafe said eventually.

"Me neither."

We both stared at the door. "We have to go in, though, don't we?" I asked.

He nodded. "It's not Jagger's fault Banjo has gone AWOL."

That was what this came down to. This rough-edged, empty feeling that had settled over the two of us in the last twenty-four hours.

"He might show up tonight, right?"

Rafe reached over and squeezed the back of my neck. "Yeah, sure. Maybe."

His words hardly sounded convincing. Rafe peered into

the rearview mirror and frowned. "I wish that car back there would turn his headlights off, they're blinding me."

I twisted to see and squinted sharply when they shone straight in my eyes. "Who is that?" I couldn't see a thing through the glare.

Rafe shrugged and got out of the car. He motioned for the guy behind us to kill the lights before coming around to my side to open the door for me. I smiled up at him. "How gentlemanly."

He held his hand out, impersonating some sort of chauffer, and I took it, letting him pull me up to my feet.

He leaned in, his lips hovering over mine, and I closed my eyes, anticipating his kiss.

The engine on the car behind us revved, and suddenly roared out from its parking spot. I yelped at the sudden noise, and Rafe instinctively pressed me against the door I'd just gotten out of. In a blinding flash of headlights, the dark-red Explorer sped past us and disappeared around the corner and out of sight.

Rafe flipped him the bird in the darkness. "Dickhead."

"Why do you boys have to show off like that?"

He raised one eyebrow. "I don't."

I mirrored his expression. "Says the boy who fishtailed out of my street on our very first date."

Rafe grinned. "Oh yeah."

I grabbed his hand and pulled him toward the door. "Come on. Jagger is going to kill us if we stay out here any longer. I think we're already past fashionably late."

I didn't bother knocking on the door, since the music would have drowned it out. Instead, I twisted the doorknob and stuck my head in cautiously, checking out what was going on.

Rafe inhaled deeply and closed his eyes. "Someone has pot."

It had been ages since he'd gotten high. I couldn't even remember the last time. But it had been a shitty twenty-four hours. I had no intentions of ever drinking at a party again. Not after that party at the beach where Owen had spiked my drink. So there was no reason he couldn't kick back a little. "I'm happy to be designated driver."

"No, I brought you here, I'll get you home."

"Perfectly capable of getting myself home, babe. And you. Go, if you want to."

I could see him teetering on the edge of indecision, but then someone called his name. He kissed me on the cheek, whispering, "I'll make it up to you tonight."

His lips brushed the shell of my ear, and I shivered in anticipation. Good deal for me.

He wandered off in the direction of the smoke, while I veered away from it, heading to the kitchen and living area beyond, where all the action seemed to be happening.

Jagger pounced on me the minute I walked through the doorway. "Did you find him?"

I shook my head, any hope Banjo might have been here deflating. Last night, we'd called everyone we could think of, looking for him. Augie. All the guys on the football team. His boss at the catering company. Jagger. Colt.

No one had seen him since the game. We'd both tried calling his phone, but it went straight to voicemail every time. We'd left messages; they'd gone unanswered. When Rafe had tried Augie again this morning, he'd confirmed Banjo hadn't come home at all. Rafe had suggested a missing person's report, but Augie had quickly shot that idea down, saying Banjo would be back. He'd seemed more concerned about his missing car than his missing brother.

Which hadn't surprised me at all. Banjo's brother was the most self-absorbed asshole I'd ever had the displeasure of meeting.

Jagger's shoulders drooped, but she put an arm around me and steered me toward the refrigerator, taking out a sealed bottle of water and passing it to me. "He'll show."

I cracked the lid and took a sip. "I hope so. I'm worried."

"We all are."

I knew that was true. But this was a party, and I didn't want to ruin it for Jagger. So I plastered on a fake smile. "How good is this? Aaron's parents aren't home?"

"It's just his dad. He's upstairs somewhere, with noise-cancelling headphones on. He's chill, though. Said we could do our thing as long as it was nothing more illegal than some underage drinking."

"Uh..." I shot a glance back the way we came. "They're smoking pot in the front room."

"What!"

I shrugged. "I left Rafe in there, searching for a joint."

She rolled her eyes and stormed off, leaving me alone with my bottle of water. I wandered around, amongst the crowd, smiling back when Aaron waved at me from the middle of game of beer pong.

"Lacey."

I stiffened at the voice behind me.

It wasn't the one I'd wanted to hear. I didn't turn around. "What do you want, Colt?'

"To talk."

I sighed.

"Please."

Well, that was new. "I'm shocked you even know the meaning of that word. Who knew you had manners?"

Colt remained stoically silent.

I rolled my eyes. "Fine. Talk."

He moved in closer, until the warmth of his breath ghosted over the back of my neck. I shivered at the attraction that always reared its head when he was around. I didn't even have to look at him to feel it. It pulsed around the two of us, something so strong it was almost tangible. Almost like an unseen danger my body couldn't help but react to.

"Turn around. I'm not talking to the back of your head."

"Then go away."

A low growl came from his chest, and then suddenly his fingers were digging into my hips. He moved around me so quickly I didn't even have time to work out what was happening, and then he'd hoisted me up and over his shoulder, like I was a goddamn sack of potatoes. His shoulder pressed into my belly, stealing my breath, and I dangled down his back, my center of gravity too far over to pull myself back up. Damn my lack of core strength.

"Colt," I yelled, thumping a fist against his back. "Put me down!"

But he was having none of it. He strode down a hallway off the main room, took a sharp left into what looked to be a guest bedroom, and kicked the door shut behind us. It slammed into place with an earsplitting bang. If anyone noticed, though, no one stopped us. He tossed me down on the big, neatly made bed, the mattress bouncing beneath me.

I scowled at him as he leaned back on the door. There was no point in screaming. Even if anyone dared to go up against Colt, they wouldn't hear me over the music. Instead, I sat up and crossed my arms over my chest.

Colt's gaze dipped momentarily to my cleavage but then

came right back to my eyes, his glare as hot as mine. "Why do you always have to be such a pain in the ass?"

My mouth gaped open. "Me? Are you serious right now?"

He gave a curt nod.

"Un-fucking-believable."

"What? I asked nicely to talk to you. You wouldn't."

"So a normal response is to toss the person ignoring you over your shoulder and lock her in a room?"

He shrugged. "You're talking to me now, aren't you?"

"Not by choice." I pushed to my feet, my anger boiling. "You're so self-centered!" I stormed to the doorway he was blocking, but he didn't budge. "Move."

"No."

"Colt." There was a warning in my tone. After last time, I probably should have been scared. But if he'd planned on hurting me, he could have easily done that when we were alone. Hell, that gun he'd given me was currently tucked safely into the purse slung over my shoulder. I could pull it out right now and aim it at him. But what would be the point? He already knew it was fake. I contemplated doing it anyway. Maybe I could just clock him over the head with it.

He softened a little and then slowly held his hands up like I was about to arrest him. "I wanted to say I'm sorry."

I stared at him for a long moment and then went to the window, lifted one of the slatted blinds, and peered out.

"What are you doing?"

"Checking to see if pigs are flying."

He scowled some more.

"Did you seriously just apologize?"

"Yes."

"See why I'm surprised?"

"Look. I realize I scared you the other day at the gym."

"No shit, Sherlock. You held a gun on me. Of course you fucking scared me. You're part psycho, I'm sure of it."

A smug smile tipped up the corner of his lips. "How was I supposed to know you'd run off crying? I thought you were made from tougher stuff."

I threw my hands up in the air. "Anyone ever tell you that your apologies fucking suck, Colt? They feel more like insults." I made for the door again. "We're done."

To my surprise, he moved aside. A tiny jolt of disappointment shot through me. Which was fucked-up. Did I actually want to stay here and argue with him some more?

Yes.

No!

I gripped the door handle, but he knocked my hand off it quicker than I could blink.

I glared at him.

He glared back. His black eyes bored into mine, challenging me. Demanding. Unyielding.

He stepped in.

I stepped back. Again and again until my back hit the wall.

Colt closed the distance between us.

There was something possessive in his stance that warmed my blood in a way anger didn't.

"We're not done," he growled, almost to himself.

His lips slammed down on mine, and my stupid traitorous body reacted immediately. I threw myself at him, my arms around his neck, my mouth frantic on his, the kiss hard and bruising as we grabbed at each other.

My head spun. His kisses were everything. The sun and the moon and the stars, all rolled into one fiery ball of heaven. Or maybe of hell. I had no idea. But it felt wicked.

Kissing him in this way would send me straight to the Devil's court.

And I couldn't get enough of it.

I drew him closer, wrapping one leg around him. He dipped slightly so his erection rubbed exactly where I wanted it most.

We both groaned, the noise lost to the pounding bass vibrating through the walls.

His tongue stole into my mouth, frantic and branding, owning me completely while I mewled for more.

And then he was on his knees in front of me, unbuttoning my jeans.

"There's no lock on the door," I gasped out as he pulled the zipper down, exposing the lace of my thong.

He grinned up at me, that devilish smile that was going to send me straight over the edge playing all over his mouth. "I like the idea anyone could walk in here at any moment."

"That turn you on?"

"Fuck yeah. You know what turns me on more, though?"

I shook my head, my legs trembling, gaze darting to the door. The sounds of people on the other side filtered in. How long would it be before someone wandered in, looking for a bathroom or a quiet place to make out?

He yanked my jeans down, taking the thong with him. He fit his mouth over my pussy, tongue darting out for a taste.

I couldn't help myself. I grabbed the back of his head and howled out a cry of ecstasy.

"That," he murmured between slow, luxurious licks. "That noise. I want to hear it again, Lacey."

He plunged his tongue between my folds, where I knew I was already wet for him.

I forgot all about the door. Forgot about the party going

on outside. All that registered was Colt's talented tongue and a rising need inside me.

I threw my head back, widening my stance as much as the jeans pooled around my ankles would allow. Colt's tongue assaulted my clit, swirling around it, then over it, tormenting and wild, until I was panting and aching and so damn wet I could feel it on my inner thighs.

One finger slipped up inside me without resistance. I clutched his hair, pure relief filling me when he added another, stretching me deliciously. In and out he fucked me with his hand, rougher and harder than Banjo or Rafe had ever been, alternating his fingers with his tongue until I was weak with the need to come. I liked that he wasn't gentle. I wanted to beg him to go harder. Rougher. Faster.

"Colt," I groaned. It was all I could manage as I teetered on the edge.

With his other hand, he gripped my thigh so tightly, holding me in place while my orgasm barreled down on me. His fingers hit that spot inside, and I went flying into a pool of bliss, the sensations rocketing up from my core and spreading out through my body like a wildfire. I clenched and pulsed around his fingers, while his tongue became lazy, circling my clit slowly, drawing out the pleasure until I couldn't stand it a minute longer. I pushed his head away.

I panted for breath, watching as he licked me from his fingers and backed toward the door. "You taste good, Lace. Really fucking good."

And then he opened the door, sending me scrambling for my clothes before anyone in the hallway noticed I was half naked and still trembling from the most mind-blowing orgasm of my life.

When I looked up again, he was gone.

*S*till flushed from everything that had happened in that little spare bedroom, I found Rafe in the front room, lounging on a couch, sharing a joint with Jagger.

I snorted on a laugh. "Didn't you come in here to tell him off for getting high?"

Jagger shrugged, taking a long drag. "He offered and I got sidetracked in my lecture. Don't tell Aaron."

I glanced over my shoulder in the direction of the main party. It was only a few feet down the hallway. "You're not hiding it real well. He could walk in here any minute."

She giggled.

"She's baked," Rafe confessed. "This shit is good."

His eyes were a little bloodshot, too. I suspected he wasn't too far off 'baked' either.

"I hate to be a party pooper, but can we go?" I asked Rafe. "I need to talk to you."

He nodded quickly. He kissed Jagger's cheek and then pushed to his feet, taking my hand. I waved goodbye to Jagger while I led Rafe to the door. As soon as we were outside, the cold night air slapped me in the face.

"Hey," Rafe said, pulling me to a stop. He seemed instantly more sober than he had inside. "You okay? Did something happen?"

I nodded, biting my lip. "Colt happened."

"Ah. I thought that might have been the case."

"Huh?"

"He kiss you again?"

I wasn't going to lie. "Bit more than that actually."

He nodded, but he didn't appear upset.

"You understand what I mean?" I wasn't sure the words I *didn't* say were getting through his pot-addled brain.

Rafe laughed and put his arm around my shoulder. "I'm his best friend. I know exactly how much he loves to go down on girls. Especially in public. Heard all about it in great detail. And I'm betting that's what happened just now, judging by that glow on your face."

Heat bloomed on my cheeks. "Well, this is awkward."

Rafe just shook his head. "Not for me."

"You sure your parents weren't hippies? You've got a very 'free love' sorta attitude."

He laughed. "Have you met my dad?"

"Unfortunately."

"I don't want what he has, you know? I don't want some rigid life and a woman too afraid of her own shadow because I'm an overbearing prick. If Colt and Banjo make you happy, then that's what I want for you."

I lifted up onto my toes and brushed my lips over his. "You blow my mind."

"If we go home, I'll blow your mind in other ways."

I grinned. "Promise?"

He tugged me toward the car with a renewed sense of urgency.

"Don't leave on my behalf."

I froze. Fear wound its way around my limbs, rendering them completely useless.

Owen stepped out of the shadows, a blonde girl following him. I gasped when I realized it was Gillian. My gaze bounced between the two of them, horror stealing my breath.

Owen didn't take his eyes off me. He stalked toward me like a panther hunting prey.

Rafe stepped between us. "What the fuck are you doing here?"

Gillian stepped up beside Owen and linked her arm through his. "I invited him."

I gaped at her. "You what? Why would you do that?"

Her perfectly shaped brows furrowed in annoyance. "How many guys do you want, Lacey? First Banjo, then Colt, now Rafe?" She screwed her face up in a sneer.

Owen chuckled darkly. "Don't forget me. She had me, too."

Rafe lunged for Owen's throat.

I yanked him back. "No!"

I knew exactly what Owen was capable of. Rafe might have been able to take him sober, but it wasn't even about that. It was about what Owen had the connections to do afterward. Owen was more untouchable than any of the Untouchables at Saint View High. I'd made a deal to keep Colt safe, but it had been making a deal with the Devil. And it had left Gillian to fall into his web.

Disgust for myself took over. But I knew where reporting Owen would have got me. It wasn't my fault he walked the streets now, a danger to women everywhere. That was on his father, a man who'd sworn an oath to protect and serve this community.

He didn't give a shit about anyone but his family's reputation.

Owen didn't give a shit about anyone but himself.

Despite how mean she'd been to me, I did care about Gillian. And I couldn't leave her alone with the guy who'd beat me half to death and attempted to rape me. I tugged on my earlobe, using it as an outlet for my worry. She'd seen me the morning after Owen's attack. Maybe I hadn't come right out and said he'd tried to rape me, but surely she'd worked it out? At the very least, she knew he'd beaten me up. Wasn't that enough to get her to stay away?

I moved around Rafe and grabbed Gillian's hand. She resisted, but I didn't care. I yanked her hard, away from the boys who stood in a silent face-off. "Don't do this," I hissed at her.

She pulled her arm from mine, shaking me off. "Do what? I'm single now. And so is he."

I stared at her. I might have hated Gillian for everything she'd done to me since starting this school, but I couldn't let this happen. I had to get through to her. "He's not what he seems. Please, Gillian. You want to get at me, fine. But do it some other way. Not with him."

"You're ridiculous," she laughed, heading back to Owen's side. "This has nothing to do with you."

I wanted to scream in frustration. "He's not a good guy."

She spun back on her heel. "You think Colt is? Oh, how quickly you looked the other way, princess. You wouldn't know a good guy if he bit you in the face."

She hooked her arm through Owen's again.

He winked at me and then turned to his date. "Shall we?"

She stared up at him with adoring eyes, leaving Rafe and me helpless to do anything but watch after them in horror.

25

BANJO

"Where the fuck have you been?"

I threw the car keys down onto the side table by the door and made a beeline for the refrigerator without saying a word. Like it even mattered.

Augie trailed after me, watching from the other side of the counter. Even with my head shoved inside the refrigerator, I could feel his annoyance. It rolled off him in waves. By the time I closed the door, with a handful of ingredients to make a sandwich bundled into my arms, he may as well have had steam coming out of his ears.

"You want to start talking?"

"Why? I brought your car back in one piece. What do you care where I've been?"

"Don't, really."

"That's what I thought."

I found a cutting board and got busy laying out the bread for my sandwich, adding a layer of mustard.

"Make two."

I glanced up.

He nodded at the sandwich, and I pulled another two pieces of bread from the bag.

"Rafe called about a dozen times. Colt, too."

"What'd you tell 'em?"

"Nothing. Didn't know anything to tell."

"Good. They call again, tell them not to come around."

Augie raised an eyebrow. "You get in a fight or something?"

"Nah. Got shit going on. Don't need them sticking their noses in." The words hurt even to say. But I'd seen Rafe after the game. He'd watched me with Coach. He probably knew exactly why I'd run off like a fucking crybaby. If Rafe hadn't told Colt, then Coach would have. I didn't need either of them pitying me or saying bullshit phrases like, "There's other schools that will want you."

I'd spent most of the night at a bar outside town. I had a fake ID, but they hadn't even asked me for it, and the bartender had been more than happy to take the rent money I'd been saving for Augie and turn it into alcohol.

I'd gotten so fucking wasted I'd had to sleep it off in the car. But even when I woke up this morning, cramp in my neck and back aching from slumping around the steering wheel, I just wanted to get drunk again.

Coach had tried to let me down easy. But the rejection stung all the same. I'd had my heart set on that college and I'd been the bomb on Friday night. It had been my best game of the season. I was supposed to be a sure thing, and I'd been so confident walking out. So sure my life was about to change.

And it had.

But not in the way I'd wanted it to. Coach's "There's other fish in the pond" speech had rolled off my stunned silence. I couldn't play any better than I had. If they didn't want me after that, there was little hope for anyone else. It had just been the icing on the cake. I'd already lost Lacey and Rafe. Who had I been kidding, thinking I could just write some dumb letter that would make it all better? It seemed so childish and selfish now. They had bright futures ahead of them. And I was just a rusted anchor that would drag them down to the depths of the ocean to drown them.

My tongue burned with the urge to ask Augie the questions I'd developed while I drank myself stupid last night. He hated my talk of college. Had taken every comment as a personal insult. He'd played that sex tape to a roomful of people without blinking an eye, just to ruin my chances with Lacey. Was it too much to suspect he might have sent copies to other people, too? Like the scouts from the school I'd had my eye on?

He was never going to let me go.

"You win," I said quietly, handing him his sandwich.

He took it from me without a thank you. "I win what?"

I shrugged. "I'll do what you want me to do. Work with you."

Augie put his sandwich back down on his plate, brushing crumbs from his hands, and grinned at me broadly. "'Bout fuckin' time, little brother. Easiest money in the world. And together, we'll make a mint."

He slapped me on the shoulder, took his plate from the countertop, and headed for the stairs. At the bottom, he paused and called back to me, "There's a woman coming tonight. I think she'd be up for it. You sweet?"

No, I wanted to scream. *No, I'm not fucking up for it.* It was the last thing I wanted to do tonight, or any night. But this had always been inevitable. "Yeah, I'll be there."

Augie whistled his way up the stairs. It was an upbeat, cheerful tune.

But to me, it sounded like a funeral march.

I spent a long time standing in the shower after Augie disappeared to his bedroom. The water cascaded over me, but no matter how hot I made it, it couldn't dissolve the feeling that settled on my shoulders. The complete and utter uselessness of my life became the thousands of tiny water droplets surrounding me. Coating me.

Drowning me.

I scrubbed every part of me until my skin turned pink. Only then did I turn the shower off. Augie had gone through my closet and chosen the outfit he wanted me to wear, though he'd frowned and murmured something about needing to go shopping before the next time. I'd just closed my eyes. The next time. How many times would there be? I'd never really thought past the first one, but one client alone wouldn't pay the bills, would it? The money was good, but not that good. I'd have to take on at least a few.

Nausea rolled my stomach. I pulled on the clothes, ran my fingers through my hair, and dabbed on the tiniest bit of cologne. Despite my outward appearance, when the doorbell downstairs rang, I was anything but ready.

Augie appeared in the doorway. "Go wait up in my room."

I hesitated, and Augie narrowed his eyes. "You wanted this, Banjo. Go."

I nodded and trudged upstairs, my heart thrumming. As each step brought me closer and closer to Augie's room, I tried to turn my thoughts around. I was no virgin. I loved sex. How hard could it be to get up there, do something I normally did for fun, and then take enough cash to pay for our rent that week? How was this any different to any other time?

I opened the door to Augie's room and gazed awkwardly about, wondering where the hell I was supposed to stand. Was I supposed to sit? Fuck. I had no idea. His room was a reasonable size but mostly filled up by an enormous bed. He didn't sleep up here unless he was working. If he was alone, he slept downstairs in the room across from mine. This one was a hell of a lot nicer than his space on the second floor. The mattress was covered in fresh, black satin sheets, the comforter folded and tucked away at the foot of the bed. A small bar sat off to one side, the mini refrigerator stocking a variety of alcohol. I'd raided it a few times, so I knew exactly what was inside.

Augie's laughter on the stairs churned my stomach. The sound of a woman's had me reaching for the window, wondering if I'd survive a three-story jump.

I wasn't sure I cared at this point.

The door opened before I could test the theory.

Augie entered first, glaring at me as if he could read my mind and knew exactly what I'd been contemplating.

The woman followed behind him, her arm linked around Augie's like a possessive snake. Her long hair fell around her face in curls, the bleached blonde obviously straight out of a bottle. She was older than Augie's twenty-eight years. Noticeably older. Not unattractive for a woman who had to be late forties. Lines marred the sides of her eyes and her mouth, but her makeup was understated, illuminating her sharp blue eyes.

Her mouth tipped up in a smile, gaze wandering over me lazily. She turned to Augie and raised an eyebrow. "I approve."

He grinned. "I knew you would."

Augie took the woman's bag and jacket, draping them over the armchair in the corner, and offered her a drink. "Your usual, Pam?"

She perched on the edge of the bed, crossing one long, slim leg over the other, and waited for Augie to hand her a wine glass. She turned to me. "You seem familiar."

I took a few steps back so I stood in front of the window. My fingers strangled the sill, while I tried to keep myself in check. If I knew her, I didn't recognize her. She could have been any rich white woman with more money than sense.

I'd asked for this, I reminded myself. This was what we Mitchell boys were good at. Augie had used his face and body to get by for years. I don't know why I'd thought I was any better. "Probably because I look like Augie."

She pondered that for a moment, then shrugged and took a sip of her wine. "I guess that could be it, the two of you are very similar. Lucky me."

She smiled at that, and Augie chuckled. I glanced between them. Augie wasn't drinking, so I assumed that meant I couldn't ask for a drink either. Though, fuck, that would have made this entire thing marginally more bearable.

"What's your name?" the woman—Pam—asked.

"Jordan," I answered.

Augie nodded at me. He'd told me to use a fake name. Why, I wasn't entirely sure. He'd mumbled something about privacy, but she was in our house, so surely it wouldn't have taken a genius to work out our real names if she'd wanted to. Augie was a nickname, one my parents had given him before I was even born. So I guessed that was why he felt comfortable using it with this woman and the countless others who he brought to this room. I didn't have a nickname to do the same with. So Jordan it was.

I sucked in a deep breath, the anticipation killing me. How long was I supposed to stand here and make small talk? I glanced at Augie. "Are we doing this?"

He shot me a steely glare. "She hasn't even finished her wine."

But Pam merely laughed. She stood and placed her glass on the bar and patted Augie's biceps. "I'm done. His enthusiasm is hot."

She crossed the room and stood in front of me, an expectant gleam in her eye.

Augie gave me an overexaggerated nod in Pam's direction, widening his eyes for emphasis. When I didn't move, he shook his head in frustration and went to Pam's back. Eyes trained on me, he leaned in and kissed the side of her neck.

Her eyes fluttered closed, and she tilted her head in the opposite direction, giving him more room. Augie sucked and kissed his way down her neck, fingers finding the zipper at the back of her dress and drawing it down her spine. He pushed it slowly off her shoulders, the silky, expensive material pooling around her stilettos. A shiver rolled over her body. Her lace bra covered perky, fake tits, the matching panties barely covering her snatch. The flat planes of her belly and toned thighs showed she worked out.

Augie shifted around her, kissing her shoulders and neck before traveling to her mouth and claiming it.

I blinked in surprise. I hadn't realized he kissed these women. It froze me to the spot.

I couldn't kiss her.

The last two people I'd kissed were Lacey and Rafe. I

didn't want this woman's mouth on my lips, erasing away the memory of them.

Pam's bra disappeared in a flash of Augie's fingers, her panties dropping a moment later, until she stood before me in nothing but her heels.

"Jordan," Augie barked at me.

I jumped.

Pam opened her eyes and studied me, then took a few steps back, laying herself across the bed. "Come here, sweetheart," she murmured. "I don't bite."

I should be hard, I realized with a start. Though she had to be twenty years my senior, she was still a naked woman, lying on a bed, waiting for me to fuck her.

I should have been hard, but I had nothing to give. I didn't feel anything. Not an ounce of attraction. Not a surge of need. In that moment, I knew nothing was going to change that. I could force myself over to that bed. I could take her nipples in my mouth, rub my fingers against her clit, get her off good.

But I was never going to be able to fuck her.

"I'm not doing this." I shoved off the wall and pushed past Augie.

He grabbed me by the shoulder, nails digging into my flesh. "The fuck you aren't. I promised Pam both of us. That's what she's paid for. That's what she's getting."

I shoved him back, eyes burning. All I could think about was Lacey. How much I wanted her. How stupidly in love with her I was.

She was the only woman I wanted to see naked. She was the only woman I wanted to touch. "I said no."

"You wanted this."

"I never wanted this, Augie. Never! You wanted it for me. You made me think I had no other option."

"You don't, big shot. You heard those scouts last night. You don't have the talent for college ball. You're as dumb as dog shit, so you sure as hell ain't getting a scholarship based on your pathetic grade point average. So what else do you have? A job at Walmart? You think that's going to keep Lacey in the life she's accustomed to?"

"Lacey?" Pam asked.

Augie and I both ignored her, the two of us too busy staring the other down.

He was the first to break. I knew he would be. Because I refused to let it be me. I would have stood there all fucking night, all week—hell, all year—if the alternative was touching a woman who wasn't the one I loved.

"Get out of my house," Augie growled.

I shouldered past him. "Gladly."

"Take your shit. Don't come back."

I whirled on him. "What?"

"You heard me. You're eighteen. You think you're too good for this life? Then go make your own."

He crossed the room and crawled across the bed to Pam, murmuring something in her ear I couldn't hear. She eyed me over Augie's broad shoulders, concern creasing her forehead. But then I was gone. I thundered down the stairs and out the front door. All I stopped to grab was my bike. There was nothing else from this house I wanted.

Not anymore.

26

———

LACEY

*R*afe and I drove back to my house in silence, both of us lost to our thoughts. I couldn't get the sight of Gillian and Owen out of my mind.

I stared out the windshield, making turns and stopping at lights on autopilot, watching the dark night outside until I pulled into my driveway. I couldn't even move. My fingers were frozen around the steering wheel. "This is my fault. I should have reported it. Maybe he would have gone to jail after all."

Rafe reached across and squeezed my hand. "None of this has anything to do with you. What happened that night on the beach was Owen's fault, not yours. The fact you couldn't go to the police? Also Owen's fault."

"I tried to warn her."

He squeezed my fingers. "I know."

"What if he hurts her?"

Rafe shook his head. "You can't think like that. Gillian doesn't listen to anyone. Except maybe Colt."

He was being kind, but it was all I could think about. Rafe got out of the car and jogged around to my side. He unclipped my seat belt, which jolted me out of my own head. I climbed from my seat, and he put his arm around my lower back, guiding us up to the front door.

"Can you stay?" I asked. "I don't want to be alone."

He cupped my cheeks between his hands and tilted my face up to look at him. Then he pressed the sweetest of kisses to my forehead. "There's nowhere else I'd rather be."

Selina stretched on the couch as we entered, a smile pulling at her lips when she noticed Rafe's arm draped over me. She was ready for bed, in a long, flowing blue robe that touched the floor, her face free of makeup.

"You two are home earlier than I expected. The party no good?"

I didn't know how to answer that. Some of the party—the bits where Colt had cornered me in a bedroom and made me come so hard I saw stars—was amazing. The last part, not so much.

"We weren't really in the right sort of mood," Rafe explained on my behalf.

Selina nodded and crossed the room, motioning to the TV. "I've got some things to do and then I'm going to bed. TV is yours if you want it. It's still early."

Rafe looked at me, and I shrugged. I flopped down on the couch and passed the remote to him. "You can choose."

"What do you want to watch?"

"Anything."

He found a rom com, we both settled back, and I rested my head on his shoulder, grateful for his warm, steadying presence. I tried to concentrate on the movie, but it was a losing battle. The minute I pushed Gillian and Owen out of my mind, Colt and Banjo rushed in. Fucking Colt. What had that been tonight? I swear it was his mission in life to confuse the hell out of me. I refused to think about what we'd done—what he'd done—in too big a detail. I didn't want to pull it apart to work out what, if anything, it meant. Hell, he'd gotten me off and then gone straight back to being an asshole, walking out of the room, leaving me half naked for anyone in the hallway to see. I was pretty certain no one had noticed, but I'd been so busy yanking my clothes back into place I couldn't really be sure. I fought back my annoyance and pushed Colt out of my head, too.

But that left Banjo and my worry over where he was.

A sharp knock came from the door.

"Can you get that, Lace? I'm in my pajamas," Selina called from the back of the house.

Rafe glanced over at me. "You want me to?"

I shook my head and pushed to my feet. "It's fine, I will." I was too antsy to sit there anyway. I needed to move. When I got rid of whoever it was at the door, I'd take Rafe upstairs and do some moving with him. That had to be a better distraction than the B-grade movie neither of us were really watching.

I strode to the door and checked the peephole.

"Oh my God." I fumbled with the locks and yanked it open, my heart slamming against my chest.

His bike lay discarded on the path behind him. His fitted pants and shirt disheveled, his cheeks flushed pink. Banjo glanced up from beneath his blond hair.

The world of hurt in his eyes tore me in two.

I'd never seen someone look so broken.

Without a word, I took two steps across the porch to stand in front of him. I lifted one hand and brushed the hair from his face. He leaned into the touch like he was starving for it, before pulling back, as if he'd remembered we weren't there anymore.

We weren't who we used to be.

He wasn't the same boy I'd fallen in love with.

But it didn't matter. Because I still loved him, no matter what.

A sob ripped from my throat, one born of the fear I'd felt for him the last twenty-four hours, plus something more. I ached for whatever had hurt him, because I knew, just from his face, it was something bad. Something that had destroyed the happy-go-lucky boy he'd once been.

I opened my arms, and he stepped into them without hesitation. He wrapped himself around me, holding me tight, face buried in my neck while I let my tears flow onto his shirt.

We still fit together the way we always had. I breathed in his coconut scent, remembering all the other times we'd stood like this, and clutched him that little bit tighter, wishing I could get those moments back.

It was a long time before either of us pulled away. Banjo was the first to move, but he barely moved back an inch, one hand tangled in the hair at the nape of my neck.

"Where were you?" I whispered. "What's happened?"

He swallowed hard, his beautiful green eyes glassy. Then he looked over my shoulder.

I followed his line of sight. Rafe watched us from the doorway, his expression unreadable.

Banjo cleared his throat. "Rafe…"

They silently battled it out for a moment before something in Rafe's expression cracked. "Fuck." He stormed across the porch, and I slipped out of the way just in time to avoid becoming a Lacey pancake. Rafe threw his arms around Banjo, and Banjo crumpled against him, a choked sob coming from his chest while Rafe held him up.

Silent tears rolled down my cheeks watching the two of them.

"Where the fuck were you, you asshole?" Rafe gritted out. "You fucking scared me."

Banjo nodded into his shoulder. "I know."

"I should punch you in the head for this."

"I won't stop you."

But Rafe made no such move. Just hugged Banjo tighter.

I went to the door. "Come inside. I'll make tea."

Rafe snorted at that and twisted to look at me with one eyebrow raised. "You drink tea?"

I shook my head with a tiny laugh, grateful for the break in all the heaviness. "No, but it seemed the right thing to say."

Banjo twisted away from Rafe, sniffled, and then choked out a laugh. "Got anything stronger?"

"I think that can be arranged."

I waited for them to both come inside and then left them in the living room while I ran down to Lawson's study to grab a bottle of bourbon. When I came back, Rafe sat in the armchair that faced the couch. I took the spot next to Banjo, sitting so close to him our legs touched. I handed him a glass and poured a hefty amount of alcohol into it before passing it to Rafe who set it aside. We both stared at Banjo while he took a swallow of his drink. Finally, his gaze lifted, bouncing between us for a moment, but then came to rest on me.

Then he spilled it all. All the details of how the scouts had rejected him on Friday night. Of how Augie's business involved more than small-time drug dealing. My mouth gaped when he told us about the prostitution and what Augie had been wanting him to do.

Rafe swore low under his breath. "Why the hell didn't you tell us?"

"What did you want me to say? Hey, my brother fucks

women, and sometimes other men, for money to pay our bills? And that he's pushing me to do it, too?"

I blanched at the thought of anyone being forced into that sort of life.

But Rafe's jaw tightened, and his fingers balled into fists by his sides. "I wouldn't have judged you. I would have fucking helped you."

"How? No one can help me out of this. Augie is right. I'm an adult. I can't expect everyone to take care of me all the time."

Rafe got to his feet and stormed the space between them, leaning down until they were eye to eye. "Bullshit. You're my brother. You always have been. Don't fucking shut me out."

Rafe's eyes burned with hurt. Banjo's with shame.

A growl of frustration came from Rafe's chest. "Don't you fucking know I love you? Lacey loves you. You come to us. We're your family. We're the people you rely on."

Banjo stared. "I thought I'd blown it with both of you. I didn't even mean to come here. I just got on my bike and rode."

Rafe fisted his fingers in Banjo's shirt and shook him roughly. "You fuckhead. I was mad. That doesn't mean we're finished." He dropped to his knees in front of Banjo and cradled his face, pulling it toward him.

They only hesitated for the briefest of moments before Rafe finished what he'd started.

A lump rose in my throat at their kiss. It was softer and sweeter than the last time I'd seen this happen. They held each other tight, fingers punishing in their grip on each other. My heart ached. They were soul mates, these two. There was no denying it, seeing the two of them like this.

I watched in silence. There were words I itched to say.

Plans I wanted to make to fix this for Banjo. I could help. But I couldn't help with the two of them. They needed to fix their relationship for themselves.

That kiss was the first step.

When they broke apart, Banjo reached out a hand for me. "Come here," he said, voice laced with gruff emotion.

I went willingly, settling myself across Banjo's lap, Rafe behind me. He pressed a reassuring kiss to my back, while Banjo cupped my face.

"I've missed you," he whispered against my lips.

My eyes filled with tears again, and I nodded, for fear of saying anything would make them spill over.

"There was something I never got to tell you, that night of your birthday. And I've hated myself every day since. I love you, Lacey. I have this entire time. I never stopped. I'm so sorry, baby. I'm so sorry I hurt you."

I pressed my fingertips to his arm. "Wasn't you."

His nod was slow and reluctant. "But I put you—both of you—in that position."

Rafe snorted on a laugh that broke the tension. "From memory, it was a pretty enjoyable position."

I blinked at him. "You did not just go there."

He grinned and brushed his lips over mine. "Yeah, princess. I did."

I let him loose on my lips but then pulled away and turned back to Banjo. I sank my fingers into his hair and pressed my mouth to his before he could apologize any more. I licked past his lips, deepening the kiss, reminding myself how much I loved him. Nothing had changed in that respect. Nothing had gone away. "I still love you, Banjo. Nothing you did, or didn't do, could stop that. I needed time."

"Have you had that?"

"Too much."

His green eyes bored into mine, and suddenly something changed within them. A fire took the place of the shame and despair that had hidden there moments earlier. "What do you need now, Lacey?

Behind me, Rafe's breathing became sharper.

"You," I whispered against his mouth. "I want to kiss you, and hold you, and remind you of what you mean to me."

Beneath me, his dick stiffened. Banjo glanced over my shoulder at Rafe, and something silent passed between them. Then Rafe was on his feet, and Banjo linked his arms around my back. "Hold on."

He stood, taking me with him. I wrapped my arms around his neck, my legs around his waist, and his hands slipped lower to my ass, supporting my weight. Rafe led the way up the stairs, Banjo and I following behind. I couldn't stop watching him, worried if I did, he might disappear again. He took the stairs without focusing on them, his gaze locked on mine.

At the landing, we made a sharp turn into my bedroom, and Rafe locked the door while Banjo took me to my bed and dropped my feet so I could stand. He kissed me again, softer this time, nipping at my lips until I opened for him, and then leisurely exploring my mouth. Our tongues moved in slow, slick motions, the kiss becoming something more. Passion mounted between us, building me up, and I moaned into Banjo's mouth, encouraging him to take this further.

He lifted my top, pulling it over my head and dropping it on the floor beside us. He dipped to kiss the swell of my breasts, his mouth lingering over my heart. I searched for Rafe and spotted him sitting in the window seat, his gaze trained on us. But he made no move to join us.

I questioned him silently, but he shook his head. "He needs this."

Banjo looked up from lavishing his attention on my chest. He glanced at Rafe and then back at me. He claimed my mouth hungrily. "I've never needed anything more than I need you right now."

My knees buckled as the kiss deepened. I heard the snap of my bra, felt the touch of Banjo's fingers at my back, and the slide of my bra as it fell away. I lifted Banjo's shirt, running my fingers across his chest, following them with kisses. I traced the outline of the freckles dusting his pecs and abs.

He was so beautiful.

And he was mine.

Ours.

He made swift work of my jeans, unbuttoning them and tugging them down my legs until I stood before him in nothing but my panties. I looked at Rafe again, and heat bloomed between my legs at his expression. He was enjoying this. His gaze raked over both of us, his attention lingering on the cut of Banjo's body as much as my curves. But then Banjo was pulling off my panties and drawing my attention back to him.

I perched on the edge of the bed, unbuttoned his fly, and fit my mouth over him.

He hissed loudly and shallowly thrust into my mouth a few times. But then he moved back to push his jeans off the rest of the way and kissed me hard. The force of his kiss pushed me back, and my eyes closed so I could no longer see Rafe watching us.

But I could feel it. And it only heightened the ache growing inside me.

My legs opened as if they had a mind of their own,

welcoming Banjo's body between them. His mouth went for my nipple, drawing it into the wetness and licking it with his tongue, while his cock notched at my entrance. Bare. Warm. Thick.

"Condom?" he asked.

"Drawer."

He found the box I'd shoved at the back after we'd returned from our night in the hotel after the Ridgemont game. He sat back on his knees, my legs spread wide around him, and rolled the condom over his length. I missed the weight of him, but it was also kind of hot, watching him palm his cock. Then he was hovering over me once more and kissing me so thoroughly my head spun.

"I need you," I whispered to him.

He understood what I was saying. I didn't want the foreplay. I wanted the connection. His lips lowered to mine once more, the kiss soft and sweet. His cock nudged inside me, inch by delicious inch, slowly stretching me and filling the void. Our gazes locked as he stilled.

"You're so beautiful," he whispered, pulling out then sliding back in.

My body was jelly beneath his touch. I raised my hips to meet his thrusts, staring deep into those green eyes I'd missed so much. The connection sparked between us, my heart doubling in size, my body welcoming him home. We'd only done this once before, but it was as if we'd done it a million times. Our bodies moved effortlessly, while his eyes said everything I'd ever wanted to hear.

I missed you.

I love you.

I'm not leaving again.

His hand reached between us, finding my clit and rubbing slow circles over it. I held his gaze for as long as I could, but eventually, the sensation became too much. My nipples beaded against his chest, and I arched my back so his cock hit me at just the right angle.

"I love you, Lace," he whispered in my ear, only for me to hear this time.

I clung to him, pressing my fingers to his broad back, clutching him closer while sparks lit up inside. They gathered between my legs, begging to be set free.

"Come for me, baby," he whispered.

I let loose, yelling out his name. The sparks flew through my body, taking a blinding pleasure with them. Banjo's movements quickened until he shuddered. He buried his face in my neck when he came, groaning my name, over and over, his body jerking and mine spasming around him. He collapsed on top of me, and I held on to him, my ankles crossed over the backs of his thighs, my arms trailing strokes down the soft skin of his back. I soaked in the feel of him.

Slowly, as I came down off my orgasm high, I remembered Rafe was still in the room. I twisted so I could see him.

Our gazes collided.

Banjo looked over, too, a lazy grin pulling at his face. "Enjoy the show, perv?"

Rafe's answering smile was smug. "You got no idea."

Banjo glanced down at me and wriggled his eyebrows suggestively. "You thinking what I'm thinking?"

He jerked his head toward Rafe.

I knew exactly what he was thinking. And I was so ready for it.

27

RAFE

*I*f someone had told me a few months ago that I'd be watching my best friend fuck the girl I was falling for, I would have called you crazy. I would have laughed, puffed out my chest, and made up some macho bullshit about how straight I was.

But watching Banjo with Lacey had my heart pounding. I was so hard I was ready to bust through the seams of my jeans, and my cock begged for attention. Instead, I'd pressed my fingers into the padded cushions of the window seat and watched Banjo's hips grind against Lacey. Listened to her moans of ecstasy. Admired the way their bodies fit so perfectly together.

Imagined what it would be like if mine joined them.

Banjo disappeared into Lacey's bathroom, but Lacey glided across the room to stand in front of me. I drank her in. Her long dark hair, cascading over her shoulders and down her back in loose waves. The pink flush of her cheeks. Her high, perfect tits, with the nipples dark and beaded, straining toward me. I couldn't help myself. I sat forward and skimmed my hand down the side of her body. Over her ribcage and the swell of her hip before drifting to the center of her body. I focused on her sweet bare pussy, and a small moan slipped from her lips.

Banjo reappeared, striding across the room, still buck naked. He'd ditched the used condom and was already getting hard again. My dick kicked at the sight of him, as turned on by Banjo's body as I was by Lacey's.

I was so not straight.

Someone needed to pass me a bisexual label and I'd wear the fucking thing with pride.

Banjo was hot. Really fucking hot.

I groaned watching the two of them, before Banjo bit out a command, "Stand up."

I did, because holding myself back any longer was a losing battle. Banjo tucked his fingers into the hem of my shirt and lifted it over my head, leaving my chest bare. He grabbed the back of my neck and hauled me in roughly for a kiss.

"Thank you," he whispered, in between hard presses of his mouth.

I pulled back, a question in my eyes.

"For her. For letting me have her."

I nodded.

Lacey fell to her knees and worked the buttons on my jeans. I glanced down at her, but then Banjo was kissing me again, and I fell into his touch, kissing him back just as hard, our mouths moving in slow, slick slides that had my balls aching.

Lacey yanked my jeans down, and then her hot wet mouth covered my erection, and I groaned at the sensation.

On instinct, one hand dropped to the back of her head, fisting in her long hair while I tried to keep my hips still. I didn't want to ram my dick down her throat, but fucking hell, she was doing a good job of swallowing me down anyway. Her mouth and hand worked in unison, and when Banjo kissed me at the same time, it was an explosion of sensation. His fingers found my nipple, brushing over it before working it into a stiff peak of pleasure.

Lacey's free hand came between my legs, cupping my balls, and it was nearly the end of me. I pulled out of her grasp, not wanting to come yet.

"Want to come inside you, Lace. Not down your throat."

I lifted her to her feet and kissed her hard, tasting my own arousal on her tongue. I walked her back to the end of her bed, so her ass pressed against the solid wooden bed frame. And then I spun her around, guiding her hands to hold on to it. She let out the tiniest of impatient whimpers, and Banjo grinned at me. He picked up a condom from the box he'd left on the bed and tossed it to me. Then he dropped to floor, moving beneath the bridge Lacey made with bed frame.

"Widen those legs, princess," he directed, while palming her tits from his position beneath her.

She moaned and did as he said. Her legs trembled. But I was there behind her, hooking my arm around her waist to keep her steady.

I loved fucking from behind. Loved how deep and raw it was. I did want to make love to her. To lay her down, have sex with her face-to-face, and confess all the feelings I harbored for her. But now wasn't that moment. Not with my dick begging to be let loose and the deep instinctual need I had to make her scream.

Maybe it was because I'd watched her have sex with my best friend. I was still a competitive guy. And a part of me did want to one-up the orgasm she'd had with him.

I gripped her tight with one hand and trailed my other

down her spine and over the sweet curve of her ass, squeezing it.

Her back arched, her legs widening again, and she pushed her ass back against my hand, encouraging me.

From his position on the floor, Banjo tipped his head back to suck her nipples. I stared down at the slick slit between her legs, so on display for me, and couldn't wait another moment. I pressed my dick to her entrance and let her pussy swallow me whole.

Her cry of pleasure had me fumbling to move faster. I dug my fingers into her hips, withdrew from her body, and then slammed back home, groaning at the tight warmth that enveloped me. She rocked back, mewling with each thrust of my hips stretching her wide.

Beneath us, Banjo shifted down toward me, and Lacey's howl of delight told me he'd moved his mouth to her clit. I slid out of her entirely, and for one hot moment, watched from above as my best friend tongued her. My gaze rolled down his body, over his abs to his cock, now fully erect again. He stroked himself slowly while devouring Lacey.

Pre-cum wept from my tip, my balls tightening with the need to come. I'd never seen anything so hot in my life. This was better than any porn I'd ever watched. Better than anything I could have dreamed up in my head. Lacey looked back over her shoulder at me, and the desperation in her eyes told me everything I needed to know. She was right there, verging on the edge of a powerful orgasm, and I was driving her wild by delaying it.

I pushed back inside, and she cried out her release, shouting my name and then Banjo's. Her pussy clenched down on me so hard I nearly passed out.

Banjo's hand wandered from his cock to my balls, and

though it startled me at first, the rush of sensation it sent cascading over me was like nothing else.

"Fuck!" I bit out, slamming into Lacey's tight heat once more.

Banjo squeezed my balls, and it was all freaking over. I shuddered, pulsing inside Lacey's body, torturing myself in the very best way, pumping in and out, her body dragging out my orgasm until I couldn't handle another moment. I froze, still inside her, unable to move while we rode out our pleasure together. Banjo's groan as he came again mingled with our chorus of pleasure.

Eventually, I pulled out and lifted Lacey's boneless body to stand. I wrapped my arms around her from behind, and her head flopped back on my shoulder.

"I'm so done," she murmured. "I think I saw Jesus."

Banjo sprawled back on the floor, gazing up at us with a cocky smile. My eyes met his, and we both grinned.

"Good?" he asked.

I chuckled at the smug prick. He knew very well how good it was. "Anytime you want to grab my balls, Banjo, go right the fuck ahead."

Lacey giggled, and I kissed her neck before walking her in the direction of the bathroom. I held a hand out to Banjo as we passed and dragged him along with us.

In a tangle of naked bodies and wet kisses, the three of us fell into the shower. And didn't come out for a very long time.

28

COLT

The smell of pancakes and bacon wafted up the stairs to my bedroom, but even the delicious aromas couldn't entice me from my bed. Downstairs, Coach said something, his voice too low for me to make out the words, but Mom's responding laugh echoed up. It should have made me smile. I was happy she was happy. I'd been a brat about it when she and Coach had first started dating two years ago, but by now, he was part of the furniture. I still had no idea why he hadn't officially moved in, when he spent more nights here than he did at his own place. But their happiness reminded me that other people in this house hadn't laughed in a long time.

Me.

Aria.

I tucked my hands beneath my head and stared at the rafters of the ceiling. I'd heard her crying again last night. And I hated there was nothing I could do to fix it for her. When it had first happened, I'd gone downstairs and slammed through the doorway, demanding to know what was going on.

She'd taken one look at me and clammed right up. It had been Mom who'd finally gotten the truth from her.

I'd lost it completely when she'd filled me in.

I tried to push the thoughts out of my head. They'd become the thing I feared the most. Not dying. Not losing the people I loved. No, it was worse when they were here, but so hurt and broken by the hands of another. I was completely powerless to do anything, and I hated that feeling. When the system failed, as it so often did in Saint View, the pent-up rage inside me had no place to go.

The sounds of Aria's tears at night shredded me. She never let me in. Never let me comfort her. And so instead, I'd spent night after night trying to drown out the noise.

It was useless. It was still there in my head. Her heartbreak always ringing in my ears, even as I slept.

I sucked in a deep breath.

I rarely slept anymore.

I closed my eyes, still so tired even though I'd been lying in this exact spot since I'd gotten home from the party last night. My dick kicked, remembering exactly what had happened there. I hadn't even wanted to go. But I'd needed to apologize to Lacey. I'd felt like an asshole, ever since the incident in the gym with the gun. But it had been necessary. I couldn't have another person's pain on my conscience, the way I did with Aria's. I needed to know Lacey could protect herself.

Even if I was the monster she needed protection from.

A tentative knock on my bedroom door had me pulling the blankets up over my lower half.

"Yeah?"

The doorknob twisted, and Aria's head poked through the doorway. "Sorry if I woke you."

"You didn't. What's up?"

She came inside, but instead of perching on the end of my bed or on my armchair, she went straight to the window. She chewed one fingernail as she gazed out. "I think someone is watching the house."

"What?"

"You haven't noticed? There's a car parked down from Augie and Banjo's place. It's been there on and off for the last few days."

I shrugged. "So? Maybe the neighbors got a new car. Or they have someone couch-surfing."

"I'd be more inclined to believe that if they ever got out of the car. Whoever owns it just sits in it."

Okay, well, that was weird. I threw the blankets off, glad I'd slept in sweats last night. I didn't normally. I padded across to stand behind Aria, peering over her head. She pointed down the road a little, at a dirty red Ford Explorer. It was old and beat up enough to fit in with the rest of the rust buckets in this neighborhood. "The tint is so dark, how could you even know?"

Aria gave an annoyed huff. "I'm homeschooled. I spend a stupid amount of time staring out these windows. I could run the Neighborhood Watch. If we had one."

That sort of thing didn't exist in Saint View. You kept your nose out of other people's business. Sticking it where it didn't belong was what got you in trouble around here.

"I swear, though, there's people inside. I've seen them when I walk past on my way to the store." She turned to me with those big worried eyes. "What if it's the cops? What if they—?"

"It's not the cops."

"How do you know?"

I didn't. But I didn't want to tell her that. There was every chance it was. But my role here was to protect her. Keep this sort of shit away from her. I'd already failed once. I wouldn't do it again.

I put on a t-shirt and an ancient pair of Nikes. "I'll handle it."

"What are you going to do? Don't do anything stupid."

I shot her an exasperated look. "I'm going to go see what's up. Nothing more."

She still seemed worried, but she didn't say anything further. I left her at the window and trudged downstairs, grunting a good morning when Mom and Coach lifted their gazes in my direction.

Outside, I jogged down the handful of steps, eyes trained on the car down the road. I strode purposefully toward it, trying to take in the details as I went. Number plate. Make. Model. None of it out of place.

But Aria was right. From this angle, with less distance between us, there was definitely something moving from within the car. The tint was dark enough I could only see shapes rather than features, but fucking hell. The skin at the back of my neck prickled with awareness. There was definitely someone sitting in that car, on a fucking freezing morning, when normally people would want to be wrapped up somewhere warm, drinking their coffee.

An engine roared to life, and the car jerked from its parking spot.

"Hey!" I picked up the pace, breaking into a run.

The driver gunned the engine and swung into a wide one-eighty before putting his foot down hard on the gas and careening out of the street.

I stopped and watched the car screech around the corner and disappear.

"Someone steal your lunch money?"

I glanced over my shoulder at Augie, coming down the

steps of his place next door with an armload of clothes. I wandered over and leaned on the chain-link fence that separated our properties. "Something like that. Whatcha doing?"

Augie dumped the load of clothes onto a pile of other mismatched items by his mailbox. "Taking out the trash."

I eyed the pile he was making. Banjo's skateboard. A box of trophies I knew came from Banjo's shelves. A pile of surfing magazines. I reached over and plucked a t-shirt from the top of the discarded clothes. "Isn't this Banjo's favorite?"

Augie lit a cigarette and inhaled deeply. "Who gives a fuck?" Barely concealed aggression was veiled within his words.

I dropped the shirt and eyed him. "Does Banjo know you're throwing out all his shit?"

"Banjo doesn't live here anymore, so he should have taken his shit with him."

Worry dumped over my head, cold as a bucket of water. I hadn't seen Banjo since Friday night. I knew Rafe and Lacey were worried about him, but I hadn't been overly concerned, knowing he'd turn up sooner or later. But now? I was officially worried. "What do you mean he doesn't live here anymore? Where the fuck is he?"

Augie took a long drag on his smoke, eyeing me. "Fucked off to the rich bitch's place, probably. Surprised you aren't there, too. Isn't it some sort of gang bang? Those fancy sluts are always up for it."

"Shut up, Augie. Don't fucking talk about her like that."

He laughed and blew a ring of smoke. "I see you're as pussy-whipped as those other two. What the fuck has Lacey Knight got between her legs that's got you, Rafe, and my brother all panting over her? Gold spray out of her cunt when she comes?"

The gasp behind me was the only thing that stopped me from launching myself over the fence and ramming my fist down Augie's throat.

"You're sleeping with Lacey Knight?" Aria's brown eyes bored into mine, her face drained of all color.

I took a step toward her. "Aria—"

She held her hand up. It shook violently. "You are, aren't you?"

I shook my head. "I swear I'm not."

But the trembles traveled up her arm and overtook her entire body. Her eyes widened. "You are! Don't lie to me, Colt. You are!"

I ran up the stairs and grabbed her by the shoulder, dragging her away from the front door and around the side of the house, out of Augie's sight. She flailed and fought with me the entire time, but I was a good foot taller than her, and she had little chance of fending me off. I gripped her by the shoulders while she tried to slap my hands away.

"Fuck, Aria. Stop it. I'm not sleeping with her."

Her eyes were a blaze with fury. "Liar."

Irritation rolled through me. "That's rich, coming from you." I loved my sister. More than anyone on this planet. But fucking hell, I wasn't going to put up with this bullshit either. Not after everything I'd done for her.

She shoved both hands against my chest. "I haven't lied about anything!"

I caught her by the wrists and shoved her hands back down by her sides. "Really? Then how about I ask you this again. Those photos Gillian put in Lacey's locker. Where did they come from?"

"How the hell should I know?"

"Liar."

Her eyes narrowed. "Fine. It was me. Happy? I put them

in her bag. What's the big deal? You know everything I wrote on those photos was true. You're a fucking traitor, Colt. You were supposed to be on my side."

My temper soared. "I am on your fucking side. I'm always on your side. Why the hell do you think I did what I did?"

But she wasn't listening. Her eyes filled with tears and quickly brimmed over. "She walked around Providence like she owned it. I hate her. I hate all of them."

Her shoulders crumpled in, and my heart ripped down the fucking middle. All the fight drained out of her. I grabbed her roughly and pulled her into my arms, crushing her against my chest while she sobbed into my shirt.

The lump in my throat threatened to choke me. I couldn't stand it. I wanted to run. Or punch something. Her shoulders shook, and I held her tighter.

"I'm glad you did it," she choked out. "I'm glad you killed him."

I opened my mouth to answer her, but then a movement to my right caught my eye.

In the doorway, Mom and Coach stared at me, horror written all over their faces.

"Colt," Mom whispered. "What have you done?"

29

LACEY

I woke to Banjo kissing my lips and Rafe's mouth between my thighs. On instinct, I widened my legs and tilted my pelvis, giving him better access while my tongue glided in unison with Banjo's. I'd lost track of how many orgasms I'd had last night when the three of us had crashed out naked in my bed. At least four.

If the way Rafe tongued me right now was any indication, these boys were hell-bent on making it a fifth before breakfast.

"Lacey?"

Banjo and I both jerked our heads toward the door Selina had called out through. I'd somehow completely managed to forget she was even home, what with the multiple orgasms. Now, in the cold light of the morning, I panicked.

"Quick," I hissed at Banjo, "get in the bathroom."

He blinked in surprise, but I was too busy shoving off the blankets to care. Rafe grinned up at me, his pink tongue darting out to swipe through my folds. Oh my God. Him and his wickedly talented mouth would be the death of me. With more than a little reluctance, I shoved him away from my now needy flesh and pushed him toward the bathroom, too. He and Banjo both stumbled inside, hushing each other none too quietly.

"Lacey?" Selina called again.

"Just a second!" I hastily grabbed a robe and drew it on, tying it tightly around my waist. The bed was a rumpled mess, and I tried in vain to make it look like three people hadn't spent all night rolling around in it, having the most mind-blowing sex ever.

There was little to be done, though, and I couldn't leave Selina waiting on the other side forever. I unlocked the door and cracked it open.

Selina gave me a bright smile. "Morning, sweetheart. Can I come in for a moment?"

I forced a panicky smile and opened the door wider, stepping to one side to allow her access. "Sure, of course. It's a bit of a mess in here...."

Selina cast her eye around my room and then focused on a spot on the floor. I died a thousand deaths when I noticed one of the guys' underwear.

"Um..."

Selina patted my shoulder. "Banjo?" she called. "Can you come out of the bathroom, please? I want to speak with you."

The bathroom door cracked open, and Banjo's beautiful green eyes shone out over a cheeky smile. "Hey, Sel."

She raised one eyebrow. "We're on a nickname basis now, are we? Shall I call you Ban? Or maybe Jo-Jo?"

Banjo wrinkled his nose at both suggestions and came out of the bathroom, a fluffy white towel wrapped around his hips.

Well, this was embarrassing. But at least she didn't know about—

"Tell Rafe to come out, too. Little point hiding in there after the racket the three of you made last night."

Kill. Me. Now.

Rafe came out wearing an identical towel to Banjo.

"So, I can explain..."

Selina raised one eyebrow in my direction. "I'm old and widowed but not stupid, sweetheart. You don't need to explain."

I had no idea whether that was better or worse. Somehow, it was both.

"All of you sit a minute. I want to talk."

I sat between the two of them on my bed, Selina standing in front of us like some schoolteacher with a point to drive home.

"If this is the safe-sex lecture, we're good on that front," Banjo piped up. "I think we used a whole box of condoms last night."

Rafe snorted on his laughter while I just stared at Banjo in horror.

"What? We did."

"You're killing me," I hissed at him.

He gave me that adorable grin that made me forgive him in an instant.

Selina blew out a breath that lifted her bangs ever so slightly. "While I'm very glad to hear that, because I have no interest in being a grandmother at my age, that's not what I wanted to talk about. I heard you last night—"

I groaned at the reminder.

Selina shot me a look. "Let me rephrase. I heard you *talking* last night, when you were downstairs."

"Oh."

She turned to Banjo, her expression becoming serious. "What your brother wanted you to do..."

Banjo dropped his gaze to his lap. "It's fine, Mrs. Knight. I can handle it by myself."

Selina shook her head. "You shouldn't have to. There's no one watching out for you."

"I am," I said quietly.

"Me, too," Rafe chipped in.

Banjo glanced at both of us. I picked up his hand and threaded my fingers between his.

"Well, now I am, too," Selina said, emotion clogging her voice. "Angelique has more work than she can handle around here, and I want to free up some of her time. I need someone to keep the pool and gardens neat and tidy and to help with a few other outdoor maintenance jobs."

Banjo shook his head. "It's okay, I already have a job, truly. I'll be fine."

"That's great, because this isn't the sort of job that pays a wage. It's a position in exchange for accommodation. We have a pool house that no one ever uses. You're welcome to it for as long as you need it, if you're willing to pitch in and help out."

My eyes widened. "Are you serious?"

Banjo's mouth fell open. "What she said."

Selina nodded. "I'm in the position to offer you a safe home. That was important to me when we took Lacey in. And it's still important to me now. It's yours if you want it, Banjo."

Banjo let out a whoop of glee and sprang from the bed. He threw his arms around Selina, picking her right up off the floor and spinning her in a circle.

"Banjo!" I yelped, as his towel began to slip from his

hips. He put her down and grabbed it before things got indecent.

Selina staggered a little but caught herself. Then a smile turned up her lips. "I'll take that as a yes, then?"

Banjo nodded rapidly, then looked to me. "Is this okay with you?"

"Are you kidding?"

He grinned and turned back to Selina. His expression morphed into something more serious. "Thank you."

She smiled and nodded at him. As she went to leave, she paused in the doorway. "Notice I said you could have the pool house? Perhaps if the three of you want to have sleepovers in the future, it could be out there? Where I can't hear you?"

***

After Selina left, the boys and I showered—separately, because who knew how long we'd manage to keep our hands off each other if we were in there together—and dressed before wandering downstairs.

I made a beeline for the refrigerator, taking out eggs and bacon and hash browns to whip us up a mid-morning feast, while the boys pulled up stools at the breakfast bar and watched the replay of some football game on my iPad. I got the bacon frying, adding extra for Selina when she reappeared, fully dressed and made up, her nose sniffing in my direction. She put her arm around my shoulders and squeezed, and I was pleased she looked happy. Happy for me, I think.

"Thanks for not judging," I said quietly, glancing over my shoulder at the boys. Neither of them paid us any attention. "And for what you did for Banjo."

"What's to judge? Those boys worship the ground you walk on. I'm glad you've sorted things out. I just want you to be happy."

"I am."

"Then that's all I care about."

I studied her for a moment. She was one of the most caring women I knew. It really was a cruel twist of fate that she and Lawson had never been able to have children of their own. Her maternal streak ran a mile deep.

A knock at the door had Selina glancing at me curiously. "You expecting a third member of your harem?"

I bit my lip because that comment immediately had me thinking of Colt. I had no idea what he and I were to each other. Enemies that made out sometimes seemed the most accurate description, but how that fit in with what Banjo, Rafe, and me had was undetermined. I wasn't even sure I wanted to try to decipher that one.

"Nope," I answered her truthfully. "Not expecting anyone."

Since I had my hands full trying to make an elaborate breakfast for everyone, Selina wandered off to answer the door.

I added bread to the toaster. "How do you guys have your toast..." I looked over my shoulder at the two of them, but the question died on my lips.

Chief Waller and two officers stood behind Selina.

She bit her lip, anxiousness tingeing her tone. "They have some news on Lawson's case."

My heart picked up. I switched the gas stove off and put the tongs down on the counter.

Banjo and Rafe exchanged a glance and simultaneously pushed to their feet.

Rafe pointed up the stairs. "We'll give you some privacy and go wait in your bedroom."

Chief Waller held up a meaty hand in a stop gesture. He eyed the boys, his lip curling ever so slightly. "You're Saint View boys, aren't you?"

I bristled at the prejudice in his tone. That fucking old prick. Where did he get off, staring down his nose at them? Especially after what his son had done. His money and fancy house hid a wealth of sins. These boys might be from the wrong side of the tracks but at least they had morals. Something Chief Waller had none of. Was it any surprise Owen had turned out the way he had, with this asshole as a father?

Banjo shot me a 'settle down' look and calmly twisted to face the policemen. "Yes, we are."

"Then you can stay and watch this footage, too. Perhaps you'll be able to identify the man on the video."

I swallowed hard. "You found video? From the night of the fire?"

"From the night of your uncle's murder, yes."

"You said you checked all the businesses on that street. No one had cameras that caught anything."

Chief Waller huffed at me, like I was a stupid kid speaking out of turn. Selina came to my side, taking my hand and squeezing it, her silent support spoken through the gesture. I tried to reel in my anger, annoyance, and complete lack of faith in our police department. If they had video, we were about to see the man who'd murdered my uncle. And that wasn't going to be easy for Selina. She needed me. Not to run my mouth, but to support her.

I squeezed her hand back.

One of the officers produced an iPad and placed it on the

countertop. Selina and I moved in beside Rafe and Banjo, the four of us crowding around the small screen.

"This is footage from the back-yard of a house on the street behind Providence School for Girls. It was brought forward only yesterday."

I ground my molars, trying to keep in the accusations that threatened to explode. Hadn't they asked the owners of the neighboring properties if they had cameras? Sure, they'd asked the stores and cafés opposite, but they hadn't thought some of the residential houses behind the school might have had security cameras, too?

So much gross incompetence. But it was hardly surprising with this yahoo at the head of the department.

Even now, he didn't look impressed by having to be here. "Press play, please."

I reached out a shaky finger and hit the little triangle button.

At first, the video showed nothing out of the ordinary. A large yard with neat flowerbeds surrounding the perimeter. A trampoline took up one corner of the screen, and children's toys were scattered about the perfectly manicured lawn. It was a night vision view, so the black-and-white image had that eerie green tinge. Nothing moved, the video so still it could have been mistaken for a photo.

But then the back fence shook, and fingers grasped the top edge. The top of a head appeared, then strong shoulders pushed the man up, his legs appearing next as he vaulted over, landing in a crouch on the other side.

He lifted his head, and the video froze.

So did my heart.

I stopped breathing.

"Do any of you recognize this man?" Chief Waller asked,

his gruff tone completely no-nonsense and full of impatience.

Selina leaned in closer, peering at the grainy footage. "No. I'm sorry. I don't. Lacey?"

I stared at the face on the screen. The face of the man who'd saved me from death and taken my uncle's life.

I knew.

I knew his eyes. His nose. His lips.

I'd kissed those lips just last night.

Colt.

I forced myself to speak calmly. "No, I don't know him."

Beside me, Banjo cleared his throat. "Me neither."

Rafe turned and shrugged at Chief Waller. "Sorry, never seen him before."

Chief Waller clucked his tongue and reached over my shoulder. He flipped the cover on the iPad and stashed it beneath his arm. "Very well. We'll continue to make inquires. Sorry to interrupt your breakfast."

Selina nodded and shook Chief Waller's hand before walking him to the door.

The boys turned wide eyes on me, and for the longest moment, the three of us just stared at each other. Banjo opened his mouth to speak, but then the scuff of Selina's slippers on the tiles grew closer, and I shook my head frantically. He closed his mouth.

My mind whirled. A million different thoughts crowded my brain. So many, I couldn't make sense of any of them. Instead, I picked up the tongs and served up the breakfast I'd made, giving a plate to Selina and then Rafe. He stared at me with his big blue eyes. I couldn't look at him. He was analyzing me, trying to work out what I was playing at. But even I didn't know. Why hadn't I told Chief Waller exactly who was on the tape? My fingers trembled when I set Banjo's plate down in front of him.

"You okay, Lace?" he asked.

I glanced at Selina who seemed as off in la-la land as I was. Her fingers trembled as she picked up her knife and fork. Did she know? Did she know I'd been making out with the man who'd murdered her husband? Had she recognized him? I wasn't sure she'd ever met Colt. I didn't think she had. They'd both been at my birthday party, but there'd been hundreds of people there that night. A crowd of nameless, faceless, Saint View kids who she wouldn't have paid any attention to.

I put the last plate, the one I'd made for myself, down on the countertop. I forced a smile. "I'm fine."

Everybody knows a woman who says she's fine is anything but.

I wasn't fine.

I doubted I'd ever be fine again.

30

LACEY

Rafe paced up and down my bedroom floor.

Banjo stared out the window.

I sat on the edge of my bed, fisting the sheets.

"I don't believe it." Rafe stopped abruptly, spinning around. "They're setting him up. They have to be."

I stared up at him. "You saw his face. Right there on the screen, Rafe. Do you think they Photoshopped it in?"

"Maybe."

I went back to twisting my sheets. "I don't think so."

I closed my eyes and let the memories of that night rush in. The heat. The flames. The smoke.

The strong arms that held me close.

Colt.

"It was him," I said quietly.

Rafe stared at me. "What are you saying? That Colt killed your uncle?"

I had no idea if that was what I was saying. I had no idea about anything.

Banjo shifted position on the window seat so he faced us again. "Why didn't you identify him?"

"I don't know."

"You do," Banjo pushed. "Is it because you aren't sure it was him?"

I shook my head.

"Then why? Why not tell Chief Waller that it's Colt on that video?"

I sucked in a deep breath, but no words came out.

Rafe knelt in front of me, peering into my eyes. He studied me for a second, then swore low under his breath. "Fuck. Are you in love with him?"

I blinked. "What? No."

He looked doubtful.

"I'm not," I said again, but hell, even I wasn't convinced. I blew out a long, slow breath, trying to steady my nerves. "I don't know what it is, with him and me. I couldn't turn him in."

Banjo stood and crossed the room, coming to sit beside me. "Maybe you aren't in love with him. But there are feelings there."

My chest got tight. The room was suddenly too stuffy, too airless. I leaned forward, resting my elbows on my knees while I fought off the impending panic attack. What the hell was wrong with me? The police had put proof right in my face that Colt was there that night. He was now the only suspect in the murder, and yet here I was, covering for him.

I glanced up at them, my heart breaking right down the middle. "I have to tell them the truth. I need to go down there and tell them who it is. I have to. If he killed Lawson..." My voice broke. "I can't cover for him. I can't!"

"You already did," Banjo said quietly.

I shook my head. "I'll fix it."

Rafe put his hand on my leg, the warmth and weight of it reassuring. "Stop and breathe for a second, and let's think this through. There's a reason you didn't say anything. And it has nothing to do with any feelings you might have for him."

I sucked in another deep lungful of air, desperately hoping he was right. I couldn't be that girl. The one who put feelings for a boy she didn't even like above what was right.

I was desperate for another reason.

"What then, Rafe? Please. If you have any ideas, I'd really love to hear them."

Rafe sat back on his heels. "Was there blood on your clothes?"

"Huh?"

"The clothes you were wearing that night of the fire. We're working on the assumption this guy who saved you is also the man who killed your uncle, right? Your uncle was stabbed to death. Surely that would have left blood on the killer's hands?"

Banjo nodded. "And if he had blood on his hands, then there would have been blood on your clothes, from when he carried you out."

Both of their faces were so filled with hope. But I wasn't as optimistic. "And what if he simply washed his hands before he lit the fire? I was at the other end of the building when the murder happened. He could have murdered my uncle, washed his hands, and watched an episode of *Supernatural* before he lit the fire for all I know."

None of us laughed. There was nothing funny about it.

Rafe scrubbed his hands over his face. "And risk being there longer than he had to be? No, at best, he would have just wiped his hands on something."

"Still doesn't help us."

"Fine. What about my dad?"

Banjo jerked his head up. "What's your dad got to do with it?"

Rafe glanced at me, and I nodded, indicating he should tell Banjo. "We worked out that Lacey's uncle and my dad went to college together. But he claims they didn't know each other, even though he signed his yearbook. I'm still suspicious of him. He's been up to something for months."

Banjo's eyes went wide. "Okay, this is getting out of hand. Why on earth would your dad want to murder Lacey's uncle? What motive does he have?"

"What if he wanted Lawson's job?"

I gaped at him. "You think he'd murder someone over that?"

Rafe shrugged. "Maybe not go there with the intention of murdering him, but you've seen my dad in action. His temper has a very short fuse, and he thinks nothing of resorting to physical violence. What if he went there to talk, but it ended up in an argument?"

"An argument that turned deadly?"

Rafe shrugged. "I have honestly no idea."

"Me neither," I said.

"Well, that makes three of us." Banjo sighed. "You know there's only one person who's going to tell us anything about this. Don't you?"

I let out a shaky breath. "Colt."

31

———

LACEY

*I*t took an hour to convince Rafe and Banjo not to storm over to Colt's place and demand an explanation. It then took the rest of the day to build up the courage to do it myself.

I wanted to do it alone. I needed answers only he could give.

But I was also terrified of what those answers would be.

I didn't want to hear him admit he'd been there that night. Or that he'd killed my uncle. I'd dreamt about this boy. Kissed his lips. Let him touch me in places that turned me pink to think about.

I didn't want to hear that the person who'd saved me from Owen's attack on the beach was capable of taking the life of another. He'd denied it when I'd asked him once before, but I'd seen his face on that screen. He'd lied.

I needed to know the truth. All of it.

As the sun went down, I drove out of the gates of Providence and into the slums of Saint View. These streets were familiar now. I'd driven them every day for months, and now I wished I had an excuse to stop to look at a map or ask for directions. Anything to slow down the time.

I turned into Colt and Banjo's street, dread creeping up my spine. The urge to turn around and flee was so strong I had to force my hands to keep the car steady, instead of spinning the wheel to hightail it out of there.

That would only be delaying the inevitable.

Someone would identify Colt eventually. And then I wouldn't get this chance to find out what he knew.

Or what he'd done.

I parked outside his house and shut my car door with shaking fingers. It didn't close properly the first time, and I cursed, opening it to try again. The slam echoed around the quiet street, and I winced at the commotion I was making. I glanced around, expecting the flicker of curtains being pulled aside in the neighboring houses, but they were all still. Nobody cared what I was doing out here. It was only me who felt as if a gigantic spotlight shone down on my head, exposing my every movement, my every thought.

I forced myself across the patchy grass of Colt's front lawn and stopped in front of his door. I sucked in gulping lungfuls of air, my stomach nauseated and my head so dizzy I was sure I was going to pass out.

This was what I'd come to Saint View for. But now I'd found it, I wasn't sure I wanted it. Not like this. Not in him.

I rapped my knuckles on the wooden door and waited with bated breath for him to answer. A moment of silence had me thinking perhaps no one was home, and for half a second, I was relieved. But then footsteps thundered down the stairs, and the door swung open.

Not Colt.

A girl with dark hair tumbling over her shoulders and eyes as black as night stared back at me. I did a double take.

There was no mistaking she was Colt's sister. The near-black eyes were a dead giveaway. Nobody had eyes as dark as Colt.

Except for her.

I shook myself out of my trance, realizing I was just standing there, staring at the poor girl. "Sorry. Hi. I'm Lacey. I thought Colt's sister was younger, so I'm a bit thrown." I tried to smile at her, though casual chit-chat when I was about to accuse her brother of murder was about as ridiculous as me having a threesome with Banjo and Rafe.

But that had happened, and so was this.

"Seriously?"

I blinked at her tone. Wow. Hostile much? "Sorry. Your mom said something last time I was here that made me think you were a child." I forced a smile I didn't feel. "I see you're not."

The laugh she let out was hard. "Of course. How stupid of me to think you'd remember me."

I blanched at the aggression. "Have we met before?" I was sure I hadn't met Colt's sister when I'd stayed here after my birthday party. I'd been groggy, but I remembered seeing Colt's mom and Coach. I definitely didn't remember this girl. "Do you go to Saint View as well? I'm sorry. It's such a big school, I can't even keep track of the senior class. Are you a sophomore? Junior?" I knew I was stalling. I should have asked for Colt and gotten this over and done with, but making small talk with his sister was easier than facing what I had to do.

She took a step toward me. She had an inch or two on me in height, so I had to raise my chin to keep eye contact with her.

"You stupid bitch. Of course you have no idea who I am. How typical. Lacey fucking Knight, queen of the fucking world—"

"Aria," Colt snapped from behind her.

He yanked her arm, pulling her roughly back inside the house while I stood with my mouth hanging open. What the fuck had happened here? Did asshole behavior run in this family? But no, Colt's mom had been nothing short of sweet.

She shook him off, eyes blazing. "No, Colt. This is all going to shit!"

He got right back in her face. "Shut up and go upstairs. I'll deal with this."

Deal with what?

I had no idea whether Aria obeyed his demands to go upstairs or not, because he stepped outside, slamming the door behind him, cutting her off completely.

"Deal with what?" I asked helplessly. I was completely thrown by the entire conversation. The whole way here, I'd prepared for Colt's aggression. I'd never thought I'd have to deal with his sister's as well.

His eyes flashed as he moved toward me. The anger there startled me, but I wasn't scared. He'd had multiple opportunities to hurt me and never had. Instinctively, I knew he wasn't that sort of guy.

But that didn't mean he wasn't dangerous in other ways. I took a step back.

"You need to leave."

I shook my head. "No. I need to talk to you."

"Dammit, Lacey. For once in your goddamn life, can you listen to me? You need to leave. Now."

Irritation replaced the anxiousness I'd felt the entire way over here. He was telling me to leave? After what I'd just found out about him? Oh, hell no.

"I'm not going anywhere without an explanation."

He threw his hands up in the air. "An explanation of what? Last night? Fucking get over it, princess. I got you off.

You liked it. That's it. If you came here for more, you're going to have to look elsewhere. Go back to Banjo and Rafe."

My blood boiled, and I clenched my fingers into fists. "Are you serious? Wow, fuck me, Colt. You are the most self-centered, cocky asshat I've ever met in my life. You ever stop to consider the whole world doesn't revolve around you and your tongue?"

He smirked. "That's not what you were saying last night."

"Oh, fuck you."

He got in close. So close my nipples brushed his chest. "That what you want, princess? You want to go right now? Back seat of your car?"

I shoved him away, fire burning behind my eyes. "Stop it. Stop trying to intimidate me with your sexual bullshit. If I wanted you, I would have had you by now."

He moved right back in, and dammit, I didn't have the strength to push him away again. His smell drifted around my nose, so clean and manly and so distinctly Colt it curled my toes.

"Then why haven't you, Lacey?"

His lips hovered over mine, our breaths mingling, fire and sparks crackling between us. That infuriating smile he seemed to save for me tilted his lips, and he lowered his head.

I closed my eyes, my body warring with my head. I wanted him. I wanted his lips on mine, his tongue in my mouth. I wanted to press against him and forget the entire morning. Forget it all and just get lost in the touch of him.

His fingers found my chin, and he tilted it up, a grumble of satisfaction that he'd won—again—rolling through his chest.

I opened my eyes and stared directly into his. "Did you kill my uncle?"

He froze.

All the good things disappeared. The butterflies in my belly. The buzzing tension between us. His warm fingers on my skin. Ice washed through my veins.

"Get in your car."

"No. Tell me. The truth this time. I'm so fucking sick of your lies. Was it you? Did you pull me from the fire at Providence?"

A muscle ticked in his jaw. "Yes."

A wave of relief flooded over me that he'd actually admitted it. But that quickly turned into dread. I shook my head, my fingers trembling, tears building behind my eyes. I fought back the urge to scream. "You killed my uncle."

He went to move, and I took a step back. But that did nothing to dissuade him. He grabbed me anyway, his big fingers locking around my arms.

I pushed at his chest. "No! Let me go!"

But he wouldn't. Instead, he kept on walking, forcing me back toward the road. "Shut up," he hissed. "Get in the car."

"No," I screamed again. This time, a sob broke free. "You killed him. Admit it. Just admit it. Please. I can't stand it."

He pushed me up against the side of my convertible and held a finger to my lips, silencing my cries. "Please, Lacey. Get in the car. I'll tell you everything."

32

COLT

With Lacey yelling her head off, for once I was glad I lived in the worst area of Saint View. Because not one person opened a door to see what was going on. Nobody questioned me as I put a screaming woman into a car and got in beside her. This sort of shit was an everyday occurrence around here. Violence was the norm everybody knew and expected. It wasn't even interesting to them anymore.

Lacey stared at me from behind the steering wheel, her eyes wild, chest heaving.

I turned away. I couldn't look at her. I glared right through the windshield, refusing to even glance in her direction again. "Start the car."

My calm tone belied the chaos erupting inside me. My entire life had already blown up in my face once today, and now it was happening again.

"I'm not going anywhere with you," she seethed.

Her eyes were glassy with unshed tears, and that got to me. I couldn't stand seeing women cry. Hated it with every inch of my being. I was so tired of tears. And of the men who put them there.

Myself included.

"Please, just drive. I need to show you something. This will all make more sense if you see it. It's not far. And then, if you aren't happy with what I have to say, you can turn me into the police yourself. I won't fight you on it."

From the corner of my eye, I watched her bottom lip quiver. She was beautiful like this. Wild and angry. Hate burning behind the tears. Riling her up had always put the spark in her eye, and so I'd just kept on doing it.

But this was different. This wasn't the two of us bantering, trying to one-up the other to see who'd crack first.

She turned the car on and tugged her seat belt across her chest as if she were putting on armor. For what I had to say, she'd need it.

"Take a left at the end of the street."

She put the car in drive and checked her mirrors unnecessarily because there wasn't another car around. She drove slowly and cautiously, shooting me tiny glances every few seconds like she was worried I'd pull a gun on her. Again.

Couldn't really blame her.

From the busier main road, I pointed out the way to a place I still remembered well. Two lefts. Stop at the traffic lights. Turn right.

This part of Saint View was no better than the street I lived on. If anything, it might have been worse. While the houses on my street were all occupied by tenants, the houses here weren't. Many lay abandoned, open for squatters or drug dens. Broken glass glittered on the cracked sidewalks.

Lacey parked outside number seventeen, though only

because I pointed it out. It no longer had a number on the rusted mailbox. She glanced around her, out the window, and over her shoulder as if she were frightened someone would jump out of the shadows and yell boo.

Around here, that person would probably have a gun. So she was right to be cautious. She moved to lock the doors, but I caught her wrist and shook my head. "Get out."

"Not a chance."

I ground my molars. She did my head in with her stubborn streak. A growl rose up my chest. "Get out."

I didn't wait for her to listen. I opened my own door and slammed it behind me, then stood on the sidewalk, staring up at the two-story building in the emerging darkness. The nearest streetlight was smashed, and the natural light of the day was rapidly slipping away. The long shadows that slid over the building did nothing to make it look more appealing.

I leaned back on Lacey's car, and it jolted behind me when she finally got out.

She grudgingly walked to my side, her entire body stiff. "What is this place?"

I glanced over at her, studying her expression for a sign she was playing dumb. But she wasn't. She truly had no idea.

I pointed at the building in front of us. "I used to live there."

She gazed up at the property, probably taking in the boarded-up windows and the overgrown lawn. "Not recently, obviously."

"No, not recently. But I was born in that house. Mom still yammers on about what a rush I was in. Didn't even give her time to get to the hospital."

"When did you move?"

I shrugged. "Dunno. When I was eight, maybe? Could have been younger."

She glanced up at me. The drive over had calmed her a little. She no longer seemed like she wanted to take a swing at my face. Now she was just...resigned.

I sighed. "None of this is familiar at all to you?"

She tilted her head to one side and looked at the house again. "No, should it be?"

I put my hands gently on her shoulders and twisted her toward the house next door. It was near identical in its disrepair. The windows weren't boarded, but there was no sign of life from within, and I suspected no one had lived there for a long time. "What about now?"

She shook off my touch, then turned to me, her irritation sparking again. "None of this is familiar, Colt. Why would it be?"

Fuck. She seriously had no idea.

"Because that," I pointed up at the house next door, "was yours."

Her eyes widened. She whipped her head back to stare at the house, then back at me. Her eyes narrowed. "Stop it."

There was disbelief in her eyes, but everything I was telling her was true. "Stop what? It was."

"How would you even know that?"

I laughed. "How? Because I lived right next door to you until you went away, Lacey. Unlike you, I haven't blocked all that out."

She shook her head. "Don't lie to me."

I grasped her chin and tilted her head toward me. I schooled my face into the most serious expression I could conjure up so she'd know, without a doubt, I wasn't trying to play her. "I'm not."

She let out a long slow breath, and I let her go. Her shoulders fell.

"I don't remember it," she said softly. "I knew I lived in Saint View. But not where. Every time I asked, my aunt and uncle said they didn't know."

"How is that even possible? They're your family? One of your parents' siblings."

She shot me a dirty look. "Thanks for mansplaining what an aunt and uncle is, asshole. Lawson was my mom's brother. They cut my parents out of their lives before I was born. Or vice versa. I was never really sure why. I didn't know them at all before I came to live with them." She tugged at her earlobe distractedly. "Do you remember my parents?"

I reached over and pulled her hand away from her face. "Sort of. You mom used to do that, too. Tug her ear when she was stressed out. We hid from her once, at the back of your yard, beneath some thick bushes. She didn't know we'd dug the dirt out and could fit beneath them. I kept shushing you because you wanted to reveal our hiding spot."

"How surprising, you were a rule breaker even back then."

I shrugged. "When we eventually gave ourselves up, your mom had almost ripped her ear off in worry. I couldn't stop looking at the red blotch while she yelled at us."

"I don't remember any of that."

I stared at her profile, taking in the high cheekbones and the pixie-ish slope of her nose that lifted slightly at the end. I'd teased her about it as kids. She wouldn't remember that. But I had. I'd known exactly who she was the minute she'd walked into Saint View High.

There was no forgetting your first love. And Lacey had

been mine. At five years old, I'd loved her so fiercely I would have moved mountains for her if that sort of thing were possible for a five-year-old.

And then she'd disappeared.

All of a sudden, up and gone, and her name was never mentioned again.

Until Aria won a scholarship to Providence School for Girls.

Realization dawned in Lacey's eyes. "That's how you knew my name. The man who rescued me from the fire knew my name."

I nodded.

Her face suddenly crumpled again. "Why?" she whispered, the words desperate. "What did he do to you?"

I knew she was talking about her uncle. I rounded on her, stooping so we were eye to eye. She wouldn't look at me. But I waited until she had no choice. She lifted her watery gaze to mine.

"I didn't kill your uncle, Lacey. I swear."

A single tear dripped down her face. "I don't believe you."

Pain punched through my chest, but I should have expected that. She had no reason to believe me.

"Why were you even there, Colt?"

I ran my hand through my hair, memories dumping down over my head. "I needed to talk to him. My mom tried first, but he blew her off. Wouldn't take a meeting with her." Gutless prick. The words were on the tip of my tongue, but I knew if I told Lacey my true feelings about the man who'd raised her, she'd never listen. She'd block out everything I'd said and go straight to the police. I had to make her hear me. "When I tried, I was turned away at the door."

Lacey gaped at me. "You came to my school?"

I nodded. "Multiple times. But his secretary always made some excuse as to why your uncle couldn't see me. I didn't have an appointment. He was in a meeting. He was off grounds. I was escorted off the property every time."

Lacey stared up at me, waiting for me to continue.

I chewed my bottom lip, knowing I had to tread carefully. Right now, I had her. She was listening. But one wrong step from me would send the entire house of cards crumbling to the ground.

"How did you know he'd be at the school that night?"

"I was watching him."

Her eyes widened. "You were what? You stalked him?"

I threw my hands up in the air. "Call it what you want. How the hell else was I supposed to talk to him?"

"Make a fucking appointment!"

I lost my patience. "Are you being intentionally dense? They wouldn't give me an appointment. They took one look at me, realized who I was and where I came from, and never gave me a chance. Your uncle wouldn't have anything to do with me. He threatened me with a restraining order. And you know why?"

My brain screamed to shut up. I was going to lose her. And that was the last thing I wanted.

"Why?"

I clammed up. *Fuck!* I'd promised Aria. Promised I'd never tell anyone.

"Why, Colt? Just tell me." Lacey shoved at my chest.

I didn't budge. If I couldn't tell her the whole truth, I'd tell her everything else and hope that was enough to convince her. "I went to the school that night to confront him. Parked on a back street and got over the fence from a neighbor's yard. I knew where he'd be. In his office. I'd been there enough times, I knew exactly where it was."

"And then you waltzed in, some demon of the night, and stabbed him?"

I shook my head, replaying every second of that night, like I had so many times over the past few months. It was all etched into my mind, never far from thought, only held back by sheer determination. "No! I got to the back door, jimmied it, praying he'd turned the alarm off. I still don't know if he had or if the fire killed it. All I could see was smoke."

Lacey stilled. "The fire was already lit when you got there?"

"Lit and well under way."

She covered her mouth with her hand, but confusion drew her eyebrows in tight. "No, you wouldn't have gone in. You would have walked away."

I stared into her eyes, begging her to believe me. "Not when I knew you were inside. I could hear you, screaming for your uncle. Screaming for help." I hadn't even thought about it. I'd smelled the smoke. Heard her screams, and then the next thing I knew I was running through the building, flames devouring the walls around me.

She rubbed her hands beneath her eyes, dashing away tears. "Why would you do that? You could have been killed."

Wasn't that the million-dollar question. The one I'd been asking myself ever since.

She wouldn't want to hear the answer. *I* didn't want to hear the answer.

This conversation was over.

"Let's go. It's dark, and the longer we stand here, the more attention we draw to ourselves. Around here, that'll only lead to no good." Without waiting for her to agree, I got back in the car and closed the door. I let out a breath that had been strangling my lungs and waited.

She stared up at the old house once more and then got in on her side.

She looked over at me. "What now?"

I had no fucking idea.

33

LACEY

I turned the engine on and let the roar drown out the pounding in my head. I couldn't stop looking up at the house that had once been mine. It had two windows on the second story. Had one of them been my bedroom? Had my parents painted the walls pink or mauve and bought me a dollhouse? Had I run from my room, down the hall, and into theirs on weekends? I couldn't remember any of that stuff. I couldn't remember my dad's face. I had vague recollections of my mother, but nothing concrete. Feelings more than true memories. I think I was happy. I wanted to have been. But if I had, then why the hell couldn't I remember any of it?

In front of me, the headlights cast a glow over the darkened street. It lit up a dirty red SUV, parked a ways down the road.

Colt stiffened beside me. "No fucking way. It's that Explorer again."

"What Explorer?"

"Drive up there. I want to ask these fucks why they're hanging around and now following me apparently."

"Following you?"

"Yeah, Aria said they've been watching the house. When I went to confront them, they took off. Go down there."

The car was vaguely familiar... "Shit." I clenched my fingers around the steering wheel. And then I jerked the car into drive and spun the wheel, making a U-turn on the wide road.

Colt slammed into the window with a grunt of surprise. "What are you doing?"

I took a left at the top of the street and put my foot down on the gas. "Are they following?"

Colt twisted in his seat, but he didn't need to answer. A flash of headlights in my rearview mirror told me they were.

"Fuck," he swore, twisting back to the front. "What's going on?"

I took another turn without indicating and shot a panicky glance at Colt. "I've seen that car before, too. At the party last night. Shit, what if it's the police? The police know!"

His eyes darkened, but I couldn't keep looking at him. I had to concentrate on the road.

"Lacey, stop. What do they know?"

I shook my head, gaze continually flicking to the rearview mirror. The headlights were still there. Farther away now, but still tailing us.

A sudden rush of certainty filled me. "They know you were there, at Providence the night of the fire. Colt, they have your face on video, leaving the crime scene. They've probably been watching you this entire time!"

He jerked around again, staring in horror at the car behind us. "You think they're the cops?"

"Oh my God, was I speaking French? Who the hell else would they be? What else are you involved with?"

"Nothing. Fuck!"

I turned down another side street, blindly driving, no idea where I was going. Colt was completely frozen up beside me.

I snapped my fingers in front of his eyes. "Tell me where to go."

That seemed to jolt him out of his trance. He took one last peek at the car behind us, and a steely determination came over him. "At the end of the street, turn left. It'll take you down to the beach. It's narrow, but this car will fit. I don't think theirs will. They'll have to get out or go around. It'll buy us enough time to disappear."

I gunned the engine again and made the turn when Colt told me to. A horrid, nails-down-a-chalkboard sound exploded from the side of my car, and I winced, knowing I'd hit the wall bordering one side of the narrow alley. "Colt! This isn't a road!"

"Never said it was."

Oh my God, he was infuriating even now. Nevertheless, I put my foot down and tried to keep the wheel straight. It was a short alley, but for the damage I was doing to my car, it might as well have been a mile long. The scraping, screeching noise didn't let up until we shot out the other side. Colt let out a holler and threw his hand out the window, middle finger saluting the car stopped at the mouth of the alley behind us.

My fingers shook, and I jerked the car to the side of the road.

Colt stared at me, eyes wide. "What are you doing? Keep going."

But I couldn't. Adrenaline was crashing my system, my heart beating too hard, and the realization we'd probably run from the cops was setting in. I stumbled out of the car, verging on a panic attack, vise-like fingers squeezing my chest.

Colt scrambled out, too, grabbed me by the shoulder, and shook me. "Hey—"

The words died on his lips. Concern replaced the irritation on his face. "Shit." He hauled me to the passenger side, half-lifting me off the ground in his efforts to get me there quickly. "Get in."

This time, I didn't fight him. I let him bundle me into the car and watched numbly as he sprinted around and got in the driver's seat. He winced as his knees hit the steering wheel column. "Goddammit, you're short."

For some reason, that was what undid me. I started laughing. And once I started, I couldn't stop. Hysterical laughter, verging on manic, that then somehow morphed into gulping sobs. It was all I could do to sit there and laugh-cry while he got the seat pushed back and slammed the gearshift into drive once more.

"Put your seat belt on," he commanded.

Around hiccups, I made a face. "You put yours on."

The corner of his mouth tipped up, but this time it was tinged with relief. "Fuck you."

"Fuck you, too."

My heart rate was slowing now that I wasn't the one in control of getting Colt to safety. We both darted glances behind us every so often, but if the car following us had gone around the alley to continue the chase, I couldn't see them. Eventually, as Colt drove us out of Saint View along the coast road, the vise around my chest loosened, and I could breathe again.

I leaned forward, resting my hands on my knees, sucking in oxygen.

"Put your head lower. It helps."

I didn't want to take orders from him, but I did drop my head, and found he was right. The dizziness subsided. When I finally brought my head up, it was clearer.

"I'm going to pull over so you can get some air. There's a cove up ahead."

I nodded, relishing the idea of the cold night on my face and the roar of waves enveloping me.

Colt took the turnoff marked by a road sign, and we bounced over the gravel into a completely deserted strip of parking. Beyond, the beach spread out, dark water disappearing into the night sky.

Colt clambered out from behind the wheel and inspected the scrape that ran the entire length of the car. "Pop the trunk. I think your shitty driving has put it out of alignment."

I shot him a dirty look he couldn't see but leaned across and pushed the button anyway. He inspected the trunk while I got out and stretched. Even though we hadn't been in the car that long, my muscles were stiff from stress, and my neck cracked loudly.

Colt winced, passing me the blanket I kept in the trunk. He moved in warily, but when I didn't snap off his hand like a rabid dog, he put his fingers to the back of my neck. They dug into the muscles there, kneading out the crick. The groan of relief I let out was bordering on indecent, and I let him soothe the ache, even though I knew I should have pulled away.

He dropped his hand and I almost whimpered in disappointment. Instead, I wrapped the blanket around my shoulders. He put his hands behind his head, stretching his own big body up to full height. His midnight eyes scanned the shoreline, lit up only by a fat full moon and a sky peppered with stars. Without warning, he took off down the path toward the water, pulling off his shirt and dropping it on the sand.

I blinked and then ran to keep up with him, scooping up his shirt from the sand as I went. When I reached his side, he'd popped the button on his jeans.

I stopped. "What are you doing?"

"Going for a swim. What does it look like?"

My shoes sank into the soft sand. I assumed Colt's were, too, but that didn't slow him down any. He made a beeline for the water, toeing off his shoes and socks, discarding them as haphazardly as he had his shirt before dragging his jeans over his ass.

I clapped a hand over my eyes. "Colt, stop. It's late, there's no one around. What if a shark eats you?"

He snorted on his laughter. "It won't."

I dropped my hand to my hip. "Fine. What if you drown?"

He glanced over his shoulder at me. "You'll save me."

"The hell I will. That water is probably freezing."

He shrugged. "Guess I'll drown then." He winked as if he didn't have a care in the world, and then yanked his boxer briefs off and ran for the water.

A breath whooshed out of me. Colt's broad shoulders tapered down to a narrow waist, and his ass was perfect. Slightly whiter than the rest of him, which amused me and gave me fuel for future verbal sparring. But also tight and muscled.

I dropped down into the sand, watching as he splashed into the dark water. If it was cold, he didn't show it. It was a nice night, but we were approaching winter. Even though our winters were mild, with snow being a once-in-a-decade rarity, I still thought he was a little crazy. Though I understood the pull of the ocean. It was strong, and there was nothing quite like it for making you forget your troubles.

A wave loomed, building in intensity. Colt dived beneath it.

I watched for his dark head to break the water on the other side, but there was nothing.

The wave crashed against the shore. He was taking too long to come back up.

I scrambled to my feet, panic surging. "Colt!"

His head popped through the surface, hair slicked back, and I breathed a sigh of relief, hoping he hadn't heard me. When the wave receded, I realized he was only waist-deep, and then felt ridiculous for being worried about him. The waves weren't big, and they were far between.

He swam out a little farther but then stopped, turning back to shore. "Come in. It's not so bad."

"Nope."

"Chicken."

"Whatever."

He made clucking noises that had me wanting to throw a shoe at him. Dammit if his taunts weren't getting to me. Without giving it too much thought, I stood and took off one shoe. But oh, fuck it. Who was I kidding? I wasn't going to throw it at him. And he knew it. He was very naked in that water, and I was missing the opportunity to see it up close.

I smiled at his hoot of glee, but I turned my face down to the sand, hoping he wouldn't see it.

"Get your gear off, Lacey."

"Turn around."

"Nope."

I shoved my hands on my hips and glared at him.

He still didn't turn around.

Fine, whatever. I took my shirt off and then my jeans,

and moved toward the water, still clad in my bra and panties. The tide washed over my feet. "Oh, holy hell!" I spun and headed straight back to dry sand. "Nope! Not today, Satan."

Because seriously. That water was icy enough to freeze straight over.

Cold, wet arms wrapped around me from behind. The scream I let out was deafening, but if it bothered Colt, he didn't let on. He hauled me to his chest, my back pressed against his front, his thick forearms and biceps locked tight around my middle.

He hoisted me straight off the sand and strode back to the water.

"Colt, no!"

He simply chuckled in my ear.

We hit the water again, and he wasted no time wading out. I yelped as the spray hit me, but God, I was so distracted by the feel of him at my back. I didn't dare think about how very naked he was. I tried to pull my feet up as we went deeper, desperate to keep my flesh away from the freezing water, but it was a losing battle.

"Can you swim?" he asked. "You couldn't when we were five, but you learned, right?"

My teeth chattered. "Yes."

"Good."

He threw both of us headfirst into the next wave. Icy water rushed over me, and I came up spluttering.

"Colt!"

He'd let go of me at some point, and I was glad. Because I was getting the hell out of this freezing water.

"Aw, come on, Lacey. Who am I going to sacrifice to the sharks if you get out?"

I didn't look back. I just threw one hand up in the air and flipped him the bird. Goosebumps prickled my flesh.

The slap of footsteps on the wet sand behind me had me picking up the pace. The last thing I wanted was for Colt to drag me back into the water. I glanced back over my shoulder and copped the full image of Colt in all his birthday suit glory. I squeezed my eyes tight and ran faster for my clothes, because hell, if the cold was affecting Colt, his body didn't show it.

We reached our pile of things at the same time and both dove for the blanket.

Colt came up victorious.

I scowled at him, sure my lips were turning blue.

He shook the blanket out, sand scattering around us, and then surprised me by putting it around my shoulders.

"Oh. Um. Thanks." The blanket wasn't particularly soft, made of tough material and more suitable for sitting on, but hell if I was complaining. The thicker fabric kept the cold out perfectly. "What about you?" I was trying so hard to keep my gaze on his face and not let them drift lower.

He shrugged. "You want to share?"

I shook my head vigorously. Not because I wanted to keep all the warmth for myself. But because the thought of having a naked Colt that close to me, and not doing anything about it, was unbearable. Plus, he was the dumbass who decided to go swimming. Let him freeze.

"Didn't think so. All good. I'll air dry. I don't really feel the cold."

We both stared out to the sea again. It seemed infinitely safer than looking directly at him. I tucked the blanket tighter around me, as if I could use it as some sort of Colt force field. Lord knows I needed it. I did wish I could take off my soggy underwear, but I didn't dare.

Instead, I breathed in the night air and let the crash of the waves fill my ears. "I love the beach."

"I know."

"No you don't."

He glanced over at me. "Actually, yeah, I do. We used to come here when we were kids. Your family and mine."

I gawked at him. "You remember that?"

"You don't?"

"Do you always answer questions with questions?"

"Do you?"

We were silent again for a long moment. But curiosity got the better of me. "What else do you remember?"

The moon and starlight danced over Colt features. His wet hair fell in his eye, but he didn't brush it aside. With his broad, bare shoulders, he was some sort of god born from the sea. I wondered how salty his lips would taste right now.

"I don't know. Bits and pieces. You, mostly. You followed me around a lot."

"Doubtful," I threw back at him, but it was with a smile. I really didn't want him to stop talking.

"True story. My mom would always try to get you to play with Aria. She wasn't that much younger than us, but because I thought she was annoying, so did you." He grinned at me. "You followed me, even back then."

"Are you implying I still follow you now? When has that ever happened?"

"You followed me right into a freezing ocean. You totally follow me."

Fuck. He had a point.

"What happened with Aria?"

He shook his head.

I toed at the sand. "Why do you hate me?"

"You've asked me that before."

"You didn't answer."

"What makes you think I will now?"

I sighed.

"I don't hate you," he said softly.

My breath hitched.

He twisted, and I looked up at him. Those black eyes held mine, refusing to let me pull away.

"I hate things that happen around you. Things you obviously don't even know about. Things that aren't your fault. It took me a long time to realize that." He paused then sighed. "Fuck. What I'm trying to say is I'm sorry."

"Excuse me? Did you just apologize for being the biggest asshole on the face of the planet?" Okay, so I was ad-libbing a little, but that's what his apology should have included.

He glared at me. "I'm not gonna say it twice. Take your win, don't fucking gloat."

I wanted to prod him about all these things he thought I didn't know. I wanted to demand he tell me everything, but the stubborn glint in his eye told me I shouldn't even bother. He might have apologized, but that didn't mean he was suddenly a different guy. He still held all the cards. And he held them so tight to his chest I knew I'd have to pry them off his cold, dead body.

I couldn't blame him. Everybody had secrets. Some were just dirtier, grittier, and darker than others.

A niggling voice in the back of my head told me to stop, because I probably wouldn't like what happened if he did confess.

34

———

COLT

a shiver shook me from head to toe, but it wasn't from the night air. I hadn't been lying when I'd told Lacey I didn't feel it.

But I did feel other things.

Like how damn close she was to me. And how if I moved even an inch to the left, my arm would touch hers.

She glanced up at me again. "You're cold." It was more of an accusation than an observation.

"Maybe."

She sighed. "We should go."

Everything in me resisted that idea. "I don't want to."

"Me neither. But you're going to get hypothermia if you don't get some clothes on."

She was right, but fuck. "If I go home, the cops will probably be there, waiting to arrest me."

Her plump, full lips drew into a line. "You didn't do anything wrong."

As if that mattered. "I know you aren't naïve enough to think that's how they're going to see it. They aren't going to care there had to be someone else there that night. They're going to take one look at the kid from Saint View with a history of getting himself in brawls and they're going to pin the entire thing on me. It's not much of a leap from street thug to murderer."

She stared at me, eyes big. She opened her mouth, but I cut her off.

"Please, Lacey. Don't. Don't try to explain it away. You know that's what's going to happen."

She closed her mouth for a moment but then said quietly, "I was going to ask if you wanted some blanket."

She held out the arm closest to me, the blanket clutched in her fist. The side profile of her body caught my attention. Her tits pushed up in a nude-colored bra. The curve of her hip covered by a thin strap of cotton. She waited for me to make a decision.

Step into her warmth and let myself get close to her nearly naked perfection.

Or walk away, go back to Saint View, and face the music.

I took the corner of the blanket from her grasp and stepped in closer, wrapping it around my shoulders. It wasn't big enough for the two of us. But for once, we didn't tussle.

Something sparked in the air between us. That same familiar attraction that always cropped up when she was around. We were too close to each other. There was no room to breathe, no way to get space.

She let go of the blanket, letting me have the entire thing. Her eyes locked with mine. Conflicting emotions flickered across her face, so rapidly I couldn't decipher them all. But one overwhelmed the others.

"Lacey," I whispered.

She swallowed hard, her eyes suddenly glassy. She shook her head. "This can't be how it ends. I don't want you going to jail and Lawson's killer going free. This isn't fair. I made that deal with Owen to keep you out of jail, and now you're going to end up there anyway? *No!*"

I blinked at the ferocity of her last word.

A tear rolled down her face.

My stomach clenched into a painful knot. "Don't," I gruffed out but then immediately softened. "Please don't. I can't handle it."

She dashed away the tear, but it was no good. They kept falling. I reached out to capture them with my thumbs, but she batted me away, shaking her head.

I dropped my hands.

Our gazes collided.

Then she pushed up on her toes and pressed her lips to mine.

When I didn't respond, she pulled back, her hands fluttering around her mouth. "I shouldn't have done that. Shit. Sorry. I thought you wanted this..." She turned to grab her clothes.

I caught her wrist and hauled her back to me. She stumbled into my chest, her palms flat against my stomach. She tilted her head back, confusion sparking in her eyes.

Everything I'd been trying to keep buried shot to the surface. Every feeling. Every need that rose when she was around. What the fuck were we doing? This back and forth arguing when all I really wanted to do was bury my face in her neck and breathe her in. "I don't want *this*," I growled. "I want *you*."

I slammed my lips down on hers, gathering her tight—too tight—and crushing her to my chest. For the tiniest of moments, I didn't think she'd kiss me back. But then she was all over me, her hands in my hair, pulling me down, scratching at my scalp. Her leg inched between mine, so we were as close as we could be. Our lips moved with bruising intensity, which only fueled the fire building inside me since the very first day. I needed her. I couldn't go away without knowing her body. Tasting her skin. Hearing her scream my name.

The blanket had fallen, but neither of us stopped to grab it, the cold completely irrelevant when heat roared between us. She ground her hips on me, getting me instantly hard, and I groaned into her mouth, savoring the taste of her lips, still salty from the seawater. Her nails dug into the skin at the back of my neck, and I relished the sting, giving it back to her by nipping at her mouth.

She lowered one hand between us, found my erection, wrapped her fingers around me and gave me two quick, fast jerks that felt way too good. I moved with her, rolling my hips into her grasp.

One snap of my fingers, and her bra came apart. She struggled to get it off while I dragged her panties over her peach-shaped ass.

Her damp underwear fell onto the sand, and I pulled away, wanting to drink her in.

She whimpered, and it was the fucking sexiest sound I'd ever heard.

"Don't stop," she begged.

But I shook my head. "Need to look at you." The shape of her curves in the moonlight was the most beautiful thing I'd ever seen. High, perky tits, with her nipples beaded and straining for my touch. Her flat torso that spread to the curves of her hips and ass. Shapely thighs, and at the apex, her sweet, bare pussy I hadn't gotten out of my head since the last time I'd seen it.

Her chest rose and fell too quickly, but she let me drink my fill. This woman wasn't the same as the one I'd rescued from a different beach, not all that long ago. This one stood with her head held tall, confident in the knowledge I wanted her body more than I wanted oxygen. I had the strongest urge to dominate her and work her until she begged for me to let her come. But I knew her. And I liked that she would never be that submissive. I could try to own her body, but I instinctively knew she'd always give as good as she got.

That was always the way with the two of us. I gave her shit. She gave me hell.

Proving my theory right, she fell to her knees before me, taking my cock between her perfect lips and sucking me deep inside her mouth. She gazed up while she worked my length, tongue stroking the underside until my balls were clenching with need. I scraped her hair up from around her face, wanting to watch the show she seemed determined to give me.

"Rub your clit, Lacey," I commanded and was rewarded with a moan of pleasure.

Fuck, maybe she *would* listen if I bossed her around. Her knees widened on the sand, and I groaned, hearing but unable to clearly see what she was doing to herself.

And fuck, I wanted to see it. I wanted to watch her make herself come, so I knew exactly what she was into, so I could do it all again, over and over, for as long as she'd let me.

I jerked from her grasp, and she stared up at me in confusion, her fingers still parting her pussy.

"What's wrong?"

I shook my head and decided to go with the brutal honesty. "I want to watch."

I had a feeling she was blushing, but then she pulled the blanket out and lay back on it, the top half of her body supported on one elbow, the other hand trailing down her stomach and over her mound. Her knees dropped out to the sides, showing me everything she had between. I sank down on the sand, barely noticing the gritty texture on my knees. I palmed my cock, the thick, heavy weight familiar in my hand, but fuck, I'd never had a sight this hot to jack off to.

Her eyes dipped to my cock, and I gave myself a good, long stroke, rolling over my cockhead and enjoying the slow slide back down. I loved the way her tongue poked out the corner of her mouth, as if she were desperate for another taste. I'd let her before this was over. I wanted to fuck her mouth and feel her tongue wrap around me. But not until I'd gotten her off. Not until I'd watched her fall apart.

Her fingers matched my speed, me jerking my dick, her rubbing circles on her clit. If she felt the cold night air now, she didn't show it. I was burning up, every cell on fire, every muscle screaming that I cover her, take her, make her mine.

But she could never be mine. Not for longer than tonight.

I pumped my cock harder, faster, and she kept up with me. Her fingers dipped lower, spearing into her pussy, eliciting a breathy moan. Her slick fingers shone in the moonlight, and dammit if I could handle it a second longer. I grabbed her thighs, holding her wide open, and took over the job for her. Pre-cum leaked from my tip at her startled shout of pleasure, my tongue making contact with her swollen nub. I was desperate to plunge in, but she tasted good. Like the ripest fruit in summer, her juice coating my tongue and rolling down my throat as her hips bucked against my hold. Her fingers grabbed at my hair, alternating between holding me to her cunt and pushing me away, only to pull me straight back when my lips left her flesh.

"Colt!" she yelled, her shout lost to the crashing waves behind us. She was so close, so on the verge.

"I need to be inside you," I mumbled. "Want to feel you come on my cock."

"Yes!"

I reared over her and took her lips hard. Our tongues tangled once more, and then there was no holding back. She lifted her hips, searching, seeking, and I plunged into her wet heat.

Her scream of pleasure ripped from her chest, filling mine, and fuck, I drank that sound down as if it were a fifty-year-old whiskey. Her pussy clenched around me, hot and tight, and I was balls deep before I even realized what we'd done.

"Fuck," I muttered, pulling out. I leaned on my hands, breathing so hard while my dick throbbed against her belly. "Wait, we need a condom." I fished one from the wallet in the back pocket of my pants, and rolled it on.

Then I lifted her off the blanket and onto my lap, sitting her on her knees, legs spread over me. "Ride me, Lacey," I murmured in her ear.

She kissed my mouth again, and then her hips rolled. Small, slow circles that became bigger with each movement. She was so fully impaled on my dick, I couldn't move for fear I'd come and this would all be over.

I never wanted it to be over.

She clutched my shoulders and rocked her body over mine. She still pulsed from her orgasm, but I wasn't done with her yet.

"Faster," I urged her. I reached between us and found her clit, pinching it while she gyrated against me, the pace slow and sensual and completely in defiance of my request for her to go faster.

Her smug grin told me she knew exactly what she was doing.

Fuck no. I wasn't letting her get away with that.

I flipped her onto her back once more, hooking one leg over my shoulder before driving home deep. We both groaned in unison, the angle so right my balls clenched again.

I fucked her hard. Slamming my hips against hers at a punishing pace that had her eyes rolling back in her head. Her fingers snuck between our bodies again.

"Yes," I encouraged her.

Her fingers slid to her clit, rubbing it hard and fast, matching the pace I set until neither of us could stand it anymore.

"Colt," she screamed again.

But I was right there with her this time, yelling her name as I gave in to the blinding sensation. I crashed my mouth down onto hers again, the kiss hot and sloppy, but neither of us cared. All that mattered was getting as much of each other as we could in this one tiny pocket where everything felt right.

If this was all we had, if I went back home and cops had my house surrounded, then this would be enough. This one night with the girl who had owned my heart for as long as I could remember.

35

LACEY

I let Colt drive us back to Saint View. My legs still trembled from the orgasms, and I wasn't sure there was any blood left in my brain for it to function. I probably would have driven us in the complete wrong direction by accident.

Or maybe not by accident. Because the closer we got to Saint View, the more realization set in. We had no idea what we'd find at Colt's place. "Maybe you should call your mom?" I asked tentatively.

But he shook his head. "No, she would have rang by now if they were sitting in our living room. They're either watching the house waiting for me to get home, or they don't have enough to arrest me."

I swallowed hard. If someone had identified him from that video, I was pretty sure they'd have enough. "We could just not go back. I've got money. We could go to a hotel..."

The corner of his mouth lifted. "You want to fuck some more, princess?"

My smile matched his, and my lady parts gave a special little throb of appreciation at the idea of screwing him again.

I wanted to reach across the gearshift and squeeze his thigh, or maybe run my hand down his biceps. But I curled my fingers into my palm instead. That wasn't what we did. We might have fucked like it was going out of fashion on the beach, and I might have screamed his name as I came, but down-and-dirty fucking was one thing. That was how everything between us was. A stolen kiss outside a gas station. Oral sex shoved up against a wall at some party. None of what we'd done gave me the permission to touch him gently. To wrap my arms around him and whisper that everything was going to be all right.

I didn't know that it was. And even if I had, that wasn't what we did.

The walls were re-erecting themselves around us, and I wanted to break them down. I really did. I wanted to slam them back into the sand and bury them where we'd dropped them. But the baggage they brought with them was back. As we rolled through the outer limits of Saint View, I felt the gap between us widen again.

He was shutting me out.

And there was nothing I could do about it.

Colt pulled the car over before we arrived at his street. He came around to my side, opening the door, waiting for me.

I didn't want to. "What are you doing?"

"This is as far as you go."

I shook my head, getting out to stand with him. "I want to come with you."

To my surprise, he drew me to his chest, his strong arms wrapping around me. He dropped his head so his cheek pressed against mine, his nose lost in my hair. He inhaled.

I waited for his kiss, for his mouth to cover mine. But instead, his hand ran down my arm. He squeezed my hand, then turned it over, putting the car keys on my palm and closing my fingers over the top of them. Our lips hovered inches apart, breaths mingling in the night air.

"Go home, Lacey."

He let go of me and stepped back stiffly. Then he spun on his heel and stalked away into the darkness.

"Colt!" My lips tingled at how close he'd been.

But he didn't stop. Didn't turn. Didn't acknowledge me at all. And as the shadows swallowed him whole, I let him go.

It was late when I got home with my banged-up car. Well after midnight. Rafe's car was missing from the spot on the driveway where it had been parked earlier, and I surmised he'd gone home. My steps were slow, my body held down by the weight of what had happened tonight, and what might be happening to Colt right now. Fatigue plagued me, and my bed called my name, but I didn't take the stairs. Instead, I made a beeline for the back doors that led out to the pool area, and beyond that, the pool house we hadn't used in years.

The door was unlocked, and I slipped inside silently. The dim light of a lamp guided me to the big bed that sat in the center of the room. I smiled at Banjo, fast asleep, his tousled blond hair spread out across the white linen. He didn't stir, and I reluctantly walked past him and into the bathroom. I closed the door quietly behind me before turning on the faucet and letting the water warm up while I shed my sandy clothes one by one. With outstretched fingers, I checked the water temperature, then immersed myself beneath the waterfall, letting the spray wash the sand and salt from my body. I squirted shampoo into my hair and bodywash onto my hands and lathered myself from head to toe, reluctantly rinsing away the memory of Colt's fingers on my skin.

I stifled back a sob, but then the bathroom door opened, and Banjo slipped in, sweatpants slung low on his hips. Our gazes met, and he dropped his pants wordlessly, opened the glass door, and stepped beneath the spray with me.

Tears fell down my cheeks, and though they mingled with the water, Banjo seemed to know. He always knew what I needed, when I needed it. He put his arms around me and held me while I cried. Soft, disappointed, guilt-filled tears that hurt my heart.

After a while, he pressed tiny kisses to my hair, then reached around and turned the faucet off. He took my hand and led me from the shower, finding two fluffy towels beneath the sink that we wrapped ourselves in, then moved back into the main room.

We dropped the towels and slid into bed together, finding each other in the dim light. He fit his front to my back, a lifeline in his muscled arm banded around my waist. I pressed back against him, seeking the comfort of his touch.

"What happened with Colt?" he finally asked.

"We had sex," I admitted, because somehow that seemed easier than the rest.

Banjo kissed my shoulder. "Okay."

I twisted to look at him over my shoulder. "That doesn't bother you?"

He brushed his lips over mine before I sank back down into the pillow.

"No," he said quietly. "You and Colt were inevitable. Nobody fights like the two of you do unless there's sexual chemistry fueling it. Rafe and I both know that. But does being with him change how you feel about me? About Rafe?"

I shook my head and felt the relief in his hold.

I lifted one of his hands from my waist and brought it to my mouth, kissing his fingertips. "Did you know? That he knew me when I lived in Saint View?"

"No. He never told me."

"The cops chased us tonight. At least we think it was them. We got away, but I dropped him back near his place. He wouldn't let me go with him."

Banjo sighed. "He's stubborn."

A half-smile lifted my lips. "Understatement of the year." But then I sobered again because none of this was funny. "What if they're arresting him right now?"

Banjo was silent

And eventually, so was I.

There was nothing left to say.

I woke to Banjo arguing with someone on the phone, while he stood outside the pool house. Realizing I had no clean clothes down here, I wrapped myself in a sheet and padded to the glass doors, pulling aside the heavy curtain that offered privacy. Banjo paced the length of the pool in his sweats, his bare feet near silent on the pavers.

"If you hear anything, call me immediately."

He looked up as I walked outside, shivering in the morning air, and came right over to me, dropping a kiss on my lips. I wanted to deepen it and pull him tight into my embrace, but my curiosity over the call got the better of me.

"Who was that?"

"Rafe."

"He okay?"

"He's fine. I was filling him in on what happened last night."

I bit my lip. "All of it?"

He gave me a reassuring smile. "Yes, all of it. He's cool. Just like I told you he'd be."

I breathed out a sigh of relief. I had no idea how I'd gotten so entangled with the three of them, but I did know I didn't want it to stop. "Has he heard from Colt?"

The smile fell off Banjo's face. "No. I called Colt and Willa and Aria multiple times. None of them are picking up."

"That can't be good."

Banjo nodded. "Probably not. I need to go over there. Can I take your car?"

"Of course."

"Get Jagger to pick you up, and I'll see you at school later, okay?"

I was baffled by how he could be thinking about school after everything that had happened, but when I considered the other option—staying home and worrying over Colt—school actually seemed a pretty good idea.

I walked him up through the main house and to the front door where he kissed me goodbye, so soft and sweet my heart ached.

"I love you," he said, pulling away.

"I love you, too."

I let him go, closing the door quietly behind him before going upstairs to message Jagger and get ready for school.

In true Jagger form, she didn't even question why I needed a lift. She just turned up at my place an hour later and beeped the horn. I yelled to Selina that I was leaving, though I really had no idea if she was even home. I hadn't seen her, and her bedroom door was still closed. I hesitated for a moment, wondering if I should go check on her, but no, if she had a migraine, she wouldn't want to be disturbed. Plus, Jagger was waiting.

I grabbed my bag from the floor and hustled outside to slip into her passenger seat. She reached over and gave me a hug.

Tears pricked the backs of my eyes, but I blinked them away.

Not quickly enough, obviously.

"You want to talk about it?" She twisted to check her blind spot and backed the car out carefully.

Her voice was full of concern, and I could tell by the looks she was shooting me that she was worried. But I didn't have the energy to explain it all again. Telling Banjo last night had been hard enough.

"How about you tell me something normal? Something easy that has no drama attached to it."

Her smile brightened. "Fall Ball is this weekend coming. Aaron asked me to go with him."

I groaned. "Shit, is that seriously this weekend?"

Jagger gaped at me. "You forgot?"

"In my defense, I've had a lot on."

She nodded. "Are you still going to help me decorate, though? We're on the committee. I signed us both up."

"What? We are? Since when do we volunteer for dance committees?"

She grinned. "Since putting up decorations meant all day Friday off classes."

"Just to decorate the gym?"

She faked an outraged cough. "Excuse me, Miss Knight. I'll have you know I take my decorating responsibilities very seriously. Gillian and her crew don't have an artistic bone between them, so if I left it all in their hands, the gym would probably be filled with rainbows and unicorns."

I wrinkled my nose. "Really?"

Jagger laughed. "I don't know. But the Fall Ball is always amazing. Last chance to wear a pretty dress before winter rolls in and makes anything strapless a high risk of hypothermia."

I hadn't really thought of it in that way.

She joined the line of cars waiting to get into the school parking lot. Then shot me a sidelong glance. "I do have one burning question for you, though."

"Yeah?"

"Who are you going to take? Rafe? Or Banjo?"

Or Colt, I mentally added. But that was stupid. Even if nothing had happened last night with the cops, and Colt was waiting on the other side of the gates, ready to go to his first class of the day, he wasn't going to suddenly start taking me to dances. "How much of a scandal would it cause if I rocked up with both of them?"

Jagger gaped at me. "You're coming out as a threesome?"

I raised a shoulder.

She slammed her palm against the steering wheel and whooped in delight. "Fall Ball is going to be lit this year."

36

LACEY

Nobody heard from Colt all week. He didn't show up at school at all. Rafe and Banjo went to his house each afternoon, but every day Banjo came home dejected, saying Colt had refused to talk to him again.

The only good news was he hadn't been arrested. That had filled me with an immense sense of relief.

But the knowledge the police had him on tape hung heavy, a silently ticking time bomb ready to explode and destroy everything in its path at any minute.

With nothing else to do other than butt my head against a brick wall, I threw myself into practicing for the recital and making decorations for the Fall Ball. Every afternoon, Jagger and I met with the rest of the decorations committee and worked on creating fall-related pretties with the limited resources we had at hand. The school had next to no budget for dances, so we scavenged what we could from the woods, turning fallen leaves and sticks into wreaths held together with ribbon we'd found in the art department. We sourced hay bales from a nearby farms and pumpkins from the local patch by begging to borrow them for a night. By

Friday afternoon, with fairy lights we'd found in a box of props from previous dances, we had the gym looking pretty good.

Jagger clutched my hand and squealed in a manner so unlike her I laughed. But she'd gotten as into the decorating as I had. Gillian hadn't shown up at all, leaving the work to her minions, who actually hadn't been too horribly obnoxious without her around. I wondered if she was off somewhere with Owen and cringed at the thought.

Jagger dragged me over to the selfie area and had me pose with her in front of the Fall Ball signs we'd painstaking painted onto poster board. She whipped her phone out, and we squished together, smiling and making faces at the camera until she was satisfied. "Time to get ready."

It really was. Decorating the gym had taken all day, and now I was dusty and dirty and in desperate need of a shower.

And in desperate need of my boys. Despite the fact I now sort of lived with Banjo, I'd barely seen either of them all week. Between me working on decorations, and Banjo and Rafe checking in on Colt, plus shifts at Banjo's catering job, we were ships in the night.

I missed them. Any nerves I'd felt about turning up at this dance sandwiched between the two of them disintegrated. I wanted to be in their arms. I wanted to kiss them beneath the fairy lights we'd strung all over the gym. I wanted one night where everything went smoothly and we got to be ourselves.

Fuck what everybody else thought. Let them call me a slut. I was so far beyond caring about that. College was looming on our horizons, and that meant getting out of this small-minded town. I had no idea what leaving Saint View would mean for the three of us, but we still had months to work that out. Who knew? Maybe this thing would fizzle out by then.

But when Rafe picked us up, and his gaze rolled down my body, any thoughts of fizzling went right out the window. There was nothing but sizzle in his stare, and when he swept me into his arms and put his mouth on mine, I damn near melted into a puddle.

"You look edible," he whispered in my ear.

I grinned, enjoying the way his teeth nipped at me. "So do you."

Rafe's fitted pants hung from his hips deliciously, his black shirt rolled to the elbows, the two top buttons undone, showing off a hint of the tanned skin beneath. His hair was perfectly brushed and styled, and his signature black-rimmed glasses perched on his nose. I bit my lip. All I wanted to do was drag him inside and take them off him.

Banjo appeared from the pool house, just as handsome, though more casual in tight, black, ripped jeans and a white t-shirt. He'd slung a tie around his neck, but he'd loosened it so much he looked like he'd just arrived home from a long day of work. He was tousled and sexy, and with his gaze raking over my body, I could have been the most beautiful woman alive.

Banjo kissed my cheek, his lips lingering longer than necessary. "That dress is smokin', baby." He ran his hand up my leg, beneath the slit in my skirt. "Easy access, too. You thought ahead. Good job."

I stifled a laugh. That hadn't been why I'd bought the tight black number, but it was an added bonus. I patted his chest and pushed him away gently. "Save it for after the dance." I was eager to get there on time and make sure the decorations were staying taped, pinned, or glued.

But the boys seemed to have different ideas. I got in the

passenger seat of Rafe's car, Banjo sliding into the back seat. Rafe got behind the wheel, started the car, and put it into gear, but then his big hand landed on my bare thigh, fingers searching for the split that ran high up my leg.

"Rafe," I warned, as his fingers found the gap in the material and slipped beneath.

"What?" he asked, all fake innocence.

In the back seat, Banjo chuckled. His clothes scratched against the seat as he shifted toward me, his hands appearing from behind and skating over the side of my boobs. I started to laugh, but then his fingers slipped inside my dress and his palm cupped around my breast.

At the same time, Rafe's fingers moved over my panties. "Lacey in lace," he groaned, eyes still on the road, one hand doing all the driving while the other pressed against my clit.

Despite myself, I whimpered, and Banjo squeezed my nipple. As if my legs took direct commands from my hormones, I parted my thighs and allowed Rafe's fingers better access.

The ride to Saint View had never gone so quickly. And by the time we got there, all three of us were turned on, breathing too rapidly, and seriously considering ditching the dance altogether. If Jagger and Aaron hadn't arrived at the exact same time, I doubted we would have made it inside at all. Instead, the boys both took their hands back. Rafe mumbled something about needing a minute, and when I glanced over at him, his erection was straining against his pants.

Despite the fact I wasn't all that far from an orgasm myself, I stifled a laugh.

Jagger stuck her head in my window and yelled, "Fall Ball! Let's go."

The slinky green number I'd bought for her when I'd

first come to Saint View clung to her curves, and she looked a million bucks. She'd put green streaks in her hair for the occasion, and the gold purse she'd slung across her shoulder glinted beneath the streetlights.

I got out, smoothing my dress down and checking my lip gloss was in my clutch.

Rafe and Banjo both got out more slowly.

Jagger was less tactful. She squinted at Rafe. "Why are you walking like you got punched in the kidneys?"

I snorted on my laughter. Rafe glared at me, but even Banjo laughed, too, though I doubted he was in much better condition. I pulled Jagger in and whispered in her ear what we'd been doing in the car. A grin lifted her lips.

"What? Tell me, too," Aaron complained, slipping his hand into Jagger's.

She grinned at him. "Pretty similar to what we were doing on the way over here."

Aaron simply held his hand up for Rafe to high-five.

I rolled my eyes and took off toward the gym. The school was different at night. Nicer, somehow. The low lighting made the exterior a little less hard and rough. It still wasn't pretty, but I was confident the inside would make up for it. Banjo and Rafe caught up with me as I joined the line at the door. We passed our tickets to the teacher on the door, and I sucked in a breath, pausing before the entrance. I searched for Banjo, and he was right there beside me, taking my hand. Rafe found my other, squeezing my fingers.

"We doing this?" he asked.

"Yep." Banjo grinned.

The three of us entered the decked-out gym together.

And nothing happened.

There was no sudden swivel of eyes. No ripple of gossip.

Aaron entered behind us. "Not exactly the commotion you were expecting huh?"

"Uh, no."

"That's good, though, right?" Jagger asked. "Guess you popped that cherry at your birthday party. I mean, compared to that, the three of you walking in here holding hands is pretty grade school."

I choked on my laughter. "Would you prefer we made a real splash? We could always go at it right there on the dance floor."

Her eyes twinkled with mischief. "That'd be one for the yearbook."

I groaned and detangled myself from Banjo's and Rafe's grasps. "I need a drink."

Rafe led the way. "Let's hope the punch is spiked."

It was. Very spiked by the taste of it. We'd set up a food and drinks table on the far side of the room, and the guys swallowed down cupfuls of the fruity liquid before one of the teachers realized and relegated us to the bottles of water sitting untouched to one side. In the opposite corner, one of the senior boys had set up his DJ equipment and was pumping out popular hits.

"You and Jagger did an awesome job with the decorations," Rafe yelled in my direction.

I grinned at him, unable to stop noticing how cute he was. It was still hard for me to believe he was mine. "Thank you. We worked hard."

He slung his arm around my shoulder, pulling me into the crook of his elbow and kissed the top of my head. We watched the dancers for awhile and Rafe downed another cup of spiked punch he'd hidden.

Loud squeals from the doorway caught my attention,

and a group of the cheerleaders rushed from the dance floor. "What's that about?"

Rafe peered over the crowd, then grimaced. "Gillian's arrived. She's not alone."

My stomach plummeted at the same time nerves exploded through me. "She came with Colt?"

Rafe squeezed my hand. "No, Owen."

Dread swamped me as the crowd of cheerleaders parted and Gillian strutted through the center, Owen's arm slung over her shoulders.

Banjo appeared at my other side, and the three of us stood frozen to the spot. Owen spotted us first and pushed his way toward us, Gillian stumbling at the abrupt change in direction.

She covered it with a laugh, but there was nothing funny about it. The possessive way Owen's arm clenched around her shoulders made my skin crawl.

Beside me, Rafe practically vibrated with tension. I gripped his hand tighter, a silent reminder not to let loose in the middle of a school dance. I knew he was itching to take a swing at Owen for everything he'd done. Hell, I was, too. But this wasn't the time or the place.

Owen trained his gaze on me, and fuck him, I only stood taller. I pulled my shoulders back and lifted my chin, refusing to cower, even though his very presence brought back memories of his attack. I swallowed down bile.

"Lookin' good, Lacey."

Banjo went to step in front of me, but I yanked his arm, keeping him in place. While I loved his protective instinct, I didn't need him to fight my battles.

"Wish I could say the same about you, Owen. But truthfully, the very sight of you turns my stomach." I dropped my gaze to Gillian. She was all sass and fire again, but something about her expression didn't sit right with me. She'd been full of attitude when she'd been with Colt, too, but that had somehow been different to this. Back then, her attitude had been fueled by confidence.

Now I suspected it was fueled by fear.

"Are you okay?" I asked her as quietly as I could.

Her bright-red lips widened into a smile. I didn't know her well enough to know if it was faked or real, though. But then she rolled her eyes as if I were completely ridiculous.

"I'd be better if it weren't for these tacky decorations. Honestly, I leave you two to your own devices for five minutes, and this is what you come up with?" She wrinkled her nose.

I took a step back. Okay, maybe I'd been wrong about the fear. Maybe I'd been projecting my own experiences onto her, and she was fine.

Jagger cut in, glaring daggers at Owen and Gillian in turn. "Let's go dance," she said to me. "You know, beneath all our tacky decorations."

Gillian made shooing motions, because she was a complete bitch. But Owen's arm shot out, his fingers gripping my wrist. I gasped, fighting back the terror that engulfed me at the very touch of his skin against mine. Anything Colt had taught me flew right out the window, and though I'd tucked the fake gun into my purse—I always did every time I left the house now—I was completely powerless to grab it. My entire body locked up in fear.

Banjo and Rafe were on Owen in seconds, and I wrenched my arm free as they shoved him up against the wall.

I blinked. It had all happened in a matter of seconds, but the fear didn't recede.

Owen just grinned. "What are you going to do, boys?

Punch me? Back off. You know you aren't going to do it, or you'll end up in as much trouble as your friend."

Rafe was livid, his eyes flashing sparks in the darkened room. "You think I give a shit?"

Owen focused on him. "You should. Or you'll end up in a jail cell, right next to your bestie."

I put one hand on Banjo's shoulder and pushed him aside so I could get closer to Owen. "What the hell does that mean?"

"Your friend Colt? I saw some interesting video footage of him today. Pretty sure you've seen it, too, haven't you, Lacey?"

I held my breath.

"What are you talking about?" Gillian asked, her hands shoved on her hips. "Who's in jail? What video footage? Ugh, did you guys make another sex tape? You're so nasty."

We all ignored her. Owen shrugged, like he didn't have a fucking care in the world even though Rafe's fist was balling at his side. Tension rippled in his shoulders as he tried to hold himself back.

"What did you do, Owen?" I seethed.

"What any good, upstanding citizen would do. Identified a violent criminal suspected of murder."

Gillian's mouth dropped open.

Mine pressed hard into a line. "The only violent criminal around here is you, Owen."

"The proof says otherwise, princess."

Blinding anger coursed through me. How dare he fucking call me that. Only my boys called me that. Banjo, Rafe, and yeah, Colt. Somehow, he'd become mine, too. And fuck if I was going to let Owen mess with him.

"Where is he?" I demanded.

Owen gave Rafe a pointed stare, and slowly, inch by inch, Rafe let up his hold.

Owen brushed himself off, straightening his clothes before answering. "No idea. As of a few hours ago, the cops were looking for him. But he was MIA."

I frowned. None of this made sense. We'd run from them a week ago now. But Owen was saying he'd only just identified Colt today?

Banjo spun to face me. "We need to find Colt."

I nodded. "Now."

Rafe grabbed my hand, and the three of us ran for the doorway. Banjo pulled out his phone as we hurtled across the gymnasium, dodging couples slow dancing and groups of friends hanging out. They all moved too slowly, like they didn't have a care in the world.

Oh, how I envied them. My gaze lingered slightly too long on a couple who stood beneath the fairy lights, their arms wrapped around each other intimately, their lips gliding together in the sweetest, most romantic kiss.

"Lacey."

I smacked into a wall of muscled chest. Strong arms caught me, and a familiar scent filled my nose. I knew exactly who it was.

Panic surged through me.

"Fuck, Colt," Rafe hissed. "You can't be here. Owen fucking tattled to his daddy, and now you're suspect number one in Lacey's uncle's murder."

Banjo pocketed his phone and pushed us into the shadows at the side of the room. "Seriously, Owen is here. The minute he sees you, he's going to be on the phone, and his dad's goon squad will be here in minutes."

But Colt only had eyes for me. They bored into mine. He shook off Banjo's hold but then turned to his best friends. "I know. Okay? I fucking know. That's why I'm here. I came to say goodbye."

"What?" Rafe hissed. "Fuck no, you aren't. Run. You aren't going to jail for something you didn't do. We all know it wasn't you."

Colt shook his head. "It doesn't matter anymore. I can't run. I won't do that. It makes me look guilty."

"So you're going to go to jail? You can't be serious." Banjo's plea was full of desperation.

But Colt wouldn't be swayed. "I'm going to turn myself in."

My mouth dropped open. "For what? Saving my life?"

He nodded. "Exactly. I'll tell them what happened. The truth. And let the cards fall where they may."

"No!"

His eyes softened, and he tucked a loose strand of hair behind my ear. But when he spoke, his voice was firm. "Not your call to make, princess."

In that moment, all three of us—Banjo, Rafe, and I—seemed to come to the same realization.

Nothing we said was going to stop him.

The fight went out of Rafe's stance. Banjo sagged back against the wall and ran a hand through his hair in defeat.

Colt glanced between them. "Mind if I dance with your girl?"

"Our girl," Banjo said quietly, glancing to me for confirmation. "All three of us."

I gave a tiny nod.

Colt cocked his head to one side, then took a step in. "Is that what I am? One of your guys?"

For once there was no scorn or sarcasm in his expression. And that gave me the courage to say what I really wanted.

"Yes."

He didn't comment, and in typical Colt fashion, his next words were more of a demand than a question. "Dance with me. Out in the middle of that dance floor where everyone can see us."

I bit my lip and looked over at the packed floor in worry. Owen was over there somewhere.

But then Colt's lips were brushing the shell of my ear. "Dance with me, Lacey. I want to show every person in this room you're mine. You get that?"

My heart squeezed. I got it.

His fingers wrapped around mine, then he pulled me into the center of the room. As if on cue, the DJ started playing a slow sexy song I hadn't heard before. The bass rolled through me, sending tingles down my spine.

Colt gathered me to his chest and buried his face in my neck, breathing me in.

I did the same right back. "This isn't fair," I murmured.

"Sssh. Dance."

It was as if the rest of the world disappeared, and it was just me and him, soaking each other in, holding tight, needing each other to breathe. I lost track of how many songs we danced to, with our arms wrapped around each other. But when he eventually grasped my chin and tilted it up, my heart ached.

He lowered his head until his lips hovered over mine and my eyes drifted closed. My lips met his in an agonizingly slow kiss that smashed my heart to pieces. It was so soft, so unlike any of the other kisses we'd ever shared, it stole my breath. An ache tightened across my chest. This kiss wasn't about taking what he wanted. It wasn't about dominance or control.

There were unspoken feelings in that kiss that wrapped

around my heart, pulling me into him, whispering secrets neither of us would voice.

When the police stormed the building and dragged him from my arms, neither of us said a word.

That kiss had already said it all.

37

LACEY

Chaos erupted around me. The music cut out and kids screamed, scuttling out of the way. The police surrounded the officer who'd handcuffed Colt, helping to haul him to the door. Rafe and Banjo both ran at them and were quickly slammed up against the wall of the gym, the police shouting something my brain wouldn't comprehend.

I stared into Colt's eyes until they were out of sight.

"Lacey!"

I blinked and registered Jagger's frantic face. Her fingers dug into my shoulders, and she shook me until I flopped around, rag doll style. "What the hell is going on?" she asked.

I jerked, realizing I couldn't fall apart. Now that Colt was outside, they'd let Rafe and Banjo go, but one officer still stood in the doorway, preventing anyone else from leaving.

Owen stood to one side, arms folded across his chest, a smug smile on his face like he'd planned the entire thing. My blood boiled. A new level of hate I'd never felt before, not even after he'd attacked me on the beach, washed over me.

He needed to pay. For what he'd done to me. What he'd done to Colt. What he was going to keep on doing if no one put a stop to it.

Principal Simmons appeared and relieved the officer of his command, while holding both hands up to the crowd of students. Behind me, a girl cried about the dance being ruined. I wanted to turn around and punch her. Colt's entire life had been ruined, and she was upset over a fucking party?

"Okay, okay. Everyone settle down. This was a very unfortunate incident, but it's being handled and—"

"Being handled?" Rafe sneered. He pushed his way forward so he stood nose-to-nose with his father. "Handled? Colt got dragged off by the police while you stood by and did nothing."

Rafe's dad blinked, and a hush fell over the crowd.

"That's enough, Rafe." Principal Simmons' voice was measured, but there was a hint of threat in it.

Rafe didn't hear it. Or he didn't care. His chest heaved with anger and frustration. "I used to think you only cared about yourself. After all, you never cared about Mom when you broke her down to nothing, or me, when you threw punches at my face. But I was wrong. You care what people think of you beyond anything else. So I have one question for you. How could you? How could you stand by and watch him go to jail for something you did?"

Principal Simmons squinted at his son. "What? Something I did? What do I have to do with this?"

Rafe's voice dropped low and deadly, threaded with the poisoned hate he'd been harboring for his father for years. "You killed Lawson Knight."

The air punched from the room.

Todd Simmons glanced around at the crowd of students

watching in horrified awe. Then turned back to his son. "I've no idea where you came up with an absurd—"

Rafe's fist connected with his father's jaw.

"Rafe," I screamed.

"Fuck," Banjo bit out, lunging for Rafe and hauling him back to us.

Rafe struggled against the hold, while Principal Simmons pressed a hand to his lip, his fingers coming away with blood. Murderous rage flashed in his eyes, and my heart stopped. I'd never really thought he could be the killer until that very moment.

In that moment, Todd Simmons showed himself for the monster he was.

He calmly straightened his shoulders, wiped his hands on his pants, and quietly said, "Get out."

He didn't have to tell us twice. Banjo hauled Rafe out the doorway, and I followed close behind, Jagger and Aaron bringing up the rear.

But Rafe wouldn't be silenced, even as we dragged him into the cold night air. "He did it! It was him. He's a fucking psychopath!"

Aaron went to Banjo's aid, trying to get the flailing Rafe into his car.

Jagger's eyes were wide, her hand clapped over her mouth. "Do you think that's true?" she hissed at me.

I shook my head. "I have no idea."

Right now, that was more than I could comprehend. A sob choked my throat at the pure distress on Rafe's face. I sat beside him on the back seat, locking the two of us inside.

Rafe's breaths were so fast and sharp I was sure he was going to hyperventilate. I got right in his face, gripping his cheeks with both hands. "Hey. Stop. Look at me."

He shook his head, but his shoulders fell. And second by

second, his gaze became clearer. The haze that had clouded them lifted, and the Rafe I knew and loved came back to me.

He blinked hard. "He did it, Lace. It had to have been him. He wanted your uncle's job. Or his life. Fuck, I don't know. He's going to let Colt take the fall."

I shook my head hard. "Sssh. No. That isn't going to happen. I won't let it."

The words hit me as hard as they hit him. We were wasting time. There was no point sitting here in a fucking parking lot, debating over who really killed my uncle. That wasn't helping us. And it sure as hell wasn't helping Colt.

"I need to go home and talk to Selina. We need to get him a lawyer. Not one of those shitty public defenders. A good one."

Banjo twisted from the front seats. "I need to get to Willa and Aria. They're going to be frantic." He glanced at Rafe. "You need to come, too. They need us. Can you get it together?"

Rafe nodded.

Jagger and Aaron still stood outside the car, hovering to see what we were doing.

Jagger jumped into action. "Rafe, Banjo, you're with us. I'll take you to Colt's place. Lacey can take Rafe's car, then we'll all meet at Lacey's later to see what can be done about getting a lawyer involved. Capiche?"

We all nodded. Banjo threw me the car keys he must have swiped from Rafe's pocket, and we all got out. I pressed up on my toes and brushed my lips against Rafe's.

He grabbed me and kissed me hard. "I'm sorry," he whispered when he pulled back an inch.

I shook my head. He had nothing to apologize for. Nothing. For all we knew, he was right, and we'd just let Lawson's killer walk back into a roomful of teenagers without a care in the world.

But that wasn't the most pressing problem. Rafe turned me over to Banjo who kissed my forehead. "See you soon."

I didn't stick around to watch them all pile into Jagger's little car. I got behind the wheel of Rafe's and peeled out of the parking lot and hightailed it back to Providence like the Devil was on my back.

Saint View High had turned into the pits of Hell tonight, so maybe he really was.

The streets of Providence were too quiet. It wasn't even that late, barely eleven, but I didn't see a single other car on the road.

Not until I reached my driveway.

I drove in too fast, too impatient to get to my aunt, my head full of all the things Colt needed, and the horrible weight of knowing he was sitting in some police interrogation room right now.

Or worse, a jail cell.

I let out a yelp and slammed the brakes on when I realized the driveway wasn't empty like I'd expected it to be. I fumbled with the keys while staring at the back of the familiar car. A rust-red Explorer.

The same one we'd seen outside the party.

The same one who'd followed Colt and me.

"Shit," I whispered. I slung my purse across my shoulder and tried to slow the rapid beating of my heart. I got out slowly, peering through the windows of the car as I walked past, but there was no one inside.

I prayed Selina wasn't telling the cops anything. If they'd

sent detectives to our house, that couldn't mean anything good. But I couldn't hear any yelling from inside. And I knew if they were here to accuse me of something, Selina would have been losing her shit.

I pushed the door open cautiously. "Selina?"

There was a momentary pause, then, "In the kitchen."

There was something in her voice that had my stomach turning backflips. Something wasn't right.

I moved toward the kitchen, gripping my purse tighter, and found Selina standing behind the counter, a stranger beside her.

I didn't give her more than a cursory glance before Selina's panic caught my attention. Her eyes widened, her mouth opening in horror.

Everything switched to slow motion.

Someone stepped in behind me and wrapped an arm around my throat.

The woman raised a gun to Selina's head.

A scream ripped from my lungs, and a meaty hand covered my mouth.

The woman with the gun glanced at me, her face full of something I couldn't read, but then she moved in closer to Selina, pressing the gun barrel to her temple.

Tears rolled silently down my aunt's face, and I shook my head, trying to breathe around the hands that held me captive and the fear sending my body into shock.

In my mind I heard Colt's scream from that day at the gym. *"Fight, Lacey!"*

I couldn't fight this guy off. He was huge. Colt hadn't taught me enough. I was no fighter. Not equipped to take anyone down after a single self-defense lesson.

The woman tugged her earlobe with her free hand. "You

stupid bitch," she hissed. "You said she wouldn't be home for hours."

Selina trembled all over. "She wasn't supposed to be. The dance doesn't end until midnight."

I slipped my hand inside my bag.

"Now you've gone and fucked the whole thing up," the woman screamed.

"Stop yelling at her," the guy behind me muttered. "You aren't helping anything."

She turned on him, her eyes flashing. "You think I wanted this? You think I planned for this?"

I didn't give a shit what she'd planned. I pulled Colt's fake gun from my purse and rammed it up beneath my captor's chin.

He froze.

Selina's eyes widened.

I'd never told her about the gun.

Blood pounded in my ears, and adrenaline crashed my system.

I yelled, but the words came out muffled from behind the guy's hand. I pressed my gun harder into the soft underside of his jaw, insistent.

At a nod from his partner, slowly, his fingers uncurled from my mouth.

"I swear to fucking God, I will pull this trigger if you don't let go of me." My voice shocked even me—the barely concealed rage there was low and deadly. But fuck this. Fuck them. I let out a scream that made Selina flinch.

The guy backed away, and I scuttled to one side so my back was against the wall. I turned my gun on the woman, my finger trembling over the trigger. Oh, how I wished this thing were loaded. I wanted it to be. I was so sick of people who thought they could walk all over me and take what they wanted. Whoever the hell these people were. Owen. The police. They'd already taken Colt. Wasn't that enough?

"Lacey," Selina said quietly. "Put the gun down."

I wasn't in control of my body. I didn't know who I was or what I was doing. It was like I floated up outside of myself and watched as this other version of me held a gun on a stranger.

"No," I screamed. I waved it again. "Take the fucking gun off my mom!"

My finger moved over the trigger. It was my last move. There was nowhere for me to go from here.

Selina didn't know that.

"Lacey, no," she screamed. "You can't shoot. She's your mother!"

To be continued...

**Get all your questions answered in the last book of the Saint View series, Twisted Little Truths! https://mybook.to/TwistedLittleTruths

**If you thought the threesome in the book was hot, you're going to want to see what happened in the shower afterwards! (Especially if you're a Rafe & Banjo fan!)
Download a free and exclusive bonus scene from the bonus content tab at www.ellethorpe.com

MORE THAN JUST SAINT VIEW...

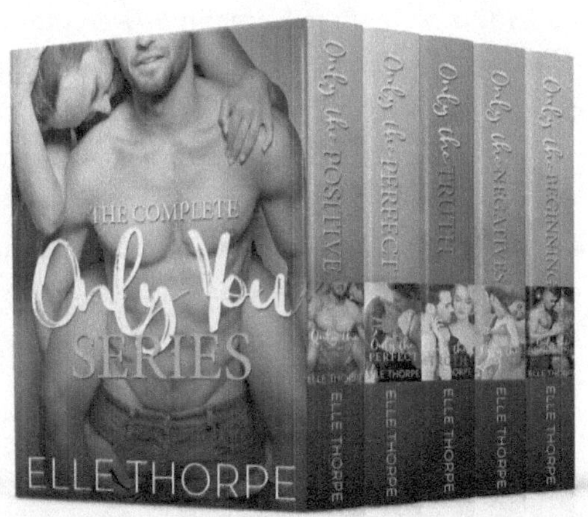

If you loved Elle's Saint View boys, try her contemporary romance Only You series. Here's a sneak peek from book 1, Only the Positive.

"Reese, stop! I have HIV."

The words exploded from his lips like a cannon blast, halting me in my tracks. The silence was deafening as I slowly turned around.

"What?" I honestly wasn't sure I'd heard him correctly.

He shook his head, one hand gripping the back of his neck. He took a step towards me. "There's a chance I have HIV. A good chance. I've had direct exposure and I'm being tested for it."

My hand flew to my mouth as my heart skipped a beat. HIV? As in AIDS?

He grimaced, his features twisting, his hurt clearly evident on his face. "And that's why I didn't want to tell anyone. I didn't want to see that look of disgust. Especially not from you."

I dropped my hand, shame creeping over me. I wasn't disgusted, but shock rolled through me like a wave, making my movements sluggish. How was I supposed to react?

"Don't worry, you can't catch it from kissing, or from anything else we've done. You're safe."

All the heat and passion between us had disappeared, and where moments before his voice had been sweet, he now sounded sharp and sarcastic. He shook his head and jogged over to his horse.

My feet were rooted to the spot. I wasn't responding the right way. I didn't need his body language to confirm that. But my brain seemed to be disconnected from my body. I had no idea how to make it move, or make it talk. No idea how to make it do anything that would salvage this situation, so we could go back to making out. I touched my fingertips to my lips.

His face was blank when he turned back to face me.

"You see now why we had to stop? I told you it had

nothing to do with you. Do you believe me now? I couldn't stay away from you. So maybe you could do me a favour and stay away from me."

Get five books for less than the price of three here: https://mybook.to/OnlyYouBoxset

ALSO BY ELLE THORPE

Saint View High series (Reverse Harem, Bully Romance. Complete)

*Devious Little Liars (Saint View High, #1)

*Dangerous Little Secrets (Saint View High, #2)

*Twisted Little Truths (Saint View High, #3)

Saint View Prison series (Reverse harem, romantic suspense. Complete.)

*Locked Up Liars (Saint View Prison, #1)

*Solitary Sinners (Saint View Prison, #2)

*Fatal Felons (Saint View Prison, #3)

Saint View Psychos series (Reverse harem, romantic suspense. Complete.)

*Start a War (Saint View Psychos, #1)

*Half the Battle (Saint View Psychos, #2)

*It Ends With Violence (Saint View Psychos, #3)

Saint View Rebels (Reverse harem, romantic suspense. Releasing in 2023)

*Rebel Revenge (Saint View Rebels, #1)

*Rebel Obsession (Saint View Rebels, #2)

*Rebel Heart (Saint View Rebels, #3)

Saint View Strip (Male/Female, romantic suspense standalones. Ongoing.)

*Evil Enemy (Saint View Strip, #1)

*Unholy Sins (Saint View Strip, #2)

*Untitled (Saint View Strip, #3)

Dirty Cowboy series (complete)

*Talk Dirty, Cowboy (Dirty Cowboy, #1)

*Ride Dirty, Cowboy (Dirty Cowboy, #2)

*Sexy Dirty Cowboy (Dirty Cowboy, #3)

*Dirty Cowboy boxset (books 1-3)

*25 Reasons to Hate Christmas and Cowboys (a Dirty Cowboy bonus novella, set before Talk Dirty, Cowboy but can be read as a standalone, holiday romance)

Buck Cowboys series (Spin off from the Dirty Cowboy series. Ongoing.)

*Buck Cowboys (Buck Cowboys, #1)

*Buck You! (Buck Cowboys, #2)

*Can't Bucking Wait (Buck Cowboys, #3)

*Mother Bucker (Buck Cowboys, $#4)

The Only You series (Contemporary romance. Complete)

*Only the Positive (Only You, #1) - Reese and Low.

*Only the Perfect (Only You, #2) - Jamison.

*Only the Truth - (Only You, bonus novella) - Bree.

*Only the Negatives (Only You, #3) - Gemma.

*Only the Beginning (Only You, #4) - Bianca and Riley.

*Only You boxset

Add your email address here to be the first to know when new books are available!

www.ellethorpe.com/newsletter

Join Elle Thorpe's readers group on Facebook!

www.facebook.com/groups/ellethorpesdramallamas

ACKNOWLEDGMENTS

Yay! You made it through the cliffhanger without breaking your kindle or tearing up your paperback. Hahahaha. I know, I know, you're cursing me right now, aren't you? But I promise, the conclusion to EVERYTHING is coming in book 3.

So for being such troopers, you guys, my readers, get the first thank you. Thank you for the way you are devouring this series. Thank you for shouting about it from the rooftops. Thank you for all your emails, and for blowing up my groups in the very best way with your excitement. You guys are the most amazing part of this job and I appreciate each and every one of you. Don't forget to come join us in my readers group if you haven't already!

Thank you to Jolie Vines, Zoe Ashwood, Emmy Ellis and Karen Hrdlicka who make up my stellar editing team. And an extra thanks to Jo and Zoe for being my author besties too! Thank you to Sara Massery for the chats, sprints, and graphic design advice. Thank you to Shellie, Karen, and Louise for your early feedback. A massive thank you to my promo and review team for really jumping on board with this series.

And as always, a huge thank you to my family. To Jira, Thomas, Flick, and Heidi. You four are the loves of my life and I couldn't do any of this without you.

Love, Elle x

ABOUT THE AUTHOR

Elle Thorpe lives on the sunny east coast of Australia. When she's not writing stories full of kissing, she's a wife and mummy to three tiny humans. She's also official ball thrower to one slobbery dog named Rollo. Yes, she named a female dog after a dirty hot character on Vikings. Don't judge her. Elle is a complete and utter fangirl at heart, obsessing over The Walking Dead and Outlander to an unhealthy degree. But she wouldn't change a thing.

You can find her on Facebook or Instagram(@ellethorpebooks or hit the links below!) or at her website www.ellethorpe.com. If you love Elle's work, please consider joining her Facebook fan group, Elle Thorpe's Drama Llamas or joining her newsletter here. www.ellethorpe.com/newsletter

facebook.com/ellethorpebooks
instagram.com/ellethorpebooks
goodreads.com/ellethorpe
pinterest.com/ellethorpebooks